Praise f[...]

**Also by *New York Times* bestselling author
B.J. Daniels**

For additional books by B.J. Daniels,
visit her website, bjdaniels.com.

B.J. DANIELS

RIVER STRONG

CANARY STREET PRESS

CANARY
STREET
PRESS™

Recycling programs
for this product may
not exist in your area.

ISBN-13: 978-1-335-50814-0

River Strong

Copyright © 2023 by Barbara Heinlein

For questions and comments about the quality of this book, please contact us at CustomerService@Harlequin.com.

Canary Street Press
22 Adelaide St. West, 41st Floor
Toronto, Ontario M5H 4E3, Canada
CanaryStPress.com

Printed in U.S.A.

This book is dedicated to Dallas Skinner,
a good friend and faithful reader. I love talking with
him about books and writing when he comes up to visit.
Also, he makes a wonderful red velvet cake and
once cooked me the best fried sage hen I've ever had.

PROLOGUE

THE MAN HAD always been dead weight. But now seriously dead, he seemed too heavy for someone who'd been so insignificant in the grand scheme of things. As the two alternated dragging and carrying his body from the back of the pickup through the darkness toward the yawning hole in the ground, the moon rose, painting the Powder River Basin golden.

A breeze stirred the leaves of the tall cottonwoods, making the trees sigh. The two stopped to listen, both on alert. Past the cottonwoods, the Powder River snaked soundlessly through a stretch of badlands; the slick surface of the water appeared cast in bronze in the moonlight. Nothing moved.

Silently, the two continued their macabre work, straining with the effort. As they neared the old abandoned well, they stopped again to listen, then looked at each other over the body as if one of them should say something.

"Burn in hell," the one said and, lifting the man's legs, the two dropped him headfirst into the cistern.

The night fell deathly silent as they stood over the large gaping black hole—one of the few wells in the basin that he would fit. They listened, waiting until they heard his head connect with the rocky bottom.

They looked at each other, a silent agreement forged between two unlikely coconspirators. Without a word, they slid the cover back over the forgotten dry well and headed for the truck, the job done—once they disposed of the man's pickup.

CHAPTER ONE

OAKLEY STAFFORD JOLTED upright in bed, the nightmare chasing her from the deep darkness of sleep into the growing light of the Montana winter day. The sun rimmed the mountains to the east, but her view from her bedroom window on the Stafford Ranch was still cast in shadow. Through the bare-limbed cottonwoods, the Powder River wound its way north, dark and silent beneath a thick layer of ice.

Even now awake, Oakley felt as if she was still spurring her horse through the darkness of the cottonwoods months earlier. The leaves created a dark canopy overhead with only slivers of sunlight filtering through, casting long shadows in her path. She raced for the county road, chased by a killer as she ran for her life. *Don't look back. Don't look back.*

She shuddered, the recurring nightmare feeling so real because it had been. She'd awoken in the hospital, shocked to hear that she'd been shot just as she and her horse had burst from the cottonwoods and onto the county road. Shot in the back, she'd fallen from her horse, striking her head so hard that it wiped out all memory of two full days of her life.

Her hand went automatically to her scar near her heart where the bullet had been removed. Even after all this time, the shadowy images still plagued her, daring her to remember. What had really happened that day?

While her memory felt like a black hole tempting her to come closer and look at what was waiting for her inside, her mind kept crying out, *Don't look back!* It made her fear that the truth might be more terrifying than her lack of memory.

Oakley started as her bedroom door opened, her older sister filling the frame. "I heard you cry out. The nightmare again?" She nodded as Tilly entered the room and sat down on the edge of her bed. "I thought after CJ confessed to accidentally shooting you, it would get better."

"So did I." But she didn't trust her older brother's version of the story. There was a part of her brain that told her there was something important she desperately needed to recall before it was too late.

"You stayed here last night?" she asked. Tilly often stayed with her fiancé at the McKenna Ranch that adjoined theirs. The river dividing their land, the two families had been at odds for years. The bitterness between the McKenna patriarch, Holden McKenna, and their mother, the matriarch of the Stafford Ranch, Charlotte Stafford, had gotten worse recently.

"Have you heard from Mother?" Tilly asked as she rose from the bed and walked to the window. Oakley saw her glance at the engagement ring on her finger, the diamond catching the early-morning light. In the distance, the mountains rose in rocky cliffs and pine-dotted hillsides capped with the last of winter's snow. Closer, the thick stand of cottonwoods stood stark along the river as it wound its way through the Powder

River Basin under a clear, cold, cloudless blue late-December sky.

"Maybe you should tell her about your engagement before she returns home," Oakley suggested, leaning against the headboard as the remnants of her nightmare burned away like morning mountain mist, leaving her unsettled.

"Mother has enough on her plate right now."

Oakley had been shocked when she'd learned who'd shot her. Her own brother. CJ swore it was an accident. She knew in her heart that there was more to it and that was what had her scared. She had to remember, because all her instincts told her that her would-be killer was waiting in fear for her to do just that.

While Oakley had been fighting for her life in the hospital, CJ had tried to flee the law. He'd rolled his pickup, almost killing Tilly and himself. Paralyzed, he'd been whisked away by their mother to a hospital in Minnesota that specialized in the care he needed. Their mother had gone with him. Oakley hadn't seen either of them since; nor had she gotten a chance to confront her brother.

"I haven't heard anything from her," Oakley said. As far as she knew, CJ was still paralyzed, needing a wheelchair, something their mother refused to accept. If stubborn determination could heal her oldest son, Charlotte Stafford would have had him walking by now and the two would have returned to the ranch.

"I can't believe that you've forgiven him," Tilly said. "He almost killed you." CJ had fired the bullet that had come so close to Oakley's heart that it had been amazing that she survived. It was his reason for shooting her that still haunted her. He'd apparently followed her onto McKenna Ranch property because he thought she was meeting someone from the rival ranch. Allegedly, he'd fired a warning shot to stop her that had gone awry.

"I don't know that I can ever forgive him entirely," Oakley said. "It was bad enough what he did to me. But he almost killed you." She shook her head. "He's never had to suffer the consequences of his actions, thanks to Mother. But this time he went too far. Not that I'd ever wish him to be badly injured. But he needs to spend some time behind bars. Not that Mother will ever allow that."

Tilly looked as if she hadn't completely forgiven their brother, either. She'd been on her way into town the day CJ found out the sheriff knew that he'd fired the near-fatal shot. Their brother abducted Tilly, taking her hostage as he raced along backroads, determined to escape punishment.

"You realize CJ will go berserk when he finds out about your engagement to Cooper McKenna," Oakley said.

"I'm not worried about CJ," Tilly said. "I'm more concerned about Mother. You know how she feels about the McKennas."

Charlotte Stafford could be scary when crossed, but for Oakley it was CJ who appeared in her nightmares, along with a nagging conviction that he was lying about the shooting. "I just worry about what she'll do, Tilly. Didn't she threaten you if you kept seeing Cooper?"

"There's nothing she can do," her sister said, sounding more confident than Oakley suspected she was.

"I'm marrying Coop and she can't stop me. As far as the ranch…"

Oakley heard the catch in her sister's voice. Tilly loved the homestead, loved working it, always thought she would be the one who kept the Stafford Ranch going for future generations. It was why she and CJ and their mother often argued about the future of the ranch and ranching. They'd especially been at odds over coalbed methane drilling on the property. CJ had talked their mother into letting the gas company drill on the ranch for the money. He'd never considered the long-term or what it would mean to future generations.

"Mother's going to need me working the ranch even more now until CJ is up and around again," Tilly said.

"If he ever is." Oakley didn't remind her sister how Charlotte Stafford handled those she felt had been disloyal. She cut them out of her life as brutally as if taking a knife to them.

"I should get moving," Tilly said. "Cooper and I are driving out to Oregon to pick up a bull. He wants to start a whole new breeding program at the ranch. Holden has offered us a section of land for a house as a wedding present. We're planning to build this summer, although I know Holden would be happy if we stayed in the main house. But with Cooper's older brother so opposed to us being together…"

"Treyton," Oakley said like a curse. "He is so much like CJ except for the fact that he hasn't shot anyone lately."

"As far as we know," Tilly said. "Holden thinks his son will come around. I have my doubts. But it doesn't matter. Cooper and I are going to be together, no matter what."

Oakley smiled. Her sister seemed to glow whenever she said her fiancé's name. "I couldn't be happier for you." Tilly had found love and like she said, there was nothing anyone could do to stop them from marrying. At least she hoped that was the case.

The sun broke over the mountains and filled her bedroom with warm golden light, chasing away the nightmare—at least until tonight. She couldn't wait for the days to get longer, the sun stronger. This winter had been harder than most and it had only begun.

"You have plans today?" Tilly asked, still standing next to her bed.

She heard the suspicion and worry in her sister's voice. "Nothing exciting. Just going into Miles City, meeting up with some friends."

"Anyone I know?"

Oakley knew exactly what Tilly was asking.

"I hope you're not still involved with that subversive group, Dirty Business," her sister said. "Stu told me that there'd been more vandalizing of the coalbed methane drilling rigs. He said the gas company is going to be cracking down."

She heard the warning loud and clear. "You still see the sheriff?"

"Don't try to change the subject. Stu and I and Cooper are friends. I was never serious about the sheriff. Oakley, you can't stop the drilling in the Powder River Basin. Sabotaging the drilling equipment will only end you up in jail or worse."

"It hurts me that you think I would do something like that."

Tilly rolled her eyes. "Maybe that works on Mother—"

It didn't. "Thank you for the early-morning lecture, big sis, but I'm well aware of all of that." She swung her legs over the side of the bed and felt that twinge around the gunshot scar. She was kidding herself if she thought she could ever forgive her brother for shooting her, especially when she couldn't shake the feeling that there had been more to it than he'd admitted. If only she could remember those lost forty-eight hours.

Unlike Tilly, she was anxious for CJ and her mother to return to the ranch. She wanted answers. She would finally get to confront her brother. She planned to get the truth out of him, one way or another. But that wasn't all she had planned as she waited for her sister to leave her room so she could call her two coconspirators about tonight.

"YOU HAVE *ANOTHER* DATE?"

Duffy McKenna turned to see the latest addition to the McKenna Ranch standing in the doorway, one hip cocked, a smile on her cute pre-teenaged face. He touched his finger to his lips and pretended it was a secret. It actually was, but he didn't want Holly Jo to know that any more than he did the rest of the family.

"You must like this one," the twelve-year-old said as she plopped down in a chair to watch him finish getting ready. "You're always looking in the mirror, messing with your hair, but you seem nervous this time."

He turned to look at her, unable not to grin. Holly Jo was sharper than some of the people in this house gave her credit for. He needed to watch this one. "You think so, huh?"

"So what's she like?" she asked, twirling a lank of her long dark hair on a finger as she studied him with those big blue eyes.

"Smart, strong, determined," he said at once. He laughed at how quickly the words had come to him and yet they didn't do Oakley Stafford justice. He realized he could have added another half dozen adjectives easily.

Holly Jo rolled her eyes. "Is she pretty?"

"No prettier than you."

She mugged a face at him, but he could tell she liked the compliment. "Are you serious about her?"

He'd never been that serious about any girl he'd gone out with. But Oakley? He realized he was dead serious. So why hadn't he done something about it? He'd been telling himself that there was plenty of time, except that he'd been thinking that for a long time now. She wasn't as close to anyone as she was him, he told himself. So of course they would be together one day. What was the hurry?

"What do you think?" he said in answer to Holly Jo's question. "You know what a serious cowboy I am."

"Exactly," she said. "Cooper says you like to play the field. That you're too immature to have a real relationship. Treyton said he doesn't understand what women see in you."

Duffy laughed. "Me neither." Great to know how the family really feels, he thought. Even his brother Treyton had weighed in.

"You going to break this one's heart?"

"Chances are that she'll end up breaking mine." That was a sobering thought.

"Elaine says it will take getting your heart broken before you find your true love." Elaine was their cook, head housekeeper, a fixture at the ranch from before Duffy was born.

"That's what Elaine says, huh? You two spend a lot of time talking about me, do you?"

"As much as anyone else except Treyton," Holly Jo said innocently enough. "Elaine doesn't see much hope for him and neither do I. But she says everyone has the potential to change and be a better person no matter their past indiscretions."

"I never knew Elaine dispensed so much good advice." He grinned at her. "What does she suggest for you?"

Holly Jo made a face. "She says I have a lot of growing up to do, but that I just need to be patient."

"I agree with her. Now, get going. I can't be late for my date. Don't you have homework to do?" He watched her shove herself up with a groan.

"Holden says I can't date until I'm at least sixteen. *Sixteen!* Do you know how old that is?"

"I do." As he watched her shuffle out of his room, he wondered what the real story was about Holly Jo. All his father had told them was that he'd made a promise to Holly Jo's mother years ago that he would take care of her daughter if anything happened to her. Had he known the mother was going to die young?

More to the point: Was there any blood connection to the girl and their family? Holden swore she wasn't his daughter. But Duffy had no doubt there was more to the story. There always was.

All the family knew was that Holly Jo was going to be living with them indefinitely. Not that the girl had been pleased about that. She'd spent months getting into trouble, trying to leave and generally fighting with their father.

Duffy liked her. It was probably the kid in him, but he thought she liked him, too. Treyton ignored her, their sister, Bailey, threatened her if she came near her room or her business, Cooper taught her to ride a horse and their ranch hand and Duffy's best friend, Pickett Hanson, was giving her trick riding lessons. Lately, she'd seemed to be settling in as if accepting the way things were. He hoped it worked out. He would miss her if she left for any reason.

Duffy turned his attention to his so-called date tonight. Who was he kidding?

It wasn't a date. It was three friends, Duffy, Pickett and Oakley, going to a Dirty Business secret meeting. Sometimes he felt like Oakley was completely out of his league even if she hadn't been a Stafford. Not just that. She often seemed to like his best friend, Pickett, more than him.

He planned to change that, he thought with a grin as he looked in the mirror. This woman was a challenge, something he wasn't used to, but that made him all the more determined. He raked a hand through his thick dark hair. Holly Jo was right, he thought with a laugh. He definitely more than liked this one.

But he also didn't want anyone else to have her—not that he was worried about Pickett.

COOPER FOUND HIS father behind his desk in the den. He saw worry etched deep in Holden's once very handsome face. Holden McKenna was still a powerful-looking man with broad shoulders. His dark hair had gone salt-and-pepper with gray, and his blue eyes seemed to have dimmed some, but there was an inner strength to him that Cooper had always admired.

"Problem?" he asked as he stepped into the room.

His father looked up from the papers on his desk. "I suppose you've heard. Inez Turner is now in hospice care. Word is that the Montana 360 Ranch will be up for sale after she passes. Her son Bob isn't interested in ranching, apparently. We could use that land, but mostly we need the water that flows through it."

When Charlotte Stafford had a coalbed methane well drilled right next to their ranch, their artesian well had gone dry. It was a loss that had put the two families even more at odds. Cooper was familiar with the Montana 360 Ranch. It had good wells and access to the river.

"You know Charlotte will want that land," he said. "If she diverts the water away from our ranch…"

His father nodded. "I've already spoken to Bob, letting him know we're interested in purchasing the ranch. We will have to top whatever Charlotte offers."

Cooper figured this would make the rivalry between the two families even worse. But it also might put the McKenna Ranch in financial jeopardy. He was pretty sure that was why his older brother, Treyton, had been pushing their father to cash in by having coalbed methane wells drilled on their ranch. Thankfully, Holden was dead set against it.

But there would also be a personal cost for his father. According to the local scuttlebutt, his father and Charlotte had been lovers when they were young. She'd thought they would marry. Holden's father had someone else in mind for his son, a woman whose ranch land the McKenna Ranch needed.

Charlotte never forgave him for betraying her. Cooper suspected his father had also never forgiven himself. There were times when her name was mentioned that Cooper had seen the pain in his father's eyes. He'd long suspected that Holden still loved her.

"Does Treyton know?" he had to ask. Since recently returning to the ranch after leaving two years ago, he suspected his brother might be planning to go behind their father's back to do what he felt was best for the ranch.

"He doesn't know the extent of it," Holden admitted. "I don't want to have another argument with him about drilling on McKenna land. We just have to make sure we get the Montana 360 Ranch. I'm afraid it's going to be a bidding war with Charlotte Stafford and probably some other ranchers in the area. Treyton seems to think I should go to the ranch, get Irma to sell to me on her deathbed." He shook his head. "I don't know about your brother sometimes."

Sometimes? Cooper had butted heads with Treyton since they were kids. Since returning to the river basin a some months ago, he'd warned his father about Treyton having been seen talking with one of the methane company bosses. He'd also told him about catching Treyton at the real estate office in town, possibly seeing what the ranch might be worth on the open market.

His brother always seemed to be angry, wanting their

father to step aside and let him take over the ranch, convinced he could run it better. Cooper feared what Treyton would do if he got the chance.

"You're headed out to Oregon, right?" Holden asked. "Taking Tilly with you?" He smiled. "Make it a nice little holiday. No reason to rush back." As if thinking the same thing Cooper was, his father asked, "Any word on when Charlotte is coming back?"

He shook his head. "As far as I know she hasn't been in communication with anyone here. I don't think CJ is healing as she'd hoped. Doubt she wants to return until he is."

His father sighed. "Charlotte hates to lose, but from what I've heard, CJ will be coming home in a wheelchair. How long he might be in one, possibly the rest of his life, is debatable. If she has anything to do with it, he'll walk again." Charlotte Stafford's iron will was legendary. "Does she know about the engagement yet?"

"Not that I know of," Cooper said. "Tilly hasn't heard from her. But the fact that her mother hasn't been taking her calls could be an indication that Charlotte *has* heard." He saw his father frown. They both feared how Charlotte would take it.

As for CJ Stafford, he and his father felt the same way about the cowboy who had almost killed both of his sisters. Cooper was hoping CJ walked again for personal reasons. He needed to settle a few things with him.

"I'm sure you've heard," Cooper said. "Charlotte's lawyers are fighting to get the cases against CJ for both incidents dropped." No one in the county who knew the Stafford matriarch believed her son would ever do any jail time.

His father said nothing. In recent years, he'd argued for peace between the families. Now he changed the subject. "Well, have a good trip. Can't wait to see this bull when you get back. Drive safely." Holden's gaze shifted to something behind Cooper. "Was that Duffy leaving?"

"Said he had a date."

His father shook his head. "I doubt he'll ever settle down and get serious about a woman—let alone working this ranch."

OAKLEY SHOWERED, dressed and headed for Miles City with a planned stop along the way to pick up her two cohorts, Duffy McKenna and Pickett Hanson. Duffy was Holden McKenna's youngest son. Pickett had been a McKenna ranch hand since all three of them were in their teens. Both were her best friends and partners in crime and had been since then. She used to sneak over to the neighboring ranch and the three managed to get into all kinds of trouble. They still did.

Both young men had stolen a piece of her heart with their good looks, their heart-fluttering grins and outrageous senses of humor. Lately, the three of them had become even closer out of their determination to stop the coalbed methane drilling in their valley.

As she pulled up to the meeting place just outside town, the two men exited the pickup they'd arrived in and walked toward her, smiling. They were both so darned handsome, cowboys through and through. For years, Oakley had watched cowgirls throwing themselves at the two of them. She hadn't been one of those cowgirls. She'd ignored both men when they flirted with her—and still did. It only seemed to make them both more determined to win her over.

She laughed now as the two wrestled over who was going to sit on the pickup's bench seat next to her. They'd made a game out of trying to court her favor. "Quit horsing around. We need to get going."

Duffy won the wrestling match, sliding in next to her, grinning and giving her a hip bump. Like all the McKennas, he had thick dark hair and incredible blue eyes with long dark lashes that made her jealous. "Hey, beautiful."

She elbowed him in the side as Pickett climbed in, slammed the door and then got the truck moving. "Tilly told me that the sheriff mentioned to her that another drilling rig had been vandalized," she said, getting down to business. Sheriff Stuart Layton was close to both Tilly and Cooper. Her sister had dated Stuart for a while before her true heartthrob Cooper had returned.

Oakley glanced over at the two men as she drove out of town and headed for the mountains they would cross before dropping down into the Yellowstone River Valley and Miles City. She loved both Duffy and Pickett, but lately Oakley felt as if something was changing. Or maybe it was her. "You know Stuart suspects us," she said, keeping to the subject at hand.

"But he has to prove it was us," Duffy said and grinned.

"I think we need to work on the ranchers," Pickett said, always the practical one. When the three of them had built a treehouse in the woods, Duffy had been convinced it was safe enough. Pickett refused to climb up until it was supported better. Duffy broke his arm in the fall when the treehouse collapsed.

"If ranchers don't let them drill on their land, CH4 will have to move on," Pickett said. "Keeping them from using their drilling equipment for a few weeks isn't stopping them."

"Neither is trying to get ranchers not to drill," Duffy said. "Too many of them need the money and if this drought continues…" It was no secret that Duffy enjoyed sabotaging the drilling rigs, but he really did want the drilling to stop. Like Pickett, he tended to joke around, making people think he didn't take anything seriously. But most people didn't know either man the way Oakley did.

"It does come down to money," Pickett agreed. "So many of the ranches had to sell their cattle earlier than they wanted because of it, our ranches included."

Oakley knew the argument too well. "Maybe someone will have a suggestion at this meeting in Miles City. We need to be careful, though. The sheriff is watching us. So are the folks at the methane gas company. It's getting more dangerous." None of them spoke until she was almost to Miles City.

"I'm not sure you should go with us to the meeting," Pickett said.

She shot him a look that she hoped sent her clear answer to that.

"I'm serious, Oakley. You're right about it getting more dangerous. I'm worried about you. Isn't your mother coming back soon?"

"What does she have to do with this?" she demanded. While she planned to confront her brother, she knew her mother would fight like a mama grizzly to protect her oldest son—maybe especially if his injuries still had him in a wheelchair.

"The next well could be on your ranch," Duffy said. "Your mother had been about to make a deal with CH4 before she left. I doubt CJ's changed her mind."

Oakley let out an oath, slamming her hand down on the steering wheel. "CJ," she said. "I'm sure he talked her into it. He'd have wells all over the ranch if he had his way. All he thinks about is the money. Doesn't care about what it will do to the ranch that our children and grandchildren will inherit." She groused under her breath for a moment before glancing over at them. "If she goes ahead with it, we're going to stop that well from going in."

They instantly started voicing their concerns about any plan that meant crossing Charlotte Stafford. "That's a little too close to home, don't you think?" Pickett said.

"Exactly," she snapped. "Duffy, you already lost a major well on your ranch because of the drilling on our ranch. You can't afford to lose another one. Eventually, it is going to destroy our own water wells, not to mention what all that salt from the drilling water is going to do to the Powder River. We have to stop it. If you don't want to help me—"

"You know better than that," Pickett said.

Duffy chuckled. "Like we would let you do this alone."

"I don't know what I'd do without the two of you," she said, meaning it even as her stomach roiled at the thought of going head-to-head with her mother and CJ. She had no idea how much time she had before her mother returned and the drilling began—let alone how they were going to stop it and stay out of jail.

IN HIS OFFICE, Sheriff Stuart "Stu" Layton sorted through the photographs taken at the crime scene. The incidents of vandalism on the gas rigs had escalated, the damage more extensive. A bigwig from the CH4 gas company was flying in today, demanding something be done and threatening to go to the feds if the sheriff couldn't handle the job.

Stu didn't like being threatened. He really doubted the feds would be interested in taking on vandalism cases, but he was no fool. Things had gotten out of hand. He had to stop it.

He sorted through the photos again, knowing full well that the group calling themselves Dirty Business was growing in numbers. It was no longer some young hotheads. Area ranchers had joined the group, trying to organize against the gas company.

The sheriff figured the vandals only made up a small portion of the group, though. He was pretty sure he knew some of them, but he had no proof. They'd been clever, making sure no one saw them and leaving no evidence as to their identities.

He studied the photographs more closely. No tire tracks. They'd walked into the site where the drilling equipment had been. But they'd also left no footprints. He figured they had to be wearing shoe coverings. He wasn't dealing with kids or hopped-up teenagers. This group knew what they were doing. He suspected they had been trained.

The only way to catch them was to stake out drilling

equipment in isolated places around the Powder River Basin. The thought of putting his new deputy, Ty Dodson, on it gave him pause. Dodson tended to throw his weight around because of the badge. Stu hated to think what the deputy might do if the vandals ran or worse, put up a fight. He didn't want anyone getting killed over spray paint and some temporarily inoperable equipment.

"Got a minute?" He looked up to find a pretty brunette smiling in through his open office doorway at him. He and Abigail Creed, the new nurse at the local small hospital, had been dating for a few months off and on. Mostly off.

From the first time he'd met her, Stu had been suspicious of her reasons for being in Powder Crossing. Also for being so friendly to him. It wasn't anything he could put his finger on, just a gut feeling that unnerved him. Maybe he just wasn't used to sweet, thoughtful women being interested in him, he joked to himself. Or maybe Abigail wasn't exactly who she pretended to be.

"Free for dinner? I hit the market in Miles City and I feel like cooking. Feel like eating?"

He searched only a few moments for an excuse to decline and then changed his mind. He felt as if their relationship was reaching some sort of climax, one way or the other. "I'd love to. What can I bring?"

"Just your appetite. Seven?" He nodded, smiling. "See you then," she said and was gone.

Stu sat for a moment chastising himself. Abigail was probably what she appeared, a lovely, caring, pretty young woman who for whatever reason seemed interested in him. Why wasn't he more suspicious of the ones who would end up leaving him for someone else?

He thought of Tilly Stafford. He'd really thought she might be the one.

She turned out to be the one all right—for Cooper McKenna, he reminded himself. Her falling for Cooper had strained his relationship with his once best friend. He and Coop had patched up their grievance, but there was some history there that they kept stumbling over. Another woman they'd both been interested in was now dead.

He pushed away the thought of Leann Hayes, not wanting to go back down that dark alley. As far as he was concerned, the case was closed. She'd committed suicide, end of story. He just hoped that he could eventually convince Cooper of that before he demanded the case be reopened. His friend was convinced that Leann hadn't killed herself.

Fortunately, Cooper was busy, enjoying his engagement to Tilly Stafford and hadn't mentioned reopening the case lately. His friend had stopped by earlier to tell him that he was going out to Oregon to pick up a bull. Tilly was going with him. "Can I pick you up anything from the West Coast?"

Stu marveled at how he and the ranch kid had become friends to begin with. The sheriff was as blond as Cooper was dark. The two of them had grown up together. Close to the same age, they'd been in the same grade in the small rural school for years. He couldn't remember when they'd become best friends. There were rough times over the years when they'd fought over ball games or girls, but they'd lasted as friends. They'd always had each other's back—even in the worst times.

Until recently.

Stu had a bad feeling that chasm in their relationship was about to widen when Cooper found out that the sheriff had been seeing quite a lot of his sister, Bailey. She would stop by his office or drop by the house to talk. She'd already told him about her brother's trip, but Stu didn't let on to Cooper that he already knew or that he'd been seeing his wild younger sister. He had a feeling that his old friend wouldn't be happy about that. It had been Bailey's idea to keep it on the down-low.

The sheriff had no idea where it was going—or if it was going anywhere. He liked Bailey's company and she seemed to find his job fascinating. She also liked to talk about the valley's history. Since Stu had taken his dad's job as sheriff, he remembered stories his father had told. Those seemed to interest Bailey, too. She was especially interested in the feud between her family and the Staffords.

"Thanks, but I don't need anything," Stu had said, touched that Cooper would ask if he wanted anything from the West Coast. "Have a nice trip. When are you coming back?"

"Not sure. Only a day or two."

He'd gotten the impression Coop had wanted to say more, but Stu had to take a call and his friend had waved goodbye as he'd left.

CHAPTER TWO

CHARLOTTE STAFFORD STUDIED herself in the small compact mirror as the plane readied for takeoff. She hated the grim line of her mouth, the lines around her eyes. Her emerald green eyes had once been her best feature. Those and her long legs. She had a flash of memory of those slim, sun-browned legs wrapped around Holden McKenna's body and snapped her compact shut.

"Are we ever going to get off the ground?" she demanded of the attendant.

"The pilot said it would only be a little longer," the young male answered. "Can I get you anything else before we take off?"

She waved away the question with a shake of her head and looked out the window before turning her gaze on her son. CJ had been lifted from his wheelchair into a seat on the private plane she'd hired. His mood appeared worse than her own.

It was its own kind of hell to see him like this. She'd been so sure that the doctors she was paying an enormous amount of money to would repair the damage to her son. She refused to believe he wouldn't walk again.

Charlotte felt the plane begin to move, finally. She looked out the window, preparing herself for returning to the Powder River Basin. In her absence, her sons

Brand and Ryder had seen to the ranch along with ranch manager, Boyle Wilson. She groaned inwardly at the thought of Boyle, who'd been employed as far back as she could remember.

She never questioned his loyalty to her since he'd made little secret of the fact that he was interested in dating her. Like that was ever going to happen. Still she didn't doubt the man would kill for her, if asked. He also hated the McKennas, especially Holden, as much or more than she did. But over the years, she also knew that he'd been collecting secrets about her and her family like gold nuggets, storing them away until one day he might want to cash them in. It was why she would never fully trust Boyle.

Charlotte valued loyalty above all else, but seldom got it, she thought as the plane taxied out onto the airstrip for takeoff. She wielded control with an iron fist, using both her money and her power to get what she wanted. Most everyone knew better than to cross her. Those who didn't quickly learned what happened if they did cross her, she thought bitterly as the plane's engines began to rev.

She closed her eyes as the craft sped down the runway and lifted off. In the months she'd been gone, a lot had happened. But she assured herself that she would be home soon to take care of things as she always had— on her own terms.

THE TALK AT the Dirty Business meeting that evening was all about the two men the gas company had brought in to guard their equipment, Frankie and Norman Lees, so Oakley hadn't been paying a lot of attention. She'd already researched both men, hearing stories about how they'd handled things in Wyoming before CH4 gas company had moved into the Powder River Basin.

She had no doubt that they were dangerous. If anything, CH4 hiring thugs had the Dirty Business group even more divided on how to go forward. As it was, most of the group had always been opposed to vandalizing the gas rigs.

Oakley tuned out the old arguments until she heard her name mentioned.

"It's not stopping drilling," rancher Ralph Jones said again tonight. "I think talking to your neighbors, making sure they know what's at stake, is still the best approach, especially when it comes to your mother, Oakley."

One of the men in the crowd spoke up. "I know for a fact that your brother CJ ordered more drilling on the Stafford Ranch."

"It will be over my dead body," Oakley assured him. There was a splattering of applause.

"I don't think that's funny," Ralph said, getting the meeting back under control. "These men they brought in, they're dangerous. I heard from down in Wyoming what they did when they caught anyone even near the equipment—let alone anyone trying to stop the drilling. You could very well end up dead."

Oakley felt her phone notify her of a text. She stepped outside the meeting room. It was from her mother. It was the news she'd been waiting for. Charlotte and CJ were in-flight back to Powder Crossing and the ranch. She was demanding to see her. She felt her heart rise to her throat. A summons from her mother was never a good thing.

"You all right?" Pickett asked as he came out of the meeting and walked down the empty hallway to where she stood. The meeting was about to break up. Several lawyers and activists had been talking at length about what they'd done in Wyoming to try to stop the drilling.

All she could think about was whether or not her mother would be at the ranch before they returned from Miles City.

But as Pickett approached, long-legged and rangy, her thoughts strayed from her mother's return and even further from methane gas drilling. A lock of his sun-streaked hair flopped down onto his forehead, drawing her gaze to the light in his eyes. He had dark blue eyes so different from Duffy's pale ones. He was harder to read than Duffy, too. The easygoing ranch hand often joked around, but when he was serious, there was an intensity that often made her heart beat a little faster.

Like now, she felt very aware of him standing so close to her. It was as if he radiated a kind of heat. Or was it electricity?

Right now his eyes were dark, his brows knitted in concern. For a man who was seldom serious, he couldn't have been more appealing than at this moment.

Her body reacted, tingling with anticipation, but anticipation for what? She turned to him, closing a little more of the distance between them, aware of the quiet, the privacy, the almost intimacy, in the empty hallway.

She felt her heart kick up a beat as her gaze took in the cowboy she never saw alone. Duffy was always either with them or close by. Pickett's worn Western shirt stretched across his broad, muscled shoulders. He'd rolled up the sleeves, exposing strong forearms, still tanned from the summer and working outdoors.

Tucked into his jeans, the shirt made her aware of his slim waist. He wore a pair of recently washed newer jeans. Like his shirt, the fabric looked soft as it gently hugged his lanky, long legs.

"Oakley?" He looked even more concerned.

She found her voice, part of her shocked by the range of emotions making her body feel light and at the same time her breasts feel heavy. "My mother's headed home," she said.

"CJ?" he asked as he leaned against the wall, casually studying her, and yet the look in his eyes warmed her to her boots. Her toes curled a little.

"He's coming with her. I can't see her leaving his side. Clearly, she had no plans to return home without him."

He nodded. "You haven't seen him since…" He didn't need to finish, but she suspected he'd hesitated because he hadn't wanted to remind her of the shooting. Or the fact that she couldn't remember the last time she saw her brother from before she was shot.

What it did remind her of was the night she'd awakened to find the ranch hand beside her hospital bed. Pickett had been holding her hand, filling her with both warmth and a sense of safety. She'd had the feeling that it hadn't been the first time he'd sat in that chair holding her hand, his head down as if in prayer. How many times had he come to her room like this in the night when her mother wasn't around to stop him?

She'd never asked him. She hadn't let on that she

knew—even after she regained consciousness. Instead, she'd closed her eyes and squeezed his hand when she'd found him in her room. When she'd awakened again, he'd been gone. He'd never mentioned it, either. It had been their secret.

"Are you going to be all right?" he asked now.

Oakley nodded, even though she wasn't that sure. Facing her brother would be one of the hardest things she'd ever done. Except maybe recovering from the bullet he'd fired into her back.

"That could move things up a bit with the drilling," he said, still studying her.

She could only nod, trying to think about the new gas well she was determined to stop. Instead, she breathed in Pickett's fresh-from-the-shower scent as if it was the best thing she'd ever smelled. She fought the urge to move even closer. She knew that if she touched his shirt, it would be soft, the arm under it solid. That was Pickett. Solid.

"You ready to face him?"

It had been months since CJ had shot her, months since she'd seen him while he was in Minnesota recovering. She had little sympathy for him. He'd almost killed both her and Tilly. He was to blame for his injuries that had left him paralyzed, but she doubted he would see it that way. He'd never accepted blame or experienced remorse for his actions from the time he was a boy.

"Of course you're going to have conflicting feelings," Pickett was saying. "He's your brother and yet—"

"And yet, he almost killed me and I'm still not sure why. I'm angry and hurt, but I also need answers." With

CJ returning, she would finally get to confront him for what he'd done to her, but she wanted more than that. She wanted to know the real story.

Pickett frowned. "I thought it was because he'd assumed you were meeting someone on the McKenna Ranch, and he fired a warning shot to stop you."

"That's what he told my sister, Tilly, but I suspect there is more to it. I just need to remember everything before I was shot. I don't even know what I was doing there that day."

"Or what your brother was doing there," he said quietly.

She looked into his eyes and felt electricity arcing between them. This was something new, something she hadn't felt before. When she looked into the depths of those eyes, she could have sworn that he was feeling it, too. She swallowed, feeling strangely self-conscious. "I have a lot of questions."

"And a lot of anger," he noted, his gaze intent on her. Pickett listened like no one she'd ever known. "If your mother is as protective of CJ as you said she is…"

She smiled and tried to still the jitters she felt being this close to the ranch hand. She'd never felt them quite this strongly before. Something was different tonight, a closeness, an intimacy, because of being alone here. If he touched her, she knew she would walk into his arms. The thought of being held in those arms, of being pressed against his strong chest, of being protected in a way she'd never known, filled her with a need so strong that it threatened to overwhelm her.

But Pickett didn't touch her—ever—not like Duffy, who often threw his arm around her, pulled her into his chest for a hug or nudged her to get her attention. Even if Pickett accidentally brushed against her in passing, she'd felt sparks fly. And suspected he had, too, and that was the reason why he tried not to touch her.

She'd never been more aware of the man than she was right now. She yearned for him to touch her with his suntanned, callused fingertips... That she yearned so deeply for his touch—let alone that she felt such an overwhelming desire tonight to be in his arms—shook her to her core.

"I need to tread lightly," she said as if warning herself not only about how she handled CJ and her mother, but also how she reacted to Pickett right now.

She blamed her emotions on the thought of seeing her mother and CJ again. That was what had her off balance, she thought, even as she knew some of it was Pickett. She couldn't trust herself, let alone her emotions, she warned herself.

"You plan to tread lightly?" He grinned. He had a great grin. "No offense, but you're not really a light treader."

She had to laugh. If felt good and lightened that tight feeling in her chest. Playing it cool had never been her strong suit. She'd always been more confrontational, speaking her mind and dealing with the consequences. "I might surprise you." Or not, she thought, realizing that if anyone knew her, it was Pickett.

He'd seen her at her worst and her best over the years. A gawky fourteen-year-old when she'd met him for the first time on one of the many occasions she'd trespassed on the McKenna Ranch. She and Duffy had been friends since they were kids. Pickett and Duffy were already headed toward being best friends, but from that day on, she became part of the threesome.

Not all that much had changed—until tonight. Which made it hard to understand her reaction to this man she'd known for years.

"It isn't like your mother doesn't already know how you feel about drilling—especially on the Stafford Ranch," he said. He had never seemed to feel the need to fill the quiet. She realized that his nerves were as tense as her own right now.

She could hardly breathe as Pickett moved a little closer. She saw the need in his eyes as he reached toward her and brushed back a lock of her hair, his gaze never leaving hers. His callused fingertips felt just as she knew they would when they brushed her forehead. "Oakley."

Down the hall, a door burst open, noise and people spilling out. Pickett looked as if there was something more he wanted to say, to do, but the meeting had ended; people streamed out, filling the hallway with raised voices and commotion. Pickett dropped his hand to his side, looking as disappointed as she felt.

Duffy joined them, throwing an arm over Oakley's shoulder as he had since they were kids and said, "We might have problems. Let's talk in the truck." He looked at her then, his gaze going from her to Pickett before he asked, "You okay? I was worried when you left the meeting."

"Fine." She looked past him to Pickett. Their gazes locked for only an instant, the moment between them gone, but not forgotten—at least not by her—as the three of them left.

ABIGAIL CREED GREETED the sheriff at the door with a kiss. The scent of dinner wafted out as she led him into the small house she rented behind the hospital. Powder Crossing was a typical small Montana town, but back in its day it had been a stage stop for travelers from Deadwood to Miles City.

Back then, there was the Belle Creek Hotel, still standing today, but little else was left of the original town. Now Powder Crossing had a community church, a café, a bar, a grocery, a convenience store that sold gas out front and muck boots, overalls, rope and feed in the back, a hotel with its own bar and a part-time post office.

Along with a sheriff's department, the town had a small community hospital, with a couple of nurses and one semiretired doctor. For serious injuries, patients were flown to Miles City or Billings.

That was one reason Stuart had trouble understanding why a young pretty nurse would want to move to Powder Crossing to work part-time at the hospital. She'd said it was because she wanted to spend more time doing what she loved—photography. But he realized he'd never seen her with a camera.

He tried to put his uneasiness about the woman aside, telling himself he and his suspicious nature made him his own worst enemy.

"Hope you're hungry," she said, giving him a smile that promised more than dinner.

"I am. It smells wonderful," he said as he followed her toward the kitchen, stopping to study a photograph on the wall. A self-portrait of Abigail? If so, she was much younger. Her gaze was lowered almost coyishly, her smile tentative. A younger sister possibly? "Is this you?"

"A friend took it a long time ago. I don't have any of mine up yet," she said from the kitchen.

He found himself staring at the photograph, trying to figure out what it was about the shot that bothered him. Maybe everything about Abigail Creed unsettled him for a reason. A nurse and an aspiring professional photographer, if true, Abigail was multitalented. So *again*, what was she doing in Powder Crossing? Also, it seemed strange that the only photo on her wall was taken of her by someone else.

But maybe what he found more unsettling was why she seemed interested in him. A small-town sheriff who'd lived his whole life here, who'd followed in his father's footsteps right into the sheriff position. Hell, he even lived in the house he'd grown up in only blocks away from here. The farthest he'd ranged from Powder Crossing was when he went to the state police academy.

Abigail handed him a glass of wine. "Dinner will be ready soon. Make yourself comfortable."

"I was just admiring your place." He moved back to the living room. There were no photographs of friends or family. With a start, he realized that there was nothing personal at all.

He reminded himself that she hadn't been in town all that long. But it had been months. Maybe she hadn't had time to put up more than the one photograph taken by a friend.

He continued around the living room, out of sight from the kitchen and Abigail. It was the first time he'd been in her house. The other times they'd either gone out or she'd brought dinner to him at the office when he'd worked late.

Other than the one photograph, there was no others anywhere in her house. He opened a door quietly, peered into her bedroom and noticed the same thing. No photos of family or friends. No knickknacks. No mementos at all. She'd always been vague when asked where she was from.

"I've lived all over. My family traveled a lot. It must have gotten into my blood." She was just as vague as to why she'd come to Powder Crossing. She'd said a job had opened up and she wanted to shoot some photographs of the area, not knowing how long she planned to stay. Maybe that was all it was.

The house was small, so it didn't take long to check out everything, including the bathroom, before he returned to the kitchen. In her medicine cabinet, he found no prescription drugs. Not much of anything. It gave him the feeling she wasn't planning to stay here long.

At dinner, she quizzed him about his work, knowing full well that he couldn't talk about any ongoing cases. "I would think murder is rare here," she said between bites. "Can't you at least tell me about one of your closed cases?"

He chuckled and said, "I'd rather hear more about you."

"Nothing really to tell. What you see is what you get." She let that hang in the air as she met his gaze with what again appeared to be a promise of something to come.

They had more wine after dinner and a chocolate mousse that left an aftertaste before they moved into the living room to the couch. She spent time looking for a movie on the television that she thought he might like before cuddling up next to him.

He felt the weight of the long day settle over him. Charlotte Stafford had been seen driving through town in a van with her son CJ in the front. Another rumor had been circulating that an out-of-town carpenter had been out at the Stafford Ranch doing some work. Everyone was curious about CJ and whether or not he would ever serve a day in jail for shooting his sister—even accidentally—and if he was walking or not.

Stu realized he was having trouble following the movie Abigail had found. The smell of her perfume was making him a little nauseated. He told himself he should go home and get some rest. It was his last thought before he fell into a bottomless sleep.

CHAPTER THREE

DUFFY WASN'T ONE to read a room well, but he thought he'd picked up a strange vibe when he'd found Pickett and Oakley in the hallway after the meeting. They'd seemed to be in deep conversation, standing so close that for a moment...

He shook his head as they walked out to her pickup. Pickett often joked around with Oakley—just like Duffy did—but the ranch hand had never made a move on her—at least not one that Duffy knew of. Pickett liked her. What wasn't to like about Oakley? Pickett, like Duffy, might even wish there could be something between them.

He glanced at the two of them. They were awfully quiet, neither looking at the other. Duffy couldn't see the two of them being anything more than friends, could he? Was there reason to be concerned?

"So what's the big news?" Oakley asked once they were in her pickup and on the road.

He'd been surprised minutes before when Pickett had stopped to kick snow off his boots and let him sit in the middle next to her without even pretending to wrestle him for the spot. He told himself he was only imaging the tension in the pickup. Sexual tension?

"Douglas Burton, the head of CH4, is coming to

Powder Crossing to demand that something is done to stop the vandalisms," he said, getting down to business. It was what had bonded the three of them together as adults. "There is a good chance he'll be bringing security, according to the speaker at the meeting. A pair of hired thugs named Frankie and Norman Lees, brothers, got into trouble down in Wyoming because of their propensity for violence. They stake out drilling equipment at sites and put vandals in the hospital or worse."

"That sounds like a scare tactic," Oakley said, shaking her head. "If they were actually killing people, we'd know about it."

"Would we?" Duffy asked. "Apparently, down in Wyoming some of the agitators were bought off. Others just disappeared and were never heard from again."

"I don't think we should underestimate the danger," Pickett said, quickly agreeing with him.

"So what are you saying? That we let my mother put in another well without a fight?" she demanded.

"Maybe we should lay low, at least until the head of CH4 is gone," Pickett suggested.

"And if there isn't time to lay low?" she asked, leaning around Duffy to look at the ranch hand. She sounded disappointed that he would even suggest such a thing.

"Sounds like we need to do what we have to do, but maybe you stay out of it, Oakley," Duffy said.

"I hope at least one of you knows that isn't going to happen." Oakley shot a look past him again at the ranch hand as she drove. Pickett was shaking his head as if afraid that whatever he said right now would get him into hot water.

Definitely a strange vibe, Duffy told himself. "Then

we make sure nothing happens to you," he said, study-ing Oakley. Her long blond hair hung in a single braid, her green eyes were narrowed and her face was flushed. From anger or something else? She gripped the wheel, her fingers tight around it as if she was strangling some-one. Or was there something else she was fighting? He leaned forward a little to look at her face in the faint light from the dashboard. There were tears in her green eyes.

What the hell? he thought and glanced at Pickett, who had leaned back, drawing his Stetson down over his eyes as if planning to sleep the whole way back to Powder Crossing.

Duffy wasn't sure what had happened out in that hallway between Oakley and Pickett, but it had him worried—and not just about their friendship.

Pickett Hanson mentally kicked himself. Standing out in the hallway earlier, he'd had his chance. He'd looked into those amazing green eyes of Oakley's, convinced that she was feeling something, too. They'd been friends for so long, he never wanted to lose that, and yet he wanted so much more.

It had been hell making small talk when all he could think about was taking her in his arms and kissing her. Just the thought was terrifying. He had no idea how she would react, let alone if she would respond in kind.

For a few minutes, before the meeting broke up, he'd felt as if there was a connection. He'd started to… What had he started to say, to do? Wouldn't the place to start have been to ask her out?

He prided himself for not being afraid of most anything. He loved trick riding and had been thrown into the dirt many times, but he'd always gotten back up. Asking a girl out had never been one of his problems.

But this was Oakley and he wanted this more than he'd ever wanted anything. There was so much he needed to tell her and that was the problem. He feared that once she knew the truth… He could lose everything.

He rode the rest of the way to Powder Crossing worrying about her. He hadn't gotten her involved with Dirty Business. But he also hadn't stopped her once she had. If anything, she'd been surprised he was one of the early members.

"I never expected to see you here," Oakley had said that first meeting. "You're so easygoing, so fun and funny. I didn't think you took anything seriously."

"It's my cover," he'd joked. "You know mild-mannered ranch hand by day, crime fighter at night." But he'd seen the way she'd looked at him differently after that. He'd laughed to himself since he'd had a crush on her since he'd come to work at the McKenna Ranch. Back then, the three years' difference in their ages had seemed like a lot. It no longer did.

Oakley had been just as surprised that Duffy McKenna had joined the subversive group. The three of them had been inseparable from the time Pickett had come to the ranch. But they'd grown apart until Dirty Business had thrown them together again. Before that they hadn't even shared how they'd felt about the drilling. Neither man wanted to put Oakley into danger.

Since joining Dirty Business, the three had spent more time together, going for beers after the secret meetings, talking about what they could do to change the world and sharing stories and laughs. They'd played off each other's senses of humor and become even closer friends. The old trio back together.

Pickett wasn't fool enough not to see that aside from joking around, his good friend Duffy was interested in Oakley as well. If push came to shove, of course she would choose Duffy over a McKenna ranch hand, Pickett told himself. Also, he hated the thought that if he even asked Oakley out, it could cause a rift between him and his best friend.

He didn't want that, but the more time he spent with Oakley, the more he found himself wanting something way beyond just friendship. But that would mean being forced to tell her things he'd kept secret for years—all the years he'd been at the McKenna Ranch. So much time had gone by with him hiding the truth, he feared how she would take it.

When she'd been shot, he'd been terrified that he would lose her without ever telling her how he felt, let alone the truth about himself. Still, he'd held his tongue, praying she would pull through and blaming himself, fearing her shooting had something to do with Dirty Business. He'd had to go to the small local hospital at night when her mother wasn't there. He would sit by her bedside. The town and the hospital were small enough that visiting hours were never observed in Powder Crossing anyway. But he also knew whoever was working and they would let him in. All he could do was hold her hand and pray that she would survive, and she had.

That her own brother had shot her had come as a

shock. He was still confused as to why CJ had taken the shot at her in the first place. CJ, his mother's favorite, had always been a cocky hothead who got the run of the ranch. But this time, he'd gone too far. Some were saying that he got what he had coming to him. Pickett wasn't that charitable. He had little regard for the cowboy. CJ could have killed Oakley.

Pickett had run across him a few times over the years and found him to be a bully and blowhard. After CJ had shot Oakley, Pickett hoped they didn't cross paths. He would be tempted to take things into his own hands, even if CJ was her brother. While he had no desire to go to prison, he and Duffy had kicked around ideas about what to do with CJ's body.

He smiled at the memory and thoughts of his good friend. Because of that, Duffy was another problem. How serious he was about Oakley was anyone's guess. Duffy was a McKenna, not that Oakley would let that stop her if she fell for the rancher, while Pickett was a ranch hand, a ranch hand with a secret.

All total, he knew he should rein in his heart. He chuckled at the thought. His foolish heart had gone rogue and was now running free having taken off with abandon. No amount of reason was going to change that. He couldn't stay away from Oakley. Just as he couldn't let anything happen to her.

The problem was how to save her from herself—let alone keep her safe from what he knew was coming. Not only was she determined to stop her mother and CJ from drilling another coalbed methane well on the Stafford Ranch, but she was just as determined to find out why CJ had shot her and see that he paid for it.

Either way, Pickett feared it could get her killed, since like her, he also thought CJ was lying about why he'd shot her. CJ and his mother would have had to have been living under a rock not to know about Oakley's friendship with both him and Duffy as kids.

What had made CJ take that shot? Maybe it was the fact that the three of them had resumed that friendship more often lately, but Pickett doubted that. It seemed more reasonable that what Oakley had seen that day was the meth lab running at the old homestead over the mountain where she'd ridden her horse.

But had she also seen CJ and known he was involved? Was that what had him worried she would remember?

Unfortunately, the lab had been destroyed by whoever had been running it before the sheriff could get any evidence out, and Oakley hadn't remembered so she couldn't put CJ at the lab. Which meant that CJ was going to get away with whatever he'd been up to—along with the shooting.

Unless Oakley remembered.

CJ must be worried about that, which worried Pickett even more.

THE DRIVE HOME seemed longer tonight, Oakley thought. Or maybe it just felt that way because she was so unsettled.

"I hate to ask," Pickett said as they neared Powder Crossing where they'd left their rigs. "You have a plan, Oakley? One that you haven't shared with us?"

After what had almost happened in the hallway, she was more aware of him than ever. She still hated that

the meeting had let out before she'd gotten to find out
what he was going to say, let alone do. She couldn't help
feeling disappointed.

She drove for a few moments without answering
since she knew neither Pickett nor Duffy was going to
approve, maybe especially Pickett. He'd been opposed
to doing anything that could get them thrown in jail.

"I'll do whatever I have to to keep them from drilling on Stafford Ranch," she said.

"That does not sound like a plan," Pickett pointed
out.

"I'm with Oakley," Duffy said. "We have to draw
a line in the sand. Seems like the place to start would
be to stop this new well." Duffy was always up for dis-
abling the equipment as a way to protest the drilling.
He'd become quite good at it.

She could feel Pickett's gaze on her as she drove. Just
as she could almost hear his disapproval without him
saying a word. He didn't understand that there was no
getting through to CJ and her mother. She knew it was
a desperate move, what she was planning to do. So desperate that she had no intention of telling either of them.

Maybe it wouldn't stop the drilling, but it would certainly make her intensions clear to her mother. It might
also make the gas company realize that it was too costly
for them to do business in this river basin before they
destroyed it.

Not that she was taking this lightly. She could get
arrested. Or worse, killed, she thought with a shudder.

"Can we talk about it at least?" Pickett asked. "Whatever you have planned, I want to know about it. Promise you won't go rogue on me and not let me know."

She smiled over at him and felt warmth rush through her. *Oh, Pickett,* she thought and then looked at Duffy, shaken by how much she loved both of these cowboys. She quickly turned back to her driving.

CHAPTER FOUR

THE NEXT MORNING Oakley drove toward the Stafford Ranch through shafts of sunlight, her mind pinballing from her mother and CJ to Pickett last night in the hallway.

After returning from Miles City, Duffy had suggested that they pick up some beer and do what they usually did after a Dirty Business meeting. They would go out to the old water tower to talk and drink. Like it had been when they were younger, it was their favorite spot to kick back, dangle their legs over the walkway ledge and enjoy the privacy as well as the view.

They'd been doing this for years, but last night Pickett had begged off and so had Oakley. Usually, their bravery and determination would be buoyed by the alcohol, making it easy to agree that they had to keep fighting the gas company even though they all knew it could get them thrown in jail—if not killed—but that they weren't going to let that stop them.

Last night it appeared that none of them was feeling it, except for Duffy. It was late enough that Oakley didn't feel like driving back to the ranch, so she'd crashed at a friend's house in town. She needed sleep in order to be ready to face her mother and CJ, but she couldn't help replaying those moments in the hallway with Pickett. She hadn't imagined that look in his eyes right before the meeting had broken up, had she? Would he have kissed her?

Those thoughts were enough to steal her sleep. She'd awakened this morning frustrated, aching to know what might have happened if the meeting had run just a little longer and she'd found out whatever it was Pickett had been about to do or say.

That was the worst part. Not knowing. Maybe it had been nothing. A spur of the moment mistake. Whatever it was, would it happen again? Only if she and Pickett were alone.

As she drove to the ranch, she tried to prepare herself. She knew that she couldn't put off the family reunion any longer. Tilly was in Oregon with Cooper. That left her brothers Brand and Ryder, who, if she knew them, which of course she did, would have gotten up early and headed out to mend fence or move cattle to avoid both their mother and CJ.

She didn't blame them. She had often done that growing up as well, but after her mother's message, she knew postponing this would be futile. Anyway, she was anxious to know what was going on with her mother. This morning she would test the waters, all the while trying to keep from alienating either her mother or CJ. She needed to bide her time before she confronted her brother—without her mother around.

After parking, she headed for the house, a little concerned. If her worst fears were correct, then CJ had tried to kill her once. What would stop him from trying again to make sure she never remembered what had happened before he shot her?

There were new wooden ramps going into the house and a van parked out front. It appeared CJ wasn't walking yet—if ever again. Not that her brother wouldn't be dangerous—even in a wheelchair.

"Where have you been?" her mother demanded the moment Oakley walked into the house. She had started for the stairs, hoping to at least get a shower and change of clothes before what she knew would be a confrontation with her mother—if not her brother. "I thought after I left you a message, you would be here when we got home."

She stopped on the lower stairs and turned back. "I spent the night at Amy's. I wasn't sure you'd be home yet. You didn't mention what time you would be arriving." She could feel her mother's gaze on her.

Charlotte was still a beautiful woman with her long blond hair that looked grayer than Oakley remembered. Her mother wore it in a no-nonsense plait that was most often wound at the nape of her neck. Her eyes, like her daughter's, were a deep emerald green, darker in anger, like right now.

"Welcome home," Oakley said as cheerfully as she could manage. In truth, it had been nice having both her mother and CJ gone from the ranch. Things had run smoothly thanks to Tilly and their brothers. It had been almost peaceful except that they'd all known it was temporary.

She waited a few moments for her mother to ask how she was doing, if she'd healed from the gunshot that had almost killed her. But even as she waited, she knew all her mother's concerns were elsewhere. "Nice new ramps out front." If she'd had any questions about her brother's health, she no longer did. "Where's CJ?"

"He's going to be staying in the guest room on this level. We need to discuss a few things."

Oakley knew what that meant even before she heard the creak of a wheelchair coming down the hallway. She braced herself, knowing that nothing could prepare her for seeing her brother again. He'd told Tilly that shooting her had been an accident, a stupid impulsive act. That his horse shied when he'd fired a warning shot at her.

But as he wheeled down the hallway, she met his gaze and knew the truth. Her mouth went dry, her chest pressed against her lungs, stealing her breath. He hadn't misfired, just as she'd suspected. He'd tried to kill her. Why?

She had to find out before he tried again.

THE SHERIFF WOKE sprawled on an unfamiliar couch in a state of mental confusion. Through the thick fog filling his brain, he looked around at the unfamiliar setting. He wasn't sure where he was or how he'd gotten there. Then he saw the photograph, the single one on the wall. He was in Abigail's house.

"Abigail?" No answer. He tried to sit up, shocked that he'd fallen asleep on the couch fully dressed and even more concerned about how woozy he felt. He didn't normally drink wine, but he was sure he hadn't consumed more than half a glass.

He glanced at the time and felt even more confused. He'd slept all night on the couch? He remembered that look Abigail had given him after dinner. Had they made love? He didn't think so since he was still fully dressed. Only his boots had been removed. He grimaced as he stood, wobbly on his stocking feet, and saw that sunlight now streamed in through the nearby window. It was even later than he'd thought.

"Abigail?" His head ached and his mouth felt like a desert. He moved toward the door to her bedroom, pushed the door open and saw that her bed was made. Either she'd gotten up early and left or hadn't slept there at all.

There was no sign of her in the rest of the small house. His brain felt fuzzy, his thoughts random and hard to rein in. Back at the couch he put on his boots, thinking that she must have gotten called into work at the hospital.

As he finished pulling on his boots and started to rise again, he considered leaving a note, still shocked that he'd fallen asleep and slept through the entire night. Also a little surprised that he hadn't found a note from Abigail. She must be furious with him for falling asleep last night.

He needed to call her. No, maybe he'd call her later when things felt clearer, he told himself. As he started for the door, he reached into his pocket and realized his keys weren't there.

He turned back to the couch, thinking they must have fallen out. He spotted his keys glittering in the sunlight from where they lay on the end table at the far end of the couch.

Stu walked slowly toward them. The fuzz in his brain shifting to let a clear thought squeeze past. Had they fallen out of his pocket? Or had Abigail taken his keys from his pocket? Why would she go to the trouble to put them on the table at her end of the couch?

As he picked up his keys, he caught a scent that made him draw the keys to his nose. There was more than a hint of her perfume on them. He hadn't smelled her perfume on his clothing—just on his keys. Something felt all wrong. Red flags were going off everywhere, especially in the less groggy part of his brain.

His last memory was falling asleep at the beginning of the movie. He'd been tired, but not that tired. He swallowed, his mouth still dry, but this time he tasted something familiar. Chalky chocolate mousse.

His heartrate jumped into high speed. What the hell had happened last night?

OAKLEY HAD TROUBLE even looking at her brother and not giving away the turmoil raging inside her. If anything, CJ looked more imposing, as if he'd been doing upper body workouts. She'd thought the result of his pickup rollover while fleeing the law might have humbled him a little. But CJ wasn't one for introspection, never had been. If anything, he seemed angrier now, as if everything that had happened was Oakley's fault.

"As you can see, there are going to be some changes around here," her mother was saying, drawing Oakley's attention thankfully away from her brother. Seeing what she had in his expression had made her shudder inwardly while at the same time, making her want to go for his throat for what he'd done to her. She was relieved not to have to look at him.

"The ramps are temporary," her mother was saying. "I want your brother to be able to come and go at will.

The van is retrofitted for his wheelchair. I'm sure he won't have to use it for very long."

"Is that what the doctor said?" Oakley asked.

Her mother glared at her. "The doctor doesn't know. None of them know anything. Of course he will walk again. Never underestimate your brother."

"Oh, I don't," Oakley said, shooting him a look. Nor should he underestimate her, she hoped her look conveyed.

"One of the reasons I wanted to talk to you is that our lawyer needs you to make a statement for the record."

She felt a current of unease move through her at her mother's words. "A statement?"

"About the *accident*."

Oakley felt her stomach roil. "Accident?"

Her mother's look hardened. "Your brother's rifle went off. It was an unfortunate accident. He never meant to shoot at you and since you have no memory of that day…" Oakley could feel the heat of the gaze. "You haven't remembered anything, have you?" There was a note of worry in her mother's voice. She could feel both her mother and CJ waiting for an answer. Oakley was struck by the fact that it appeared neither of them wanted her to remember.

She glanced over at her brother again. He had his head down, but she knew he was watching her out of the corner of his eye, waiting to hear what she had to say. "No, I can't remember any of it." She saw relief loosen the tension in CJ's shoulders.

As his head came up, she was even more convinced there was something he definitely didn't want her to recall.

CHAPTER FIVE

HOLDEN MCKENNA RAKED a hand through his hair as his eldest son stormed out of the dining room. He and Treyton had gotten into the same old argument at breakfast; the last of his son's words had trailed after him as he slammed out the front door.

You're so clueless, so completely ill equipped for these times, you have no business running this ranch, old man.

The ranch head housekeeper and cook, and Holden's closest confidante, came into the room as Treyton's words died away. Elaine was a small, slim woman with bright blue eyes and a cheerful demeanor, who was close to his own age. He didn't know what he would do without her and her usual sage advice.

But right now, sitting here at the large dining room table alone, he felt the heat of embarrassment rise to his face knowing that she'd overheard what Treyton had said. *Old man.* At almost fifty-six, he often felt old. Maybe he was clueless as well. He definitely felt ill equipped at times, especially when it came to dealing with his family.

He glanced at Elaine as she began to clear away the dishes from the big ranch table and saw that her face was tight with fury.

"Don't listen to him," she said, anger making her bite out the words. "He doesn't know what he's talking about."

"Doesn't he?" Holden wasn't so sure.

"There is nothing wrong with you or your judgment," she assured him. "Someone just needs to knock Treyton down to size." As furious as she was, the slight good-tempered cook looked as if she would be happy to do the job.

He smiled in spite of the sick feeling he had after the argument with his son. "I'm sorry you had to hear that."

She waved his comment away. "I'm sorry your son is such a jackass."

At a knock at the front door, she'd scurried away with the dirty dishes, and he'd pushed himself up to answer it. Standing on his doorstep was a large man with an unmemorable face and buzz-cut gray hair. "Can I help you?"

"Holden McKenna? Jason Murdock. If you have a minute…"

"What is this about?"

"I'm a private investigator. I've been hired to look into Dixon Malone's disappearance."

Holden had heard rumors about a PI asking questions around town about Dixon. But it had been years since Charlotte's second husband had disappeared. Why now?

"I'm afraid I wouldn't be of much help. I didn't know the man," he said, uninclined to let the PI past the doorstep.

"I promise not to take much of your time. I understand you have a Malone working for you as a ranch hand. Rusty Malone?"

Holden saw that the man wasn't going to give up. Maybe it would be best to nip this in the bud now before the PI talked to Rusty. Unfortunately, Rusty believed every conspiracy theory he'd ever heard and often made up a few. Who knew what the ranch hand might tell this man. "Please come in. I'll help any way I can." But he didn't offer the man a seat, preferring to stand in the hopes this would be short.

His thoughts went to Charlotte and were quickly accompanied by that old ache of regret. He hated that this PI would bring back a time in her past that she, like him, wanted to forget. They'd both jumped into second marriages after losing their spouses—both living to regret it.

He blamed himself for hurting Lottie, as he'd fondly called her, years ago when they were teenagers. Even now, after breaking her heart and his own by marrying someone else all those years ago, he still wanted to protect her. But he couldn't any more than he could protect his own heart from the pain of his past mistakes.

"Like I said, I can't imagine how I could be of help," Holden said, shifting impatiently on his feet. "Rusty Malone is a distant shirttail relative of Dixon's. The two never even met. Rusty lived in Texas, coming to work for us long after Dixon left."

"What makes you think Dixon left?" Murdock asked, pulling out his notebook and pen and looking expectantly at him.

"I heard he left in the middle of the night."

"After an argument with his wife, Charlotte," the PI supplied.

"I wouldn't know about that. I heard that he was

seen in town at the bar saying it was over and that he was leaving town."

Murdock nodded. "All hearsay. I can't seem to find anyone who actually saw him drive out of town. Who's to say that he didn't go back to the ranch that night?"

"Charlotte Stafford," he said without hesitation. "I understand she never saw him again after he left the first time."

"One dead husband. Another one disappears?" He raised a brow. "Some might find that suspicious."

"People do sometimes die. I find nothing suspicious about it." Then he added, "I lost my wife some years ago."

"You don't think it's suspicious that Dixon Malone was never heard from again? While I believe your ex is alive and living in Miles City."

Don't remind me, Holden thought as Murdock considered his notes for a moment and said, "Lulabelle Braden McKenna. She didn't disappear."

Lulabelle wouldn't disappear for love nor money. She planned to stick around just close enough to drop by occasionally to remind him of what a fool he'd been.

"I believe Dixon was the kind of man to disappear. More than likely he changed his name and has a whole different life."

Murdock eyed him. "I thought you didn't know Dixon."

"It's a small community. I heard rumors. But I'm curious. Who hired you to find him after all this time? Someone he owes money to? Or another wife he ran out on?"

"Actually, his daughter, Birdie Malone… I see from your surprise you weren't aware he had a daughter."

He shouldn't have been surprised. "I've always suspected he had a past he was probably running from. But I do wonder why this daughter is interested in finding him now. Clearly, he ran out on her as well." He narrowed his eyes at the PI. "I'm also curious why you so readily supplied the name of your client."

"It's no secret. She doesn't mind people knowing that she hired me. Birdie came into some money and was finally able to afford a private investigator to look into her father's alleged disappearance. She's never believed that he left the Powder River Basin."

Holden wondered about the woman and how she'd come into money. "Are you sure her father wasn't the one to give her the money?"

"Grandmother left it to her."

Holden wanted to ask if the PI knew that for a fact, but asked instead, "How old is this daughter?"

"Twenty-five."

"So she was a child when Dixon left her—and his wife."

"They were never officially married," the PI said. "Birdie took her father's last name."

"Look, Mr. Murdock, it seems clear to me what kind of man Dixon Malone was. I seriously doubt he's changed over the years." Holden walked to the door. "I'm afraid that's all the time I can give you since all I know about him is like you said, hearsay. Fortunately, I never spent any time around him."

The PI slowly put away his notebook and pen.

"Thank you for your time. I'm looking forward to speaking with Charlotte Stafford."

"I doubt his ex knows anything that—"

"Not ex. Charlotte might have gone back to using her first husband's name, but she and Dixon are still married. The marriage was never legally terminated. Don't you think it's odd that she never tried to divorce him or have him declared legally dead?"

"Not if she never planned to marry again."

"Also, she went back to her first husband's name quite quickly after he allegedly left. But you wouldn't know anything about that, either, right?"

Holden smiled. "I'm sure you heard in town that Charlotte and I are rival landowners who don't share confidences. But I suspect she wanted to put that particular mistake behind her."

"Not just rival ranch owners," Murdock said with a chuckle. "Former young lovers, I believe is what I was told about you and Charlotte. You married someone else, broke her heart and she promised to hate you forever. Nothing like a woman scorned, I believe people in the area say. Seems they blame you for making her into the kind of woman she is today."

His first impulse was to take offense, to defend Lottie, the lover he betrayed and never got over. But he held his tongue, seeing that the PI was trying to get a rise out of him. "Let me show you to the door."

Even as he did, though, he hated to think of what people in this river basin said about him and Lottie. Worse, this man was headed for the Stafford Ranch. "I doubt you'll find Charlotte at home. You might have heard about her son's injuries—"

"I guess you haven't heard. She's returned with her son."

"That doesn't mean she'll want to talk to you about old history," he said.

Murdock smiled. "No, I'm sure she won't, especially if she has something to hide." His smile said that wouldn't stop him. "Interesting, the way you're trying to protect her." Holden began to close the door on the man, forcing him to move.

The moment the door shut, he was tempted to call and warn Charlotte. But good sense stopped him. It would be humiliating enough for her without him calling to make it worse. Sometimes he felt helpless. Maybe Treyton was right. Maybe he was too old and useless to be running the ranch.

As he looked up, Holly Jo came clunking down the stairs dressed in a skimpy top, jeans and pink cowboy boots. Her jeans appeared to have been in a dogfight. "Where do you think you're going dressed like that?" he demanded of his new ward.

Twelve going on thirty, she had moved in last summer after he'd promised her mother years ago that if anything happened to her, he would take care of the girl. It was a promise he'd been bound and determined to keep—even if he hadn't been prepared to raise another child this late in life—especially this headstrong almost-teenager. She had turned out to be tougher to rein in than he recalled it had been raising his daughter, Bailey.

"I'm going to…school," Holly Jo said, giving him her famous "are you dense" look. "You do know I go to school, right?"

"Attitude," Elaine warned as she came into the room.

Holly Jo sighed. "Tell him that this is the way all of the kids dress nowadays."

Elaine groaned. "I'm afraid it's true, though since it's still December I'd suggest changing the top." Holden motioned for her to go back up to her room and change. He nodded to Elaine, thankful for her help. Holly Jo listened to Elaine, as well as Cooper and Duffy, more than she did to him.

It was one reason he hoped Cooper would stay on the ranch after he married Tilly Stafford. But he could understand if he wanted to build his own house at some point. So far it was undecided where they would live since Tilly hadn't yet told her mother about the engagement. Holden feared how that would go. He hated to think of the trouble Charlotte might make for Cooper and Tilly because of her hatred for him.

"I thought you were cooler than this," the girl called back down the stairs to Elaine before going into her bedroom and slamming the door. She wasn't in there a minute before her door opened and she yelled, "Don't forget, Holden, you promised I could redo my room." With that, she slammed her bedroom door again. The next time it opened, she'd put on a sweater and now came down the stairs, stomping loudly the entire way. Without a word, she grabbed her coat and disappeared through the front door for the walk to the bus stop.

He shook his head as he looked at his housekeeper. "Never a dull moment."

"No," Elaine agreed. "But I like having her here," she said, smiling.

"I do, too," Holden agreed. "Join me for a cup of coffee?"

Elaine sat down as if she could tell something else was bothering him.

"It's Treyton," he said. "I think he might try to go behind my back on more than methane well drilling on the ranch." She didn't look surprised. His worry over his children and ward was growing daily. Treyton had always been a difficult child, resentful of his siblings, always afraid he wasn't getting as much attention or possessions or responsibility as the others. He especially resented Cooper and always had.

Cooper's return to the ranch after being gone two years seemed to have made Treyton even more resentful. Holden worried how far Treyton would go in his desire not only to take over the ranch, but also to show up Cooper—and his father. His brother Duffy had never been a threat since Holden's youngest son seemed to have no interest in ever running the ranch.

"I'm sorry, Holden," Elaine said. "I hate to see you so worried. But Cooper and Tilly will soon be getting married. You have a wedding coming up to think about instead of worrying about Treyton."

He chuckled. "If there even is a wedding now that Charlotte has returned."

ALREADY LATE FOR WORK, the sheriff started to leave Abigail's house, but stopped before reaching the door as a thought struck him. He felt woozy, the taste in his mouth making him feel sick to his stomach. He stood for a moment, trying to collect his thoughts in the fog still whirling in his head.

One thought broke through. It wasn't that he'd drunk too much wine.

He turned back to the kitchen thinking about the chocolate mousse and that chalky taste. He'd eaten it all at Abigail's urging. She'd said she'd never made it before but had made it special for him, making it impossible to leave a bite.

Stu hated the path his thoughts were now taking, but the lawman in him made him return to the kitchen in hopes of finding his dirty dish in the sink. He recalled her saying she would do the dishes in the morning and ushering him into the living room after he'd helped clean off the table.

But in the kitchen now, he saw with regret that the sink was empty. When he opened the dishwasher, he saw that it had been run. She'd cleaned up everything. There was no proof to go with his growing suspicion. On top of that, it made no sense. Why would she drug him if that was really what he thought she'd done?

His cell phone rang. He fumbled it out of his pocket. "Sheriff Layton." The moment he answered, he regretted not checking the screen before he picked up. He wasn't ready to talk to Abigail. He needed a clearer head before he did.

Fortunately, it wasn't her.

"Those damn vandals hit another of our drilling rigs last night, Sheriff," Tick Whitaker snapped. Alfred "Tick" Whitaker was a geologist from Texas. Stu had always suspected the man was more invested in the CH4 gas company than he let on.

"Give me the location. I'll send a deputy out to photograph the damage."

"The head of the company, Douglas Burton, is flying in this morning. Howie's gone to pick him up along with several of his security personnel. He wants to meet with you at one this afternoon."

It didn't sound like a request, but Stu didn't feel like arguing. "Fine. You know where my office is." He disconnected and started for the door when he noticed a calendar on the kitchen wall by a small desk. Abigail had marked the days she was working this week. She was off today. So where had she gone so early?

If she wasn't at the hospital, where had she gone? Either way, he was going by the lab to get a workup of whatever might be in his bloodstream. He wanted to find out before he met with the gas company executive and his associates—let alone dealt with Abigail Creed.

CJ GRIPPED THE arms of the wheelchair. He'd hoped that Oakley wouldn't be a problem, that their mother could keep her in line. He'd watched her, studying her. He could understand her anger. That wasn't a concern. He was angrier with her than she was with him; that he knew for certain. This was all her fault. Their mother was convinced that Oakley would do whatever she told her to do. Once she talked to the lawyer and agreed that the shooting had been an accident...

But when he'd looked into his sister's eyes, he'd seen the truth.

Oakley was starting to remember. He could see it in the way she looked at him. How long before she remembered everything? How long before she brought him down, sent him to prison, took from him the one thing he would kill for—the power and money their mother wielded? One day it would be all his.

But only if his sister didn't remember.

She and their mother were glaring at each other in a standoff. He felt sick to his stomach as he focused on his sister. Oakley was a ticking time bomb. She could remember and go off at any time. Hadn't the doctor said she probably would never remember those lost forty-eight hours because of the concussion after falling from her horse on the hard-pack of the road—after he'd shot her?

But there was always a chance, the doctor had said, that her memory might return. And that was the hell CJ had been living with, was still living with, waiting for the explosion that would destroy his life.

He blamed her for all of it, especially the pickup accident that had him in this wheelchair. He wouldn't have been running from the law if she hadn't butted into his business and he'd had to shoot her. She'd brought it on herself. He'd warned her to stay out of his business.

The only thing he regretted was that his aim had been off. At least dead, she would never have been able to tell what she'd seen that day and he wouldn't be waiting and worrying about her remembering.

Oakley had always been a pain, even when they were kids, he thought as he tuned out his mother and Oakley arguing. She was the one who stood up to him, tattled on him, fought him at every turn. Their younger brothers, Brand and Ryder, were smart enough to stay out of his way. Tilly had tried to mother him for a while, but had lost interest when he wasn't the sweet boy she'd thought he was.

Speaking of Tilly, he thought as a vehicle pulled up outside. "Well, look who's here," CJ said, making both his mother and Oakley turn to look. Another traitor. It amused him that Tilly was about to fall from grace. Once their mother heard what she'd been up to, getting engaged to Cooper McKenna, that would be the last of her. Another burr under his saddle would be gone from the ranch.

He glanced at Oakley, who had moved to the window to peer out. *You're next*. Soon, both sisters would be out of this house. He still needed Brand and Ryder to work the ranch, but Tilly and Oakley wouldn't be missed.

CHAPTER SIX

Oakley saw her sister pull up in one of the ranch trucks. She couldn't be already back from Oregon, could she? She must have changed her mind and not gone for some reason. Oakley watched as their ranch manager, Boyle Wilson, came out of the barn with two ranch hands to help unload the supplies Tilly had brought from town.

As her sister started for the house, Oakley saw her look at the van parked out front, then at the ramps up the front of the house. Their mother thought they were temporary, but Oakley couldn't help wondering if even her mother's determination could make CJ ever walk again.

She realized that Tilly could have been told about their mother and CJ arriving today. Which meant that their mother must have sent her a summons as well. Which meant that their mother already knew about the engagement. As her sister approached, Oakley saw her hesitate. Had Tilly had time to prepare for their mother's and CJ's return? Like her, Tilly must have conflicting feelings toward their brother. He'd almost killed her, too.

"I thought you were anxious to go change?" her mother said, suddenly beside Oakley.

Not a chance, she thought. Tilly was going to need all the support she could get. Oakley didn't move.

Her mother's voice grew sharper. "I said—"

"I heard you." She stepped to open the door, giving her sister a warning look. Oakley saw that Tilly was wearing the engagement ring Cooper McKenna had given her. Given the way Charlotte hated Holden McKenna, Oakley was worried for her sister.

"Mother and CJ are back," she said as if Tilly hadn't already heard, let alone figured that out. She saw trepidation in her sister's features for a moment before she straightened her back and determination took its place.

"Oakley was just leaving to go upstairs to change," her mother said from behind her. "She's done enough damage to this family."

Oakley spun around. "You aren't seriously blaming me for what CJ did, are you?"

"Your brother would have never been there, never had his rifle misfire, if you hadn't been on the McKenna Ranch," her mother said, green eyes hard with anger. "Your brother wouldn't be in that wheelchair, facing possible jail time. You brought this on our family."

Oakley had promised herself that she was going to bide her time. She didn't want to show her true intentions. She'd been determined not to let her mother or brother know that she wasn't taking this lying down.

But all that changed in an instant. Her mother had always made excuses for CJ. Not this time. "This is probably a good time to tell you that I intend to find out the truth," Oakley said, looking past her mother to where CJ sat looking smug. "I'm going to find out why CJ really shot me—I know it wasn't an accident, except for the part where he missed and didn't kill me—and when I do, your precious son is going to prison."

"That's enough. Either go upstairs or leave," her mother said. "I need to speak to your sister alone."

"It's okay, Oakley," Tilly said. "I need to talk to Mother."

Oakley feared for her sister. Big sister Tilly liked to believe that she could handle anything. She also liked to believe that there was good in everyone. Oakley knew better as she let her gaze move from her mother to CJ. She pointed her finger at him and mouthed, "I'm coming for you." He paled, that smug look gone.

She turned toward the door, not wanting to spend another moment in this house for fear of what she would do. "I'll borrow something to wear from Amy when I get to town," she said over her shoulder. As she passed her sister, she squeezed her arm. "Good luck. Call if you need me."

"You aren't seriously suggesting that Oakley is responsible for her own shooting," Tilly said as Oakley left and she turned to her mother. "Remember he almost killed me, too, when he took me hostage and rolled the truck."

Her mother waved away her words as if they were pesty flies. "That's all water under the bridge. We have other matters to discuss. CJ, please leave us."

He shot Tilly a self-righteous look that told her exactly how this discussion was going to go as he slowly turned and wheeled back down the hallway.

She felt her stomach roil as she looked at her seething mother. She had almost talked herself into believing that she could reason with her about the engagement and upcoming marriage. What had she been thinking? Clearly, she'd been daydreaming. That her mother blamed Oakley for getting shot and CJ getting injured told her exactly how this was going to go.

Tilly swallowed, determined to keep control of her emotions. She wouldn't let her mother get the better of her. She moved to hand her mother the ranch bill for the supplies she'd picked up in town.

Instead of taking the bill, her mother grabbed her left hand, twisting it painfully as she examined the engagement ring. "That's her ring, his mother's."

Tilly was surprised that she would recognize the ring as Margaret Smith's, the woman Holden had chosen over her mother—what had started this feud between the families all those years ago.

She flung Tilly's hand away. "I want you out of this house." Her mother seemed to be having trouble breathing.

"Aren't we even going to talk about this?" Tilly asked calmly.

"We talked about it. I told you to stay away from him. You didn't." Her mother started to turn away.

"I love Cooper. He isn't his father."

"He's a McKenna," her mother cried, spinning back around to glare at her. "They're responsible for all of this."

Tilly drew back, shaking her head. "I guess I see where CJ gets it, blaming everyone for his problems. Now the McKennas are responsible for CJ shooting Oakley and almost killing me?" Tilly couldn't hold back even as good sense warned her not to. "No, Mother, your hatred that you passed on to CJ is responsible for this. Aren't you sick of playing the woman scorned? It's over. Or are you still in love with Holden and that's why you can't bear the thought of me marrying his son?"

"I won't have you marrying one of them," her mother said, her voice shaking.

"You hate Holden McKenna that much?" Tilly asked. "Or it is that you love him that much? Either way, I feel incredibly sorry for you. I love Cooper and he loves me and we're not going to make the mistake the two of you made. We're getting married and as much as I love this ranch and believe I'm the one who should run it someday, I won't let you blackmail me into becoming you."

"Get out!" her mother screamed. "I never want to see you on this ranch again."

"I will as soon as I pack up my things."

"No, you won't. I'll have your things sent to the McKenna Ranch in the back of a cattle truck. You are no longer my daughter." She raised her voice dangerously as she advanced. "Get out!" She raised her arm as she approached Tilly.

Tilly saw that her mother intended to strike her, and she would have if not for the front door opening and a man stepping in calling out, "Hello? I knocked but you must not have heard me."

She saw her mother's stricken expression as the man took a few steps into the house. "Jason Murdock, private investigator. I've called a few times, left messages, but you never returned my calls." He stepped farther into the living room. "I decided to stop by so we could talk." He was smiling at her mother. "I'm looking for your missing husband, Dixon Malone."

All the color had drained from her mother's face. She lowered her arm, appearing to be struggling to breathe.

Using this interruption to her advantage, Tilly turned and headed up the stairs. "I'm going to get a few of my things."

Her mother was fighting to regain control in front of the PI as Tilly walked past her. "You'll regret this," her mother bit out under a ragged breath.

"So will you," she said and headed to her room. Her heart threatened to explode. She'd known what her mother was like. This shouldn't have come as a surprise. She'd known there was a chance it would come to this. Her mother's fury, though, had been far worse than she'd imagined. She'd known she would be angry but not this furious. She was throwing her daughter out, disowning her, taking away something that Tilly loved—the ranch.

She refused to cry as she began to pack her things. She didn't know where she was going. She would have to find a place to live until the wedding. She didn't want to move into the McKenna house until she and Cooper were married and while their house was being built.

Just the thought of the wedding made her eyes fill with tears. Had she really thought there would be one with a flowing white dress, the church crowded with family and friends? No, she and Cooper would have to elope, go to a justice of the peace, not have a proper wedding. It didn't matter, she told herself. All that mattered was that she would be with Cooper, the man she loved.

She packed what she could carry. Taking her suitcases out the back way, through her private entrance, she headed for her pickup, glad that after college, she'd earned money doing the books for other ranches so she could buy her own truck. Her mother had said it was a waste of money since they had ranch trucks for her to drive. Had Tilly intuited that one day she would need her own vehicle, her own money, because she couldn't stay here any longer?

She put her suitcases in the back and opened the driver's side door. As she did, she glanced back, taking one last look through her tears at the house that had been her home.

OAKLEY WAS WAITING down the road from the ranch for her sister. She was still shaken by what her mother had said to her. She couldn't even imagine what Charlotte had unleashed on her oldest daughter about the engagement to a McKenna. But she figured it wouldn't take long before Tilly would be coming down the road.

Just as she'd suspected, she spotted her sister's truck headed her way. That had been quick. Had their mother even let Tilly get some of her things? She felt her anger rising along with her determination to find out the truth and to stop her brother and her mother from destroying the family and the ranch because of their bitterness.

Oakley got out as Tilly pulled up behind her truck. She walked back. Her sister whirred down her window. "You okay?" she asked, even though she could see that her sister was devastated.

"She kicked me off the ranch," Tilly said between the sobs she was fighting so hard to hold back. "She said she never wanted to see me again."

"I'm so sorry." She reached in to pull her sister into a hug. Oakley figured it wouldn't be that long before she was in the same predicament.

"I can't believe anyone could be so…bitter, so…mean and hateful." Tilly took a ragged breath and let it out slowly. "Did you see that man who came to the house? If he hadn't walked in when he did, I think she would have hit me."

"I passed a truck on the road. I figured it was her lawyer, the one she wants me to talk to so they can clear CJ of any wrongdoing."

Tilly shook her head. "It was the private detective who's been asking questions about Dixon Malone's disappearance. You should have seen Mother's face when he came in and told her who he was and why he was there. From what little I overheard on my way upstairs, apparently, Dixon and Mother are still legally married. She never did the paperwork to have him declared legally dead. But seriously, she looked…guilty as sin. You don't think…"

"That she believes she's above the law? Or that she could have killed him?" Oakley shook her head. "I wouldn't be surprised. I think our mother is capable of just about anything. Except forgiveness."

"Unless you're CJ." Tilly wiped at the tears that spilled down her cheeks. "I need to find a job and a place to live. I'm embarrassed to even tell Cooper about this, let alone Holden. He really hoped that Cooper and I getting married might bring the families together. Instead, it's going to make things worse."

"No," Oakley said. "It's going to be all right. Let's get a place together for the time being. I have some money saved. Unless you and Cooper want to elope and skip a wedding."

Tilly wiped her eyes. "No," she said emphatically.

"I was just thinking about it. I'm not going to let her force me into running away like Cooper and I have done something wrong or have anything to hide," she said, biting at her lower lip for a moment in anger. "Okay, let's get a place together. I have money saved as well. Cooper and I will have a real wedding come hell or high water."

"That's my big sis," Oakley said, hugging her again and silently promising that their mother would regret this. "I saw a sign at the café. That upstairs two-bedroom apartment over the general store is for rent. It's going to be okay." The words sounded hollow but they made Tilly smile.

"She isn't going to change her mind. She'll never let me back on the ranch."

Oakley knew what a powerful force her mother could be. But soon, Charlotte Stafford would be fighting not just the McKennas, but also her own blood. "In the meantime, we plan your wedding and have some sister time." Fortunately, she was still able to come and go at the ranch. She had to keep it that way—at least for now.

She didn't tell Tilly what she was planning to do—or who was going to help her. Things were bad at the Stafford Ranch, but they were going to get much worse. She was thankful Tilly wouldn't be there—in the middle of it—when everything hit the fan.

CHAPTER SEVEN

THE SHERIFF FELT a little better by the time he reached his office. He was anxious to hear from the lab on his blood test. He hadn't been at the office long when Douglas Burton, the head of CH4, marched in with two large men who looked like thugs. He said they were his security.

Burton seemed to take in the small office, the small sheriff's department and Stu himself before he removed his coat, told his two flunkies to wait outside and sat down with a heavy sigh. He was a heavy-set man with an air of superiority that made Stu inwardly bristle. He'd seen the way the man had taken in the office and the sheriff himself before dismissing both. Clearly, Burton had come here to kick some butt, starting with the local law.

"What are we going to do about this problem, Sheriff?" the man demanded.

"Given what happened in Wyoming with your company, why wouldn't there be people trying to stop the drilling?" Stu said. "Residents complaining that their water turned black and smelled like gasoline, orphaned wells by the thousands leaking arsenic and methane into groundwater, cities finding fracking chemicals in their main water supply and taxpayers expected to foot the bill to clean up your mess. And you're surprised a group of concerned citizens are trying to stop the drilling here in the Powder River Basin of Montana?"

Burton leaned back in his chair. "Well, I think I can see what the problem is now, *Sheriff*. No wonder you haven't caught and jailed these vandals. You're probably one of them."

"No, Douglas, I do my job as sheriff. Unfortunately, we are short-staffed. As I saw you notice, we are a small department. I believe other gas companies have hired security to keep their drilling equipment safe, but I have to warn you, if your thugs step out of line, they'll end up in my jail behind bars."

The gas executive let out an angry breath before getting to his feet. "It's people like you who are the problem. You want your homes warm in the winter. You use the gas, the oil, but you don't want the drilling. Wait until it's forty below and you can't heat your home, your office. When people can't afford the gas and want to know why it costs so much, I'll have to tell them that it's because I've been forced to keep repairing vandalized equipment, forced to hire security to protect that equipment, raising my costs so I can get that gas to them. Then you're going to wish that you hadn't made it so hard for me to do my job."

As Burton stormed out of his office, Stu's cell phone rang. He picked up and listened as the lab tech informed him that his blood test showed a small amount of a drug that could have knocked him out in a larger quantity, but not enough to definitely say he'd been drugged.

He disconnected and sat for a moment trying to breathe, his mind racing. There was no doubt in his mind that Abigail had drugged him just as he suspected. Why, though? He thought of his keys on the end table farthest from him and the lingering scent of her perfume on them.

His heart began to pound as he looked around his office. Had she come down here last night? She had keys that would have gotten her into the back door, avoiding the dispatcher on duty. Keys to his office.

If so, what was she looking for? He tried to remember if his computer had been on when he'd come in this morning. His brain had still been foggy. With a curse, he remembered that he'd put his latest password on a piece of paper in his wallet.

He pulled out his wallet and caught the lingering scent of Abigail's perfume on it. It took only a moment to see if his password was still in the wallet. It was, but not where he usually kept it.

Touching his keyboard, his computer screen lit. He moved the cursor to Files and clicked. The sheriff's department computer program kept track of all files visited, organizing them based on the user. He checked to see which files had been opened and felt his heart drop like a meteor from space. Only one had been opened. At two in the morning.

The file on Leann Hayes's suicide.

His already upset stomach roiled, making him fear that he would hurl before he regained control. Why would Abigail be interested in Leann Hayes, a woman he'd dated? What had Abigail been looking for to go to such extremes as to drug him? *He was the sheriff, damn it.* Why take a risk like that? Head aching, he had another thought. Had the office been the only place she'd gone last night?

After picking up his keys and pulling on his winter coat, he left the office and headed home to his nearby house where he'd grown up and now still lived. He'd been tricked, drugged and used. Worse, Abigail was interested in a case that he had hoped would go away. So what was her interest in Leann Hayes? What had she hoped to find in the case file? What in his house—if he was right and she'd gone there as well?

But the big question remained. What was he going to do about it?

CHARLOTTE WATCHED THE PI drive away, anger and bitterness and fear making her chest ache. Why hadn't she had Dixon declared dead? Clearly, she should have. But she'd wanted to forget him, to put it all behind her as if it had never happened. The only reason she'd married Dixon was to show Holden.

Had she really held out hope that after his first wife, Margie, had died that he might come back to her? The thought turned her stomach. When she'd heard that he was with Lulabelle, she'd reacted out of spite by marrying Dixon—and it had come back to bite her in that behind that he had loved so well.

Now Tilly thought she was going to marry Holden's son? Over her dead body. She wanted to scream. Cooper was like his father. Tilly couldn't trust his love. Tilly couldn't trust any McKenna.

Why couldn't her daughter understand? Because Tilly had never had her heart ripped from her chest.

She'd never felt that kind of betrayal, that kind of pain that would blacken her heart, turning it slowly to stone.

A thought struck her like the blade of a shovel slamming into her skull. There would be a wedding. A big wedding. Knowing Tilly, it would be at the large church in Powder Crossing. Charlotte could see it filled with people. Everyone would be there to see Tilly in a white wedding dress, her sister, Oakley, next to her, and Cooper McKenna and his brother...not Treyton, Duffy, next to him as the two said their vows or his best friend, the sheriff? And Holden. Holden would be there. Still handsome.

She squeezed her eyes shut against the imagined sight, wanting to crawl into a hole and never come out. She couldn't do this. She wouldn't. It felt as if she'd lost control of everything as she paced the floor.

Just the thought of the PI made her feel even sicker. He'd caught her arguing with her daughter. He'd seen her at her worst. She'd clocked his shocked face as well as his self-satisfied look at seeing her flared temper. He'd been convinced that she could commit murder.

If it was that easy, lucky for the PI that he wasn't now buried in the woods behind her house. She could tell that he was satisfied he knew exactly what had happened to Dixon. All he had to do was prove it. Or find the body.

Charlotte hadn't heard the creak of the wheelchair until CJ spoke.

"That was ugly," he said behind her, startling her out of her thoughts. "You know he won't give up. He'll be back." She wished she didn't agree with him.

"But we have more important things to worry about,"

CJ said. "Inez Turner is in hospice care. We have to act now. Are you listening to me?" he demanded.

She turned to look at him blankly, lost in thoughts of the past and the growing horror of the future, each thought like a stone lodged in her throat.

"The Montana 360 Ranch. Mother, we can't let Holden get that ranch."

The name of the ranch didn't register. Her mind was on the PI, on Tilly and that damned engagement ring. She remembered the first time she'd seen it—on her best friend's finger. It wasn't until Margaret "Margie" Smith had told her who had put that ring there that her world had shattered around her. Living on neighboring ranches, she and Margie had been good friends.

Later, Margie swore that she didn't know about Charlotte and Holden, but how could she not have? The wedding was planned. There was no way Margie or Holden could back out. It was too late. They had no choice, Margie said. The day Margie married Holden was the darkest of Charlotte's life and a turning point that had sent her life to hell.

"The Turner place is part of some of the old Smith Ranch," CJ was saying loudly as if he thought she'd gone deaf. Or wasn't listening. She hadn't been. "It once belonged to Margaret Smith's grandparents."

Just hearing him say Margie's name made her bare her teeth. Margie had taken Holden away from her, dangling a piece of the Smith Ranch property in front of him—but not all of it. Her parents weren't stupid. They held back some of the ranch so Holden's father couldn't get the property. But the old, greedy son of a bastard had put pressure on his son to marry the woman for it. That much was true.

Still, Charlotte would never forgive Holden, whom she felt had betrayed her for the worst piece of the Smith Ranch. And the rest of that ranch had become the Turner Ranch and was now up for grabs. Old man McKenna must be rolling in his grave to think that Charlotte might beat his son out of the place. Charlotte, the woman Holden's father had looked down on. Not good enough for his son because she didn't come with a land dowry. At least not as large a piece of land as Margie Smith had come with.

Swallowing down the bitterness that rose in her throat, she turned her attention to her son. What would she do without CJ? She'd almost lost him. She still had to keep him from going to jail or worse, prison. Without CJ, she had no reason to go on.

"We have to get that ranch, no matter what we have to do," CJ was saying more forcefully. As if her son had to tell her that the Turner place was the missing piece between her ranch and McKenna's property on the two sides of the river. She'd been waiting for years to obtain that land—putting the final nail in old man McKenna's casket and his son's at the same time. Without water, Holden and his ranch couldn't survive.

"I will take care of it," she said to CJ. He didn't even know what was at stake if they didn't get it. "Let me change. I'll go to see Inez on her deathbed if that's what it takes."

"I heard Bob isn't letting anyone in to see her but family and close friends," CJ said. "Maybe I should go with you." He touched the wheelchair as he said it as if he thought his disability would open doors that she couldn't. He might be right, but she couldn't let him do that.

She shook her head. "I won't let her son stop me. Inez will see me. I'll get that land. Whatever it takes." She couldn't let Holden or anyone else get that ranch. Over her dead body would she ever let her former lover have it.

THE SHERIFF UNLOCKED the front door of the house he'd been raised in with trepidation. He'd been left the house and the sheriff job when his father had died. Not that he hadn't had to run for the office, but everyone had liked his father when he was sheriff, so Stuart had won easily. Truth is, no one else wanted the job, which is why no one had run against him. He'd had the house and the job ever since.

As he stepped in, he couldn't imagine why Abigail would have taken his keys and gone to his house last night. What had she hoped to find after her visit to his office? Something that connected him to Leann Hayes's death?

As he moved deeper into the house, he lamented the price of living in a small town, miles from anything. People knew things about you that you wished they didn't. Everyone had speculated on why Leann had killed herself. The prosecutor in Miles City had suspected the man Leann had taken up with after she'd left the sheriff—Cooper McKenna. Cooper had spent a little time behind bars, but without any evidence, Leann's death had been ruled a suicide. End of story.

Or it would have been, Stuart thought with a curse.

Then Cooper McKenna had returned to town after being gone for two years and found what he thought was evidence that Leann had been planning to run away with someone in Powder Crossing. His theory was that either the person had killed her and made it appear to be a suicide, or someone else didn't want her leaving town and had murdered her.

Cooper wanted the case reopened, something Stuart had been dragging his feet about doing, hoping it would blow over.

And now Abigail Creed was snooping around the case?

He stepped in expecting to catch the lingering scent of Abigail's perfume and wasn't disappointed. The scent made him queasy. He moved quickly through the small place, checking his bedroom, then the bathroom, then the living room, not even sure what he was looking for. Everything looked as he'd left it. But would he know if she had gone through his things?

Going back to the bedroom, he opened his bureau drawers. He wasn't one to roll his socks or fold his briefs. As he checked each drawer, he told himself he was wasting his time. He couldn't prove that she'd gone through anything.

But when he opened the bottom drawer, his heart fell. Old photographs. He kept them in a shoebox at the bottom of the deep drawer. He quickly pulled off the old T-shirts that had been covering the box and carried it over to the bed.

As he lifted the lid, he tried to remember the last time he'd looked inside. They were old photographs back before everyone used their cell phones and hardly ever had their photos printed.

But Leann had gotten a Polaroid instant camera for her birthday before he met her. Everywhere they went she would ask people to take a photo of them. She loved it when he took photos of her with her camera. So it wasn't surprising to see a snapshot of her mugging a face at him right on top of the pile.

There were more of the two of them, so many that he couldn't tell if some were missing. Leann had liked to take photos. Her apartment had framed ones that she'd taken before moving to Powder Crossing. He thought of the photograph in Abigail's rented house—the only personal thing in the entire place. Also, the only photograph in the home of a woman who said she was a photographer. She'd said the framed photo on her wall had been taken by a friend. Leann? He felt his chest compact, his breathing suddenly ragged.

He knew without any evidence that Abigail had found these. Why had he kept photos of Leann after she'd broken up with him and immediately gone to Cooper? That old resentment and feeling of betrayal clutched at his chest. He hadn't loved Leann. He knew that now. But it didn't make it hurt any less.

His first instinct was to destroy the photos now, but he stopped himself. The photos weren't incriminating. Leann was just someone he'd dated. There'd been no harm in keeping them, especially since everyone in town knew he had been with Leann before she'd moved on to his best friend.

After slamming the lid back on, he returned the box to the drawer, covering it with one of the old T-shirts.

He closed the drawer, fighting to convince himself that there had been nothing to find—not in Leann's file, not in his house. So why couldn't he stop shaking inside?

Because he didn't like being lied to; worse, being drugged and duped. From the moment he'd met Abigail, he'd warned himself to stay clear of her. Why hadn't he listened? Now he knew she wasn't who she was pretending to be. But what was she looking for? And why? What had really brought her to Powder Crossing, Montana? All his instincts told him the answer. Leann.

He had to find out what her connection was to Leann Hayes. Meanwhile, he couldn't let her know that he was on to her. He pulled out his phone as he reached his patrol SUV, gave himself a minute before he called her.

"Hey, you should have awakened me this morning," he said.

There was that moment of hesitation in her voice before she caught herself. Had she feared that he would realize he'd been drugged and call her on it? "You were sleeping so soundly I couldn't bear to wake you. I got called in early for work." Another lie.

"I have a big day as well. Just wanted to say thanks for the dinner. I'm so sorry I fell asleep. I thought we were going to…get together last night."

"So did I. But clearly, you were exhausted."

"I was and I'm not going to have gas station tacos at lunch anymore. They didn't agree with me."

"Oh, I'm sorry. I hope it wasn't something I cooked." She must think him a complete fool, but for now he would let her.

"Not a chance," he said more jovially than he felt,

given the sour taste in his mouth. "Got to go. Just wanted to hear your voice. Have a good day."

"You, too."

He disconnected, his pulse thundering in his ears. Abigail Creed had no idea who she was dealing with. But then again, neither did he.

CHAPTER EIGHT

OAKLEY AND HER sister rented the two-bedroom furnished apartment over the general store. She could tell that Tilly was heartbroken at the thought of never being allowed on the Stafford Ranch again. It had been her life—much more than it had ever been Oakley's.

"Is that Cooper calling again?" she asked when her sister's phone rang again. "You need to talk to him. I'm sure he's worried."

"It's embarrassing to have a mother like her."

"She definitely wears her bitterness on her sleeve. Answer the phone. I need to get going. For the time being, let Mother believe you're staying here alone. I need to be able to come and go at the house—at least for a while."

"Oakley, what are you planning?" her sister called after her.

"Call if you need me," she hollered back and rushed out. Not even Duffy and Pickett knew what she had planned. She'd kind of hoped that she might hear from Pickett this morning. She knew it was wishful thinking. Nothing had really happened between them. So why did she feel that it had changed things between them?

As she headed back to the ranch, she passed her mother's SUV. She saw no recognition, as if Charlotte

Stafford was in her own world. It gave her pause as she wondered where her mother was off to. Oakley couldn't imagine her leaving CJ unless it was very important. The staff was at the ranch if CJ needed something. Also, their brothers, Brand and Ryder, were somewhere on the ranch, but with their mother home again, Oakley was sure everyone was keeping his distance from the house.

Which meant CJ was alone.

She drove down the county road toward the ranch, anxious to have that long delayed talk with her oldest brother when their mother wasn't there to protect him.

THE MOMENT COOPER heard that Charlotte and CJ were back, he'd wanted Tilly not to change her mind about coming with him to Oregon.

"I need to get this over with," her fiancé had argued. "Mother wants to see me so she knows about the engagement. I'm sorry about the trip."

He'd gone on to Oregon alone to pick up the bull, hating that she would have to face her mother alone. He'd tried to reach her repeatedly this morning. His calls went straight to voice mail. He couldn't help being worried. They both knew Charlotte wasn't going to be happy about the engagement.

He was about to leave another message when she picked up. "What's wrong?" he asked at once, already hearing hurt in her voice. He groaned inwardly. "You've seen your mother."

"Yes."

"Oh, Tilly," he said, hearing so much in that one word.

"She kicked me off the ranch."

"Where are you? I'll come get you. I drove straight through and just got home. I didn't want you to have to face your mother alone."

"Oakley was there. We got an apartment over the general store in town for now—at least until the wedding."

He raked a hand through his hair. "You know that wasn't necessary. My father told you—"

"I know I'm welcome out on the McKenna Ranch, but I need this time. I have a wedding to plan."

"So…we're going through with a big wedding?"

"We most certainly are. That is, if you're game."

"You know I want what you want," Cooper said and heard her fighting tears. "It will be the best wedding anyone in this county has ever seen."

"Thank you," she said through her tears. "I'm not going to let her ruin this for me, for us."

"Good," he said, hearing the pain in her voice and wishing there was something he could do to lessen it. But while confronting Charlotte might make him feel better, it wouldn't help the situation. "Maybe she'll come around."

Tilly laughed. "We both know better than that. It's better she won't be at the wedding or CJ, either. Anyone who doesn't support our love isn't invited."

"That's my girl," he said, hoping to lighten the moment. "When can I see you?"

"What are you doing right now?"

OAKLEY DIDN'T SEE anyone around as she parked in front of the ranch house. Her brothers Brand and Ryder wouldn't be coming back until lunch—if that. The staff would be busy, always giving the family a wide berth when possible. With luck, she would have CJ all to herself.

As she climbed out of her pickup, she caught movement from the corner of her eye. She turned to stare at the guest room window, the curtains open, the sun glinting off the glass.

For just a moment, she thought she saw CJ standing there. She stared at the window and realized it had to have been a trick of the light because there was no one there. CJ couldn't have been standing there watching her drive up because he couldn't walk or stand, could he?

A little shaken, she hurried up the steps, across the porch and opened the front door. The house had felt oddly empty without her mother's domineering presence during her absence. It felt even emptier knowing that she'd left CJ alone. What had been so important that her mother would do that?

"What are you doing here?"

CJ had startled her as she'd stepped into the living room. So he had seen her drive up.

"I thought you were in your room."

A satisfied grin played at his lips as he saw that he hadn't just surprised her. He'd startled her. He'd always like scaring her and Tilly with every gross thing he could find to shove into their faces.

There were cowgirls around who thought her oldest brother handsome. They only saw the chiseled face, the thick ash-blond hair, the green eyes. They didn't see beneath the veneer or get a glimpse of the sneering, brittle coldness behind those eyes like Oakley did right now.

"I live here." At least for a while. "Where's your guard dog?" she asked as she took a step toward him. He'd never been able to intimidate her, even when they were little. She'd refused to cry when he'd hurt her. She'd learned early on not to go to their mother for help. CJ always lied and Charlotte always believed him over the rest of them. Her brothers had learned to keep their distance from CJ and still did. Since he never really "worked" the ranch, their paths seldom crossed.

The twinge from her gunshot scar should have been warning enough of how dangerous CJ had become since they were kids. But Oakley didn't back down as she closed the distance between them, putting her hands on the arms of the wheelchair to lean her face close to his.

"I know you lied about the shooting," she said. "I thought that with just the two of us here at the ranch you'd have the courage to admit the truth."

His expression said it would be over his dead body. "How do I know you aren't wearing a wire?"

She laughed. "I'm not, but you being worried that I am confirms what I've suspected. You have something big to hide that you're terrified I'm going to remember, don't you?"

"I'd be careful if I were you," CJ said. "You shouldn't go around making accusations without any evidence."

She felt her scar pull with another warning. But that didn't stop her. "Evidence? I know you meant to kill me and when I remember what we were both doing there that day, you're going to be spending the rest of your miserable life behind bars." She caught a satisfying glint of worry dim his gaze before she shoved from the wheelchair to walk away from him.

She could feel his gaze boring into her back. She couldn't help thinking that turning her back on him was probably a mistake since last time he'd shot her when she had.

"I doubt anyone would believe you since you don't remember anything about that day," he said, attempting to sound unconcerned. "Our lawyer would say that you're making it up because you're angry at me for the accident."

She turned slowly to smile at him. "Got it all figured out, have you? One problem. My memory is already starting to come back and when it does, I'll know exactly why you are so terrified that I will remember. Then I'll be coming for you because we both know the truth, even if you don't have the guts to admit it to my face." She put her hand over the scar so close to her heart.

With that, she turned and walked out. Behind her she heard him crash his wheelchair into the coffee table as he tried to come after her.

Just before she slammed the door, she heard him yell, "Next time I won't miss!"

She was shaking by the time she reached her pickup. He'd confirmed what she already knew, but hearing the words come out of his mouth… As she started the engine, she glanced back at the house. She'd poked the bear, and everyone knew how dangerous that can be.

As she stared at the living room windows, she thought again of what she'd glimpsed in the guest room—what appeared to be her brother standing in front of the window. She knew from experience to expect the worst from her oldest brother. But if he'd recovered from his injuries, why would he be pretending he hadn't? she asked herself as she drove away.

Not even CJ would stoop so low as to fake an injury that had him trapped in a wheelchair. Or would he?

CHAPTER NINE

CHARLOTTE DROVE INTO Powder Crossing determined she would talk to Inez Turner. The moment she drove up, though, the woman's son came out and stood next to her car.

"No reason to get out of your car, Charlotte," Bob said as she put down her window. "I know why you're here, but you won't be seeing my mother."

"I'm sure Inez will see me." She started to open her door, but he closed it again.

"Bob," she said with more patience than she felt. "Your mother and I have known each other for years."

"Everyone knows you, Charlotte."

She gritted her teeth at what he was insinuating, but planted a smile on her face. "I know she must be worried about what will happen to her ranch once she's gone."

"Not really. We've discussed it at length."

"Come on, Bob. I know you're in a position where you have to sell the ranch. Your wife doesn't want to live here, and you don't, either. Not only that, think of what you can do for your family with that money. I'm offering more than the ranch's value so you can avoid the hassle and expense of a real estate agent."

"You really need to leave, Charlotte." He turned on

his heel, walking away, even as she was getting out of the car.

She started to follow him, but when he reached the front door, he made a show of locking it behind him.

Her face flushed with anger. What a fool. He couldn't treat her like this. If she didn't need that piece of property, she would walk away and not come back.

Climbing into her SUV, she sat for a moment, fuming. Bob had always been a wuss. Inez had been the strong one. There had to be a way to get around him to his mother.

A thought struck her. What about that new nurse in town? Brand had kind of been interested in her until it became clear that she was only interested in the sheriff. What was her name? It started with an A, an old name like Angela. Abby. Abigail. That was it.

But getting to Inez before she kicked off wasn't the only problem. There'd been so many unforeseen expenses with Oakley's accident and then CJ's. The specialists for his care were costly enough, not even counting the lawyers she'd had to hire to keep him out of jail and attempts to get the case against him thrown out. Plus installing the ramps and other construction costs for the additions that had been made to accommodate his injury. CJ owed her big time.

Because of all of it, she was going to have trouble making an offer larger than Holden McKenna's. But she'd be damned if she wouldn't hock everything, including the ranch if it came to that. She had to have the Montana 360 Ranch. Realizing that Inez could go at any time, she had to contact that nurse.

With a start, she'd forgotten that there was one sure-fired way to get more money and quickly. She'd move forward with drilling more coalbed methane wells on the ranch as CJ had been encouraging her to do.

As a passing thought, she briefly considered how the rest of what was left of her family would take the news—especially Oakley. Then she reminded herself that she was running this ranch and she would run it as she saw fit. She put in a call to Douglas Burton to contract more wells before she went looking for Abigail.

The nurse wasn't working at the small hospital today. In fact, they said she wasn't working for the next few days unless there was an emergency.

It didn't take much after that to find out where she was living. The house was small, tucked behind the hospital on the edge of town. Luck was with her. The nurse's car was parked next to the house. But when Charlotte knocked, it seemed to take longer than it should have to get the woman to answer the door. Not that she was about to give up until she talked to her.

"Mrs. Stafford," Abigail said in surprise as she finally opened the door little more than a crack.

"We need to talk," Charlotte said impatiently, seeing that the woman wasn't anxious to let her in.

"If this is about CJ's injuries—"

"Are you going to leave me standing out here in the street?" she demanded.

Abigail seemed to realize that she wasn't going away and swung the door open wider. "Why don't you come in."

Stepping into the neat little house, Charlotte wondered what the woman had to hide. Something, that was obvious. A man? Possibly. The bedroom door was closed. So was the bathroom door. But why hide any-one unless she didn't want someone else knowing who she'd been with? Then again, maybe it wasn't a man the woman was hiding.

She shoved all thought of Abigail's secrets away as she turned to her. A young woman with secrets was often vulnerable—and ultimately for sale. "Are you involved with hospice and Inez Turner?"

"No."

"Can you be?" she asked. "Offer to help? Get in-side? Find out if she is well enough to sign something?"

Abigail blinked. "What exactly are you asking me to do?"

Charlotte heard it in the young woman's voice. She'd already taken the bait; all Charlotte had to do was set the hook. "I need Inez to sell me her ranch." She reached into her purse and pulled out the buy-sell agreement she'd had drawn up on her computer before going to the Turner house this morning.

The nurse didn't look shocked in the least. Charlotte recognized the expression and smiled. "Don't worry. I'll make it more than worth your time and effort. All you have to do is get into that house. Something tells me you can get to Inez if you put your mind to it."

NEWS OF CHARLOTTE STAFFORD's return swept the county. Holden hated that some people were saying that she and her son were getting what they deserved.

He wasn't surprised when Bob Turner called. "Char-lotte came by demanding to see my mother." He could hear the anger in the man's voice. "Everyone else has been kind enough to leave my family in peace during this difficult time, you included. I just wanted to thank you for that. If Charlotte comes back, I'm calling the sheriff."

Holden realized that Bob wasn't just calling to thank him for not trying to convince Inez to sell him the ranch from her deathbed. He wanted him to keep Charlotte from coming back. The thought almost made him laugh. He'd never had any control over the woman—even when they were lovers. She'd been what his father had called a dangerous headstrong wild horse. Charlotte was the kind of woman no one could rein in—let alone break to ride. It was one reason his father had been so adamant against him wanting to marry her—and not just because she had such a small ranch to bring to a marriage. Holden had said he didn't give a damn about any of that until his father and grandfather had threatened to send him packing without a penny if he didn't marry Margie Smith.

He'd been young and foolish and madly in love, but a part of him had known that the threat was real. Kicked off the ranch without a penny, Holden had feared that Charlotte would no longer want him. It had been that fear more than anything that had led him to the altar with Margie. He'd told himself he had no choice.

Margie came with a ranch that connected on the west side of their own and was a good, kind woman who'd given him four children. He'd loved her.

But never like the way he had loved Lottie. She was the love of his life—and the thorn in his side.

"Bob," he said now. "As far as Charlotte, you know my telling her to stay away would only make things worse. But I do want to talk to her about the two of us going together and making an offer on the land, splitting it since your ranch borders both of ours. Would you consider not selling until I talk to you about it?"

The man sounded relieved. "Thank you, Holden, because right now I'd rather sell it at a loss than deal with that woman. Truthfully? My mother hasn't made up her mind completely. She might go for something like that if the idea is coming from you."

"I'll get back to you." He disconnected, worried that he'd promised more than he could deliver. He placed a call, confirming that Charlotte had returned to the ranch from town, and had gone straight to the stables to saddle up for a ride.

After Bob Turner's call, Holden knew she'd had a rough day so he thought he'd know where to find her. She'd always been a creature of habit. When she was upset, she'd get on a horse and go to that spot along the creek. He knew it well. He knew her well—even after all these years apart.

As he headed to the stables to saddle up and ride over to the Stafford Ranch, always safer than driving over there, he saw his son Duffy and Pickett Hanson deep in conversation. He knew the two had become friends over the years and, knowing his youngest son, doubted they were discussing ranching.

KNOWING THERE WAS nothing more she could do for now, Charlotte had returned to the ranch. She was worried about CJ, even though there was staff available if he needed anything. He'd been in an odd mood all the way home to Montana. She worried that he was depressed and feeling guilty. She feared he might do something to himself.

In the house, she went at once to the guest room. She could hear him talking and for a moment wondered who was in the room with him. As she carefully cracked the door open, she saw him sitting in his wheelchair at the window, his back to her. She felt a wave of relief to find him on the phone, apparently talking to a friend, from the tone of his voice.

She quickly closed the door. For a moment she felt lost and helpless and unsure what to do next. When she got like this, she headed for the stables for a ride. It was the only thing that calmed her.

After changing her clothing, she went out to saddle her horse. She was anxious to hear from the nurse and hoped she'd been right about the woman. Someone had to get to Inez before she died. She had a feeling Abigail Creed could succeed if anyone could. Charlotte was counting on her to get that land before Holden McKenna got his hands on it.

DUFFY AND PICKETT saw Holden coming and completed their conversation, both concerned that Charlotte Stafford would drill a new well and Oakley would try to stop it without keeping them in the loop. Duffy had promised he would let Pickett know if he heard anything.

Pickett waved to his boss and headed toward the barn. "Going for a ride?" Duffy asked his father.

"Thought I might."

He didn't like the way Holden was studying him almost as if he thought he and Pickett were up to something. "Want me to saddle your horse?"

"I'm still quite capable of saddling my own horse."

Duffy raised both hands in surrender.

"Sorry," his father apologized. "I haven't seen much of you lately."

"Pickett and I rode fence this morning. Found a couple of strays we got back in." Fortunately, the ranch hand had been his old self today. Duffy hadn't brought up last night and neither had his friend. He told himself that he'd imagined whatever it was he thought he sensed between his friend and Oakley. "I need to go into town to get more wire. Not sure what keeps tearing up that stretch of fence near the river."

"I know you're working," Holden said. "I didn't mean to insinuate differently." He shook his head. "Have you seen Treyton?"

"No." But Duffy had been hearing rumors about him. His older brother was heading for trouble. Nothing new there.

His father nodded distractedly, clearly having more on his mind than Treyton as he told him he would see him later and headed for the stables.

Duffy was tempted to saddle up and follow his father. He was worried about where Holden was headed. He knew how important purchasing the Montana 360 Ranch was to their family. He also knew Charlotte Stafford would be doing everything in her power to outbid him—if not cheat—to get the land. This war between the two had been going on long before Duffy was born. He wished now more than ever, though, that it would end. If he was interested in Oakley, he didn't want to go through what Cooper was going through. He couldn't imagine what it would take for the families to bury their axes and put the past behind them.

After his father rode off in the direction of the Stafford Ranch, he knew it would be a mistake to follow him. Treyton treated Holden as if he was old and going senile. Duffy knew better. Just offering to saddle his father's horse had made him bristle. Following him—especially in the direction he'd gone—would be more than an insult.

Still, he wondered what business his father might have with Charlotte Stafford—the woman Duffy suspected Holden still loved in spite of everything.

ABIGAIL TAPPED AT the Turner's door. She'd worn her hospital scrubs. She'd prepared a story. The question was why do this? She didn't like Charlotte Stafford. She didn't like most of the people she'd met here. She was already taking so many chances, why do this?

The door opened. The man blocking the entry was tall, slim, with a scowl on his face. He'd opened his mouth as if already knowing what he planned to say. But his lips clamped, locking the words inside as he saw her and her attire.

She smiled and started to speak, but he beat her to it. "You're late."

That was not what she was expecting.

"Come on, my mother is in pain." He turned then and headed back through the ranch house. Abigail followed, debating when to tell him that she wasn't the hospice nurse he'd been expecting.

She decided to ride it out and see what happened.

He was the one who had it all wrong. She was a nurse whose job it was to help people. If she could relieve Inez Turner of her pain, then she was just doing her job.

The moment she saw the elderly frail woman in the bed, she turned to him. "I can take it from here."

He seemed to hesitate but only for a moment before he turned and walked out. She closed the door behind him and rounded to face the woman. Inez might be dying but she was still very alert. Her dark eyes latched on to Abigail with suspicion as the nurse advanced on her.

"I don't know you," the elderly woman said.

"No, you don't, but I know you." She moved to the side table and the drugs lined up there. "Let's have a little chat as I get you something to relieve your pain."

Duffy McKenna had come into town for supplies, but decided to have an early lunch while he was there. He'd barely sat down when he saw the man enter the café and head to his table. He had the feeling that the man had been following him—and maybe not just into the café.

"Duffy McKenna, right?" the man said as he pulled out a chair without being invited. "I'm Jason Murdock. I've been wanting to talk to you." The waitress came up to the table and cocked a hip, grinning at Duffy. She was a pretty blonde whom he'd gone to school with but had never dated.

"Let me guess. The usual, right, Duffy?" Penny asked and chuckled as he nodded, then turned to the man.

"Just coffee. Black. Thanks." He took off his Stetson and put it on an empty chair as if planning to stay for a while.

As Penny left, Duffy said, "I don't know who you are but—"

"I'm a private investigator. I would appreciate it if you allow me to take a few minutes of your time to talk to me," the PI said. "I've been hired to look into the disappearance of Dixon Malone. He's still married to Charlotte Staf—"

"I know who he was, but I know nothing about his disappearance. That was years ago, almost before my time."

Murdock smiled. "But not your father's. I understand he and Charlotte Stafford were close years ago."

"Look, I don't know what you're getting at—" he did know exactly what the man was implying "—but people come and go in this river basin."

"Exactly," the PI said as Penny returned with his coffee. She slid a plate of pancakes and a side of bacon in front of Duffy, who preferred breakfast over lunch. "Dixon isn't the only person who's gone missing around here. I found missing persons going back to the 1800s."

"Finding all of them should keep you busy for a while, but if you'll excuse me, I'm hungry and I'd like to eat in peace. I really don't care about ancient history." He slathered his pancakes with butter then drowned them with syrup before taking a bite.

Murdock chuckled as he watched him, but didn't leave. "How about more recent disappearances. Ever heard of a gas company employee by the name of Rory Eastwood?"

Duffy shook his head. "Sorry, not interested and as you can see, I'm eating."

"Would it interest you if you knew that Rory Eastwood's disappearance might involve your brother Cooper?"

He felt his stomach twist but took another bite of his breakfast.

"Eastwood gave his notice with the gas company CH4, saying he was leaving here to make a new life with his new lady," Murdock said. "The bartender down at the Wild Horse said he was all excited, but secretive about this woman he was running away with because she had a boyfriend she hadn't told yet. He left the bar that night to go pick her up and was never seen again."

"How do you know that he didn't leave town with her?" Duffy asked, pushing his plate away. The café made the best pancakes he'd ever had but this morning they tasted like cardboard. He just wanted to settle his bill and get out of the café, far away from this man and what he was insinuating. But at the same time, he knew that he should probably hear this so he could warn his brother.

"Maybe Rory did leave," the PI conceded. "But what's interesting is that this new woman Rory had fallen for? Some people think she was Leann Hayes."

The pancakes he'd eaten felt like lead inside him.

"If true, then the boyfriend that Rory mentioned was your brother Cooper. They'd been an item, I heard, until she allegedly killed herself or was murdered. So what happened to Rory? Some think they were caught together and killed, making Leann's death look like a suicide and disposing of Rory's body to make it look like he'd left town."

"That is a whole lot of supposition," Duffy said with

a shake of his head as he motioned to the waitress for his bill.

"You are so right," the PI said with a laugh. "Rory Eastwood could have left town, keeping a low profile after what happened to Leann. But Dixon Malone didn't get out of town that easily. You're wondering how I know that. I just have this itch I get with certain cases. I say he's still here in the Powder River Basin."

"Should be easy to find, then."

"Much harder to find them when they're six feet under."

Duffy had nothing more to say to any of this. He regretted not throwing the PI out. He hadn't wanted to hear any of it. But at the same time, he needed to let Cooper know what the PI was digging into.

Murdock leaned toward him over the table and lowered his voice. "People around these parts tell me that if anyone can get away with murder in this river basin, it would be Holden McKenna and Charlotte Stafford—or one of their offspring. Word is they can even shoot one of their own and get away with it."

Duffy met the man's gaze. "Don't believe everything you hear." Out of the corner of his eye, he saw Oakley pull up out front. He'd had enough of the PI. The man was starting to worry him. If there was something to find and Murdock kept digging, he could turn up evidence that would hurt not just his family, but Oakley's as well. Everyone knew that Charlotte and Dixon Malone's marriage had been a battleground. Dixon hadn't made a secret of it on the nights he drove into town to talk about his impossible, irascible wife.

As for the death of Leann Hayes, even Cooper believed it hadn't been suicide. Cooper suspected there had been a man in her life, one she was planning to leave town with, but something had gone wrong, and the man had killed her.

It appeared Murdock thought the same thing—only worse. The PI's theory was that the murderer had also killed and disposed of Leann's alleged lover, a man named Rory Eastwood.

If true, Duffy knew it could mean trouble for his brother. Cooper had already been suspected of murdering her by an overanxious prosecutor. What Duffy couldn't understand was why Murdock had been investigating Dixon Malone's disappearance but now was on the trail of another missing person—a trail that could bring him right to the McKenna Ranch.

CHAPTER TEN

OAKLEY LEFT THE RANCH, but she didn't go far. The more she thought about it, the more she was convinced that CJ was somehow faking his injury. Maybe it had gotten better, but he was keeping it from everyone. Even their mother?

She parked her pickup in a spot down the county road and cut across Stafford Ranch property to sneak back to the house. Entering her and Tilly's separate entrance, she climbed the stairs, then listened. Hearing no sound, she carefully went to the top of the main stairs and looked down into the living room.

No CJ. But still, she waited to make sure he was in his room before she descended the stairs and moved quietly down the hallway. She'd been unable to forget what she'd thought she'd seen—her brother standing in front of the window. It could have been a trick of the light. Or CJ would be trying to dupe them all. If she had to put money on it, she'd bet on the latter.

Nearing the door, she heard him talking to someone. She took hold of the doorknob and carefully turned it. The door opened a crack. She could see him sitting on the side of his bed, his wheelchair nearby.

"This isn't a social call. You have information for

me?" CJ snapped into the phone. Quiet, then, "Duffy McKenna?" She heard her brother swear. "I don't care about the ranch hand. I can buy and sell a dozen ranch hands. But Duffy? What the hell? First Tilly and now Oakley? Fine, whatever. I told you I'll get you the money. Just keep me informed any time you see Oakley over there." He shifted on the bed as if about to rise, when he looked up and swore as their gazes locked.

Surprise registered on his face followed quickly by fear, then fury. He was wondering what she'd heard and afraid that she'd probably heard too much. He reached for his wheelchair, drew it closer and awkwardly lifted himself into it. Once seated, he lifted each leg into place and spun it around to face her.

"Are you spying on me?" he demanded accusingly.

She laughed, leaning against the doorjamb as she studied him. "Talk about the pot calling the kettle names. You're paying someone to spy on me? Someone on the McKenna Ranch? Let me guess. Rusty Malone. I hope you're paying him enough."

"I don't know what you thought you heard but—"

"I heard plenty and I've seen plenty. You don't fool me, CJ. You never have. Maybe Mother's in the dark, but I'm not."

"I don't know what you're talking about, but wait until I tell Mother that you're seeing Duffy McKenna."

She shrugged. "Not half as appalling as when she finds out that you're only pretending to be paralyzed."

"Have—have you lost your mind?" He slammed a hand down on the arm of the wheelchair, his voice rising dangerously. "You think I would pretend to be in this?"

"Oh, I definitely think you would. I think you'd milk this for all it's worth if you thought it would keep you out of jail."

He shook his head, wheeling the chair around as if he was going somewhere but quickly wheeling back to glare at her. "Tell Mother and see where that gets you."

She smiled. "You've always lied to get out of trouble. But this time you've really stooped low. I saw you standing in the window earlier. Now I'm wondering how long you've been lying about everything, especially why you shot me."

"You're delusional." But he looked away when he said it, making her even more convinced he was lying about all of it.

"I have to wonder why you would stay in that chair, though, if you don't have to. Bet once the charges are dropped, you will miraculously rise to your feet. What a moment that will be."

"Get out of my room. I can't stand the sight of you."

"At least we have that in common, even though I've never shot *you*. But there is always a first." She shoved off the door frame. "But I promise I'm going to find out not only why you really shot me, but also what you're still up to. I'm watching you, CJ, the way you're apparently spying on me." With that she turned and walked back down the hall.

She heard him throw something that shattered against the wall and smiled to herself. She hadn't been wrong. CJ was lying about everything.

But how far should she keep pushing? Far enough that he made a mistake.

HOLDEN WISHED HE and Lottie could do business like reasonable ranch owners and sit down at a table and hash this out. Unfortunately, that wasn't possible, he knew as he rode up into the meadow and reined in his horse at the sight of her.

He'd known he would find her here. She sat on a large rock that the sun had bared of snow. The past few days they'd gotten a break from winter. He loved it when the days began to get longer, the sun stronger. But spring was still a long way off. Days like this, bright and almost warm under a cloudless sky made winter in Montana bearable.

But he wasn't fooled. The weather could change in a heartbeat. Snow could start falling and keep falling until everything was blanketed in deep cold white, and spring seemed like it would never come.

Holden dismounted and approached Lottie slowly. It had been a while since she'd taken a bullwhip to him. She'd threatened to shoot him the next time he rode up on the spot where they used to make love. He often wondered why she came here if it caused her so much pain.

He thought he knew what she was doing here today. Even from a distance, he could see worry lining her face as she turned up to the sun's rays. CJ was her firstborn son. Of course she would be heartbroken over what he'd done as well as his injury.

Worse, she was the type of woman who liked to believe that she had the power to fix anything. While she might be able to get CJ out of legal jeopardy, only God could get him out of that wheelchair if his injuries were as bad as Holden had heard. That alone had to be tearing her apart.

He cleared his voice. She turned her head slowly, not seeming at all surprised to see him.

"What took you so long?" She sounded tired and defeated, as if she didn't have the energy to rise from the rock where she sat, let alone fight with him.

Holden wasn't fooled as he walked slowly toward her. Her own horse was a good distance away in the trees, but that didn't mean that she wasn't armed. He stopped a few yards away.

"I'm so sorry."

"About anything in particular or just generally?" she asked in that same almost bored tone.

"About CJ. I know how hard that must be for you."

Her lips bowed a little as if amused. "It would be for any parent."

"You're not just any parent." He met her gaze and, for a moment, thought he saw the shine of tears before she blinked and turned her head away.

"What do you want, Holden?"

He sighed as he sat down on an adjacent rock the sun had dried. These warm days teased Montanans, giving them hope and quickly taking it away. He'd lived here long enough to know better and yet he wanted to believe winter was waning. He missed the color green, the smell of new grass, the hot sun lolling in all that blue above him as the cottonwoods leafed out and the air took on that feel that reminded him of days spent with Lottie in this very spot. But for now he relished in what little warmth the sun provided.

"I have a proposition for you."

She laughed, turning back to him, her smile fragile and not in the least convincing. "I can't wait to hear."

"I want this war between us to end."

Lottie huffed at that. "Doesn't sound like much of a proposition."

"We need to join forces."

Her eyebrow rose. "What exactly do you have in mind, Mr. McKenna?" There was a teasing in her almost seductive tone now and a light in those green eyes that had been missing only moments ago.

"I think we should pool our money and buy the Turner Ranch together."

She registered shock, followed quickly by anger as she rose to her feet. "I should have known." Her lips formed a straight line, her green eyes glittering now with malice.

He hurried on even though he doubted she would hear a word of reason. "It makes sense, Lottie. You take the portion next to your ranch, I take the land along my ranch border. We both get water. We both get what we want."

She cocked her head and frowned as if confused. Or was it amused? "We both get what we want?" She laughed. "You think I want the Turner Ranch for the land, for the water?" Her laugh echoed through the bare-limbed cottonwoods. When she sobered, she glared at him, no humor left. "I want that land and that water because you want it."

Holden shook his head. "How long do you want to do this? Hate me. I can see that you do. But please let's stop dragging our kids into it. No good has come from it. Can't you see that? *We* are the only ones who can stop this. We can rise above it."

Charlotte shook her head slowly. "Such big talk. Such gallant talk. Where was that man all those years ago?"

"He was young and foolish. Now he's just old and often foolish still. But the last thing he has ever wanted is for the two of us to be at such odds because he still loves you, will always love you."

She brushed angrily at the tears that fell with that admission. He saw her swallow and take a ragged breath. "You need to get off my property," she said quietly. "I've warned you about coming here." Her gaze locked with his. "Next time, I *will* shoot for trespassing."

"If the Turner property means this much to you, then you can have it. I won't stand in your way." He turned to walk away, not all that sure she wouldn't make good on her threat this time.

"You know you've lost. That's why you came here with your *proposition*," she called after him. "I've already won."

He could hear the emotion in her voice as if it would take so little to break the restraint she was fighting to keep. He stopped to turn back to her. "Oh, Lottie, we have both lost and it breaks my heart."

He reached his horse and turned to look back at her. She was hugging herself as if trying to hold her anger and hate in. He felt so bad for her, so guilty. He'd created this woman, this woman he would love until the day he died.

His biggest regret was that he had no idea how to reach her, how to ease her pain, how to erase the past so they didn't have to feel the way they did until their dying days.

After mounting his horse, he tipped his hat and reined around to head home, his own eyes filling with tears of pain.

CHAPTER ELEVEN

PICKETT HANSON STARED at his phone as another text came in much like the others he'd been getting recently. He'd ignored them and did the same with this one. He'd put his past behind him when he'd come to Powder Crossing. It had been so many years that he'd almost forgotten about that part of his life and who he'd been.

He was a ranch hand on the McKenna spread. The thought made him smile because he was happy being that man. He'd learned to be good at the job even though when he'd started he didn't know the front of a horse from the back. He laughed to himself as he stood in the barn doorway and looked out toward the river and the thick cottonwoods, limbs dark and tangled-looking like his thoughts of the man he used to be.

The day felt almost spring like. Was that why he was in this mood? He stared at the phone, wanting more than anything to hear from Oakley. He thought about calling her. Another text came in, this one more urgent. He killed it, telling himself if he kept ignoring them, the woman sending them would get the hint. He had nothing to say.

"Pickett, please can you teach me that one trick where you hang upside down from the horse?" said a young female voice behind him.

He turned, already smiling before he saw Holly Jo standing there all duded out in her Western attire. Like him, she'd come a long way since being dropped off here on this ranch. He was happy for her, knowing what a place like this could do for a person. Fresh air, horses, wild open land, a reason for existing.

"Shouldn't you check with Holden first?" he asked.

"I did and he said, 'You just be careful.'"

"He say this before he rode off?" Pickett quizzed, grinning. "Girl, you have a tendency to stretch the truth more than I do."

She laughed. "I know if he was here, he'd be fine with it as long as we were careful." Just then they both heard a rider approaching and turned to see the man in question.

"Looks like we're about to find out," he said, his grin widening as Holly Jo sighed in disappointment. They both knew what Holden was going to say.

"You could tell him it's not that dangerous," she suggested before his boss reached them.

"I could, but then I'd be a bigger liar than you, squirt."

STILL UPSET AFTER her run-in with her brother, Oakley drove back into Powder Crossing. She felt at loose ends. She hadn't been able to get Pickett off her mind. Had she just imagined that he'd been feeling what she had? She feared that might be the case.

When she saw Duffy's ranch pickup parked in front of the café, her heart leaped at the thought that Pickett might be with him. It was almost noon and she hadn't even had breakfast. Her stomach growled as she swung in and parked.

As she pushed open the café door and spotted Duffy, she saw at the same time that he wasn't alone. Disappointed, she realized that his companion wasn't Pickett. With a jolt she recognized the man as the one who'd passed her on the road to the ranch—the PI Tilly had told her about. She started to head for the counter when Duffy called her over to his table.

She approached saying, "If you're busy—"

"No, Mr. Murdoch was just leaving," Duffy said pointedly.

The man nodded with obvious reluctance and rose. "You must be Oakley Stafford." His gaze bored into her for a moment before he glanced at Duffy, then back to her. "I didn't realize you two…" He let that hang.

"We're friends," Oakley said. "You have a problem with that, Mr. Murdoch?"

He smiled. "You remind me of your mother."

"Those are fighting words," she said in warning. "I'd be careful throwing them around."

He laughed. "Yes, Powder Crossing is a dangerous place. At least it was for your mother's second husband." He tipped his hat to her as he headed out the door.

She looked to Duffy questioningly as she sat down. "A friend of yours?"

"Hardly," Duffy said, watching him leave. "He's been in town for a while asking questions."

She felt a chill. "Tilly saw him earlier out at the ranch. He's asking about Dixon Malone, the man my mother was married to."

"Is apparently still married to," Duffy said. "He also

seems to be interested in a man named Rory Eastwood." When he saw that she'd never heard of him, he asked, "Hungry?"

She eyed what little was left of his pancakes. "Late breakfast?"

"Something like that," he said with a grin. She could feel his gaze on her as if he could read her moods.

"Penny," she said to the waitress when she passed by, "I'll have—"

"The usual?"

She smiled and nodded. "Thanks."

"We are such creatures of habit, it seems," Duffy said as Penny took away his dishes and refilled his coffee cup. "Rough day already?"

DUFFY WATCHED OAKLEY fiddle with her napkin. He often felt blindsided by how pretty she was. Her ash-blond hair was long, often corralled into a single plait that fell to the middle of her back or tucked up under her hat. Her eyes, mostly green like her mother's, changed with the light. At five-five she was slim and athletic-looking as if ready to take on anything. But her real beauty seemed to come from within. This morning her cheeks were flushed, her eyes bright and her lips… He almost missed what she said.

"I got into it with CJ earlier." He pushed away thoughts about how much he liked her and listened. A run-in with CJ was enough to upset anyone, but Duffy could tell it was something more and waited.

Avoiding his eyes she said, "When I drove up to the ranch house earlier this morning…" She shook her head. "It was probably just the sunlight on the guest room window, but…" Her gaze rose to lock with his. "I thought I saw him standing at the window. He disappeared at once as if he saw me. Or maybe he wasn't there at all. I just don't know."

"You think he's faking his injury?" It would be just like the cowboy.

"How could he, though? The doctors would know, wouldn't they?"

"Depends on his prognosis," Duffy said.

"According to my mother, he will walk again. But you know how she is. If it took only her iron will he'd be up running around. If he's lying… I can't believe even CJ would stoop so low as to pretend he had to stay in the wheelchair."

"Then again, he probably has a better chance of dodging jail as long as he's in that chair, don't you think?"

"Yes, unfortunately. I even had the thought that maybe Mother's in on it and once he gets away with shooting me, he'll miraculously rise and walk." She sighed. "I don't want him to go to jail let alone prison. But I also don't want him to think he can get away with what he did."

"The PI was just saying that people in town think our families can get away with murder—or shooting each other," Duffy said. "I hate to think it might be true."

"I haven't mentioned this to anyone else—" Just then her cheeseburger and fries arrived. She took her time putting ketchup on the burger and cutting it in half.

Duffy feared she was changing her mind about telling him whatever it was she'd been about to say. He hoped she trusted him, but he was a McKenna and there was nothing he could do about that.

He reminded himself that she wasn't the only one hesitant about telling secrets. He was keeping what the PI had suggested about Leann Hayes and his brother Cooper from her. "If something's bothering you that you don't want to talk about…"

She looked up. Her gaze softened. "I keep having these disjointed dreams that I think are memories about the day I was shot. But they don't make any sense. I just can't throw off this feeling that there's more to it. That CJ is lying about why he shot me. Worse, that shooting me wasn't an accident, that the shot he fired wasn't a warning shot that went awry. He practically admitted it earlier." Her gaze locked with his. "I think he was trying to kill me, to stop me permanently from… That's the part that's so frustrating. I can't imagine what I could have seen or done that he was so terrified I would tell someone."

For a moment Duffy was speechless. Did she really think CJ had fired that shot to kill her? "Even if he was involved with the meth lab—"

"It wouldn't have been enough to kill someone over, right?" she said, nodding. "I know. But CJ is obsessed with Mother thinking the best of him."

"Is it possible something else was going on that day at the old Smith Ranch homestead besides the meth lab that you might have seen?"

"Maybe. I don't know. I don't even know what I was doing there to begin with. Did I even find the meth lab or did something else happen back in that ravine? If I could just *remember*." Cooper and Tilly, while trying to find out what she might have seen, had stumbled onto the meth lab. Unfortunately, it had been destroyed before the sheriff could bust it.

Duffy reached over and placed his hand on hers for a moment. "Don't try so hard to remember. Just let memories come if that's possible. In the meantime, be real careful of your brother. As if I have to warn you of that. But it sounds as if you're baiting him. I wouldn't do that." He knew how CJ had tormented her and their siblings growing up because of the stories she'd shared over the years.

"I don't want him thinking he's safe." She looked miserable. "Even the thought that he might have been trying to kill me…"

Duffy couldn't imagine, his hand still on hers. "Are you sure about staying out on the ranch?"

"Tilly and I rented an apartment here in town, so I won't be staying there any more than I have to, but I don't want to burn that bridge yet. I feel like I need to stay close where I can keep an eye on CJ. I suppose you heard. Mother kicked Tilly off the ranch for getting engaged to your brother."

"I heard. I'm sorry." He squeezed her hand before drawing it back.

"Tilly knew it could happen," she said with a shrug. "She's determined to go ahead with the wedding. I hope she isn't thinking that our mother will come around. I can't see that ever happening."

Duffy couldn't, either. "Eat your burger before it gets cold," he said and stole one of her fries, hoping to lighten the conversation. "If you don't want all that burger…" he joked as he helped himself to another fry.

He wasn't hungry, but he didn't want to leave. He kept thinking about her and Pickett.

"Help yourself to my fries. I never eat them all anyway." She smiled and picked up one half of the burger to take a bite as his cell phone rang.

"I'm here if you need me," he said as his phone rang again. He checked to see who was calling. It was Cooper. Worried something was wrong, he said, "I have to take this. I'll be right back." He rose and walked out of the café to take the call. He needed to tell his brother what the PI had said.

AFTER A RESTLESS NIGHT, Pickett had awakened thinking of Oakley. So he was caught off guard when his cell phone rang, otherwise he would never have taken a call from a number he didn't recognize. "Hello?"

"I'm in town at the hotel."

Just the sound of her voice made his blood run cold—let alone what she'd said. *She was in Powder Crossing?*

"I shouldn't have to spell out what happens next if you don't meet with me."

He had hit the brakes at the sound of the woman's voice. He'd been on his way into town to pick up supplies for the ranch, but now pulled over. His mind raced. She was in town? He didn't trust himself to speak for a few moments.

While he knew exactly what would happen if he didn't meet with her, he wanted desperately to do just the opposite. Rebelling came second nature to him. That was how he had ended up working on the McKenna Ranch all the way out in Montana all those years ago.

"You can no longer run from this," she said.

With a sinking heart, he knew it was true. Had he really thought this would never happen? That he'd put the past behind him, but that one day it wouldn't come looking for him? He pulled back onto the narrow county road. "I'm on my way."

"Room 403."

He squeezed his phone so hard he feared it would break before pocketing it. Hadn't he worried that he'd be found one day? He realized he probably should have answered the texts she'd been sending him. Now she was in town at the hotel. How had she found him?

Silly question. With her resources? The only surprise was that she hadn't come looking for him sooner.

Pickett swore as he drove the rest of the way into Powder Crossing, turned the ranch pickup into a parking spot and got out. He'd always felt invisible here. Just another ranch hand. The day he'd hired on at the McKenna Ranch was the best day of the beginning of his new life. He'd actually thought they'd never find him.

As he climbed out of the pickup, he looked up. With the afternoon light on the fourth-floor windows, he couldn't see if she was watching him, but he wouldn't have been surprised. Bracing himself, he headed inside.

Walking through the hotel lobby as he had many times before, he was glad to see that Willow Branson wasn't behind the reception desk. He took the stairs three steps at time. With his long legs it didn't take him any time before he reached room 403.

For a moment he stood in the hallway lecturing himself to keep his cool. The woman on the other side of this door didn't know Pickett Hanson since he wasn't the person he used to be. He had no idea what she was doing here, but he knew it didn't bode well for her to track him down, then come all the way out here from New York to see him.

Whatever she'd come for, she was clearly determined to come so far. But he was equally determined not to let her destroy what he'd built for himself out here.

The thought almost made him laugh. She wouldn't be impressed by what he'd felt he'd accomplished. She would only see a ranch hand driving someone else's truck. She wasn't going to understand. Not that he gave a damn what she thought.

But he couldn't have her blowing his cover. He thought of Holden McKenna, who'd hired him without any experience. Holden had taken a chance with him, not asking any questions of the kid he'd been, as if he'd seen the desperation in Pickett's eyes.

He thought of his life on the ranch that he loved. He thought of Oakley. He had so much to lose if the truth came out.

He took a breath, let it out and knocked.

OAKLEY COULD TELL her mother was having a bad day the moment she answered the phone.

"I need to see you," Charlotte said impatiently. "Where are you?"

After finishing her burger, she and Duffy had parted ways. She was now at the furnished apartment that she and Tilly had rented together. But now didn't seem like the time to mention that to her mother. "I'm in town. What's wrong?"

"We need to talk. How soon can you be here?"

She sighed. "I'm on my way." As she pulled on her

coat, she felt as if she should be wearing armor. All her instincts told her that her mother wanted to talk about CJ and what Oakley might say to a judge or an attorney.

What could she say since she didn't remember? While she knew at gut level there was more to the shooting, she had no evidence to prove it. CJ was going to get away with this.

Unless she remembered.

When she reached the ranch, her gaze went straight to the guest room window. The curtains were closed.

"I don't know why you think you can reason with her," she heard CJ saying as she came in the front door. "She'd love to see me behind bars. She's had it in for me since we were kids."

Stepping out of the foyer into the living room, she said, "Behind bars is where you deserve to be and we both know it."

"Oakley," her mother snapped. "I don't want to hear that talk ever again. He's your brother."

"And I'm his sister and he shot me. I was the one in the hospital all that time. I'm still in pain." She narrowed her eyes to him as she advanced on him.

"What about me?" CJ cried, slamming his hands down on the wheelchair's arms.

"You brought that on yourself," she said before her mother stepped between them.

"CJ, go to your room and let me talk to Oakley alone."

For a moment Oakley thought he would defy her. With obvious reluctance he wheeled down the hallway, but she suspected he left the guest room door cracked where he could hear.

"Let's sit down," her mother said, her voice tight no doubt as she struggled to be patient. Could she really not see the man her son had become?

Oakley sat on the edge of the couch, warning herself not to get kicked off the ranch. If she ever hoped to learn the truth about the shooting—let alone do anything about the drilling of another methane well—she needed to be able to come and go here. Tilly was already exiled. Because of the time she spent openly with Pickett and Duffy, she needed to be careful or she would be banished next.

She did wonder why her mother had never said anything about her hanging out with Pickett Hanson and Duffy McKenna. Because they'd been friends for so long? Or because she didn't think her daughter would ever be serious over either of them?

Her mother took a chair across from her. "As I mentioned, one of my lawyers will be talking to you about the unfortunate accident." Oakley had to grit her teeth not to correct her. "I need you to stop fighting with your brother. Can't you see how hard this is on him?" She groaned inwardly, teeth clenched. "Once we get through this and your brother is exonerated, you can go back to arguing with him as you always have, but for now…"

"Does it bother you at all that he shot me?" Oakley asked, more curious than defiant.

"Of course it bothers me. I stayed by your bedside for days praying you would pull through and furious at whoever had done this."

"But that was before you knew it was CJ who had shot me."

Her mother took a controlled breath. "Nothing about

this is easy for me. Fortunately, you survived. You're going to be fine. But CJ—"

"What did the doctors say about his condition?"

Charlotte looked annoyed to be interrupted but answered. "He has a neck injury, but fortunately his spinal cord wasn't severed. The doctors are optimistic he will walk again."

Oakley nodded. "So the wheelchair is just temporary. Until you get the charges against him either dropped and changed to community service or some such slap on the wrist."

Anger sparked in her mother's eyes. "If you're insinuating—"

She rose to leave. "I was just wondering if he's pulling the wool over your eyes as well as everyone else or if you're in on it with him."

"Oakley." Her mother was on her feet now, too. "Why do you want to argue all the time?"

"Because my brother has never taken responsibility for what he's done."

"What about you? If you hadn't been on the Mc-Kenna Ranch that day, none of this would have happened."

Oakley sighed. Arguing with her mother was getting her nowhere. "Don't worry about what I'll say to the attorney. You might recall that I don't remember what happened."

"That's good," her mother said. "Our attorney is flying in. I'll let you know the time and place to make your statement."

She nodded as she studied her mother. "I should warn you, though, that bits and pieces of that day are starting to come back. CJ is worried, which should tell you something."

With that, she started for the door and heard the squeak of the wheelchair down the hall. He'd been listening, just as she knew he had. "I'll tell the attorney that I don't remember," she said over her shoulder. "Unless I remember before I talk to him."

She smiled to herself as she left. But as she climbed into her truck, she looked back at the house and knew that if she didn't remember soon, CJ was going to get away with everything.

Meanwhile, she'd practically waved another red flag in front of her brother, as if daring the bull in him to come after her. Was she really hoping he could try to kill her again so he would get caught this time?

THE OLDER WOMAN who answered Pickett's knock at hotel room 403 was thinner than he recalled. Sarah Johansen's hair had turned from blond to steel gray, but that stern, determined look in her blue eyes was just as he remembered. She was dressed in an expensive-looking gray suit, crisp white blouse and heels, and couldn't have looked more out of place here in this old hotel in a small, isolated town in eastern Montana.

That was worry enough since he couldn't have people wondering who she was or what she was doing here. He had to get her out of Powder Crossing as fast as possible.

"At least you were prompt, Archibald," she said and stepped aside to let him enter.

He walked to the center of the room and turned to face her. He didn't bother to ask how she'd found him.

She worked for a multibillion-dollar corporation with more resources than the president of the United States. "What are you doing here?"

"I could ask you the same question," she said and closed the motel room door. "If you had responded to any of my texts, you would already know. Sit down."

He'd taken orders from her for years and almost obeyed without question just as he had as a child. "I won't be staying that long. What are you doing here?"

She seemed to study him then, frowning as she took him in. "You've…changed," she said, moving closer. It wasn't a compliment.

He had changed from the scared teen he'd been. And he didn't jump when she said jump, but then again there was no question about who had the power in this situation—and she knew it. Still, he was determined to wait her out.

Sarah cleared her throat and never having been one to mince her words said, "Your father is ill. It's time for you to come home."

Pickett could hear the emotion in her voice. He'd long suspected that she'd been in love with his father from the day she became his personal assistant all those years ago. For all he knew or cared, they might even have been lovers at some point between his father's ill-conceived marriages.

"I'm sorry to hear that he's ill, but my father and I said all we had to say a long time ago."

She didn't seem surprised by his response. "I don't believe you understand. If you do not return and take your place as his only son, you will be disinherited."

He laughed. "I thought he'd already done that. If

that's his best shot, it missed the mark. I don't want it. I never did."

"Archibald—"

"It's Pickett Hanson now."

Sarah actually rolled her eyes, something he'd never seen her do before. "You have always been impulsive, stubborn and foolish, but you've never been cruel. Your father is dying. He wants to make amends for the past and the disagreement between you."

He studied her, not trusting that she was telling the truth. "He's dying?"

Emotion welled in her eyes. "He doesn't have much time. He knows that you aren't interested in taking over what he built for you." Her voice broke. "He just wants to see you before it's too late."

Pickett turned and walked to the window to look out at the land he now called home. He knew his father thought he was living a lie out here, but this had been where he'd found his true self. He didn't want to lose that.

"Please come back with me," Sarah said behind him in a pleading tone he'd also never heard from her before.

He slowly turned to look at her. "I have to let my boss know. You should go on ahead. I'll catch the first flight I can." He also had to let Duffy and Oakley know. He thought of what he would tell them. Anything but the truth.

CHAPTER TWELVE

WHEN THE DISPATCHER told Stuart a federal agent was on the phone, he swore under his breath before picking up. He hoped this call wasn't about another meth lab popping up in his county, but he wouldn't have been surprised. In such an isolated place with more cows than people, there were too many old homesteads, empty farmhouses and mining shacks hidden back in the hills. The land here ran open for miles bordered by pine-covered mountains, gullies and deep ravines hidden by rocky cliffs, places you could hide a 747.

"Sheriff Layton," he said, taking the call and bracing himself for the worst.

The agent introduced himself, then said, "We did some aerial photography when we were over in your county. I was just going through it and I found something."

"Another meth lab?" He was surprised that the drug dealers had brazenly set up another one so quickly.

"We spotted something in a reservoir on one of the unoccupied ranches," the agent was saying. Out-of-staters had been buying up the west, determined to take the land back to how it was in the 1800s by not doing anything on it. It made some ranchers fear that it would be the death of ranching, especially family-run ranches that weren't making a profit. Easier to sell out and retire.

In the Powder River Basin it was on open invitation to anyone who knew the area to use the land for something other than ranching or farming since the landowners weren't here.

"In a reservoir?" At least it wasn't a meth lab, Stuart thought with relief.

"It looks like a vehicle. With this drought, the water in the reservoir dropped enough that you can see it some feet below the surface. Doesn't look like it's been there all that long."

The agent gave him the directions to the spot and Stuart said he'd run out and check. But when he realized the location, he felt a start. The reservoir was on the Turner Ranch—the one that he knew both Holden McKenna and Charlotte Stafford wanted to buy because it bordered their ranches and had plenty of water.

He swore and looked up to find Deputy Ty Dodson lounging in the doorway with a cup of coffee in his hand.

"Come on. We need to go check on something," the sheriff said as he rose and reached for his hat and coat. "You own a swimsuit?"

Dodson frowned. "It's winter in Montana."

"Then you might need a wetsuit as well, but that's only if this reservoir isn't iced over. I wouldn't worry. I believe there is a natural spring that flows into this one. The water could be open and all of forty degrees," he said as he motioned for the deputy to ditch the coffee cup and get moving. He found himself almost happy since it hadn't been a call about a meth lab. Also, that he wouldn't have to go into the water himself. He didn't like water that came up higher than his knees.

A vehicle in the reservoir on Inez Turner's ranch? He didn't kid himself that this might turn out to be just as bad—or worse—than a meth lab.

"DID YOU KNOW Pickett had family back east?" Oakley asked.

Duffy shook his head. They'd both gotten texts with little explanation, making Oakley realize that Pickett had never talked about family.

"He wasn't very old when he arrived at the ranch looking for a job, according to my father. He's just always been with us," Duffy said.

"But he's coming back, right?" Oakley asked, and Duffy shrugged. "So are we still going to the emergency Dirty Business meeting without him tonight?"

"He'd want us to," Duffy said a little too quickly.

She laughed. "Pickett told us not to go without him."

"You know how jealous he is of you and me being together alone." Duffy grinned like he was kidding, but he seemed to be happy about the idea.

"I'm sure that wasn't why he didn't want us doing anything without him," she said. "He's worried about those men the CH4 hired to catch the vandals."

"Don't worry. I will protect you."

She gave Duffy a shove. "I'll protect myself, thank you very much."

He laughed. "You're no damsel in distress, that's for sure. But it makes it hard to sweep you off your feet."

She shook her head. As if that was what he was trying to do. She was used to Duffy flirting with her, but

Pickett was usually around. She knew how Duffy was with women. She didn't take him seriously, not with his reputation.

Still, the three of them had become a team. Tonight it would be just the two of them. She'd miss Pickett and couldn't help worrying about him. He'd gone because of his family? What if he didn't come back?

"Want me to pick you up at the usual time and place?" she asked. She always drove only partly because she liked driving. Her nondescript pickup was better to take to the meetings than a McKenna Ranch truck.

Duffy grinned. "Can't wait."

She hoped this wouldn't be weird, reminding herself that it was Duffy. He was just goofing around as usual.

THE SHERIFF STOOD on the edge of the reservoir, trying to see into the water. The natural spring had kept the reservoir from freezing, but he knew the water would still be freezing cold. Picking up a rock, he chucked it toward the middle. All that accomplished was making a circle of small waves that eventually lapped at the shore.

He turned to Dodson. "Ready?"

The deputy mugged a face and mumbled something under his breath that Stuart didn't care to hear. Thanks to the local volunteer fire department, the deputy was attired in a rubber suit for cold-water rescues.

"All you have to do is make sure there is a vehicle in there and that it's not so old that we're wasting our time," the sheriff said.

Nodding, the deputy pulled the hood over his head and began to walk out into the reservoir. Stuart watched, a hitch in his chest. He couldn't shake the bad feeling that whatever they found wouldn't be good. Like the rock he'd thrown into the water, he feared this could cause a ripple that would spread even beyond the Powder River Basin.

Dodson disappeared for a moment below the water, but quickly resurfaced to stand on what was apparently the top of a vehicle four to five feet under him. He waved his arms excitedly. Stuart's stomach dropped.

WHEN PICKETT HAD told him he had to fly back east because his father was ill, Holden had been surprised. In all the time the young man had been at McKenna Ranch, he'd never mentioned family or left to return home.

"I hope he's going to be all right," Holden had said. "Is there anything I can do? Do you need an advance on your pay?"

"No, I'm fine," he'd said. "But thank you. I won't be gone long."

"Take as long as you need. We'll miss you, though. Holly Jo will be bummed. She's determined to learn to trick ride as well as you." What Holden wanted to say was, "Come back." Pickett had become like another son to him.

"Tell Holly Jo I'll be back with a whole new trick for her," Pickett said and left, driving his own pickup instead of a ranch truck.

Holden couldn't help worrying about him. The young man hadn't been himself. When Elaine walked in, he was standing at the window watching Pickett drive away.

"Is everything all right?" she asked.

"I'm not sure," he said and turned to smile at her. "Pickett. His father is ill. He's flying back east. Said he'd be back, though."

"Really? I just assumed he didn't have any family still alive," she said.

"I think we all thought that. Seems odd, doesn't it?"

"He's just always been here. I'm guessing that when he arrived looking for a job, you simply hired him and didn't ask any questions."

"You know me so well," Holden said with a laugh. "He was a kid, but there was something about him…" He shook his head. "I'm a sucker for strays, aren't I?"

She laughed. "It's one of the things I love about you." Their gazes met and held for a moment before she looked away. "Maybe if you knew something more about him, you wouldn't look so worried. Pickett Hanson is a unique-enough name, it should be simple enough to put your mind at ease."

"You're right," he said and headed into his office. Within minutes, though, he discovered no one with that name existed a few months before he'd hired the young ranch hand. Instead of easing his mind, he was more worried than ever.

THE SHERIFF MADE the call and two hours later, divers hooked onto the pickup and the local wrecker pulled it from the reservoir. He'd expected to find remains behind the wheel, but the cab of the truck was empty except for a suitcase behind the seat, along with more personal items and tools, as if the driver was either coming to Powder Crossing—or leaving.

Once the mud had been wiped from the license plate,

Stuart ran the number. The pickup was registered to Rory Eastwood of Colorado Springs, Colorado, an employee of CH4 gas company. One phone call and Stuart solved at least one mystery. Eastwood had quit his job with the local CH4 company and was leaving town more than two years ago.

How his pickup ended up in the reservoir on the Turner Ranch remained a mystery—as did where Rory Eastwood was now since the team dragging the small reservoir found no remains.

The pickup had been taken to the sheriff's department fenced yard. With everyone gone from the reservoir, Stuart had stayed for a while. He had a lot on his mind, Abigail Creed at the top of the list. He still hadn't decided what to do about her. They hadn't talked since he'd called her after she'd drugged him.

He was wondering if that would be the end of it and if he should let it go unless he planned to arrest her. But since there wasn't enough evidence that she'd drugged him…that really wasn't an option.

As he started to get into his patrol SUV, a pickup came roaring up to the reservoir. He hesitated as a large man with closely cropped gray hair climbed out. Private investigator Jason Murdock.

Groaning, the sheriff waited as Murdock headed for him.

"Let me guess, Rory Eastwood's pickup," the PI said. "Was he in it? Never mind, I would have passed an ambulance with the body if he had been. So that leaves us with him still missing. Just like Dixon Malone. I'm right. You didn't happen to find him down there, did you?"

Stuart sighed. "Sounds like you already have your answer." He turned back to his rig to leave.

"Imagine my surprise to find out that Dixon Malone wasn't the only person who's gone missing around here. You knew Rory, right, Sheriff?"

"No, sorry, never met him," he said, his back to the man.

"Seems Rory Eastwood gave his notice with CH4, indicating that he was leaving here to make a new life with a new lady," Murdock said. "The bartender down at the Wild Horse said he was all excited, real secretive about this woman he was running away with. Some speculate the woman was Leann Hayes. You remember her since the two of you were an item, I understand, Sheriff. Leann allegedly commits suicide and *poof*, Rory Eastwood is never seen again. And here's his pickup in this reservoir."

Stuart sighed and turned around. "If you have any information about Mr. Eastwood, you should come down to the office and make a statement."

"Over two years ago I hear the drought in these parts was just starting. This reservoir would have been much higher. I would imagine that's why the perpetrator dumped the truck here, don't you think? Almost seems like it had to be someone who knew the area and knew how to cover his—or her—tracks, huh."

"Nice theory," the sheriff said. "But why not dispose of his body with the truck?"

The PI nodded. "That is a good question." He glanced at the reservoir, making Stuart think about the truck as it was pulled from the water. He hadn't wanted to find what was left of a cadaver after two years underwater.

The mud had been scraped from the side window, offering a view of the cab. He'd expected the body would be inside. He'd never been so glad to be wrong.

"I just passed the wrecker with the pickup," Murdock said. "Looked like all his belongings were in there. Not much room for someone to drive the pickup—with a body in the cab." Murdock smiled as he turned back to Stuart. "Guess the killer had to find another place for Rory. Must have worried about putting him in the bed of the pickup. Wouldn't want to be driving around with a body in the back of the pickup—at least not very far. Appears they disposed of the body first, then the pickup." He glanced around. "I'd say he was probably somewhere here on the ranch or not far from here. Guess you'll be looking for a grave."

"If he's dead," Stuart said, hating this man's arrogance, even though he agreed with him. "We don't know that for a fact."

Murdock scoffed. "He's dead and we both know it, Sheriff. Makes me wonder why you don't want to admit it."

"I don't have time for this." The sheriff opened his car door, but the PI kept talking, clearly having more to say. He wished he didn't feel that he should listen.

"The thing about Powder Crossing, such a small town, everyone knows everyone else and their business," Murdock was saying. "I'm betting someone around here knows how that pickup got in that reservoir—just as they know what happened to another missing man, Dixon Malone. Someone in this river basin has something to hide. Strange part is both disappearances seem to be connected to two ranches in town, the McKenna and the Stafford ranches. The way I hear it, people around these parts say if anyone can get away with murder in the river basin, it would be Holden McKenna and Charlotte Stafford—or one of their offspring."

Stu shook his head and climbed into his patrol SUV. He'd had enough of Murdock. As he started to pull away, he noted that the PI had walked out to the edge of the reservoir and stood looking into the water's depths as if he could see the truth lying down there in the mud.

The sheriff didn't even pretend that he didn't know exactly what Murdock had been implying. Nor did he kid himself that if the man kept digging, he wouldn't turn up something. So far all the PI knew for certain, it seemed, was that Dixon Malone had been in a tumultuous marriage with Charlotte Stafford before he disappeared.

As for Rory Eastwood... Murdock had been fishing, dangling Leann Hayes as bait, Stu told himself. So what if some people in town were speculating that there was a connection between Leann and Rory Eastwood. The PI wanted to believe it. Maybe Leann had told someone in town that she was leaving with a mystery man at about the same time Rory Eastwood was shooting his mouth off down at the bar.

Murdock was trying to fit the pieces together. Leann had been dating Cooper McKenna—before her death. Before that, she'd been with Stu. If the PI could prove that Leann and Rory had died on the same night, he would be pointing the finger at not just Cooper, but Stu himself.

He swore as he drove back to his office. Once behind

his desk, he couldn't help but worry. How long would it be before all hell broke loose? At the time of Leann's death, the county prosecutor had been convinced that her sometime lover, Cooper McKenna, had killed her. Even when the coroner had declared her death a suicide, not even Cooper had believed it and wanted the case reopened.

Cooper would be even more convinced now that she'd been murdered. Rory Eastwood's pickup turning up was bad news, especially if someone could prove that Rory Eastwood had been the mystery man Leann was leaving with.

He called Deputy Dodson. "When you're finished locking up the pickup until the state forensic boys get here, I need you to go back out to the ranch. Start at the reservoir and begin searching for a grave or a place a body could have been hidden two years ago."

Since they would be searching a nonworking ranch, the body could be anywhere—even in an outbuilding. "Let me know the minute you find anything."

He disconnected and leaned back in his chair, feeling the weight of his job pin him down. If the case was reopened, Cooper McKenna would look more like the jealous lover who killed both the girlfriend and her new man. And with Eastwood's pickup being found in the reservoir, there would be no stopping Murdock, who now had the bit between his teeth when it came to both the McKennas and the Staffords, and he was running with it.

Just when Stu thought his day couldn't get worse, he looked up to find nurse Abigail Creed standing in his office doorway.

CHAPTER THIRTEEN

NEWS OF THE pickup dragged from the ranch reservoir spread like all juicy gossip in the basin. When Duffy heard the pickup was registered to a former employee of CH4 gas exploration named Rory Eastwood, he felt a chill run the length of his spine. The PI had just been talking about Rory at the café.

Duffy had warned his brother when they talked earlier. But now that Rory Eastwood's pickup had been found... He hated to upset Cooper when maybe there wasn't a problem.

He reminded himself that PI Jason Murdock had no proof that the man Leann was allegedly leaving town with was Rory Eastwood. Or that Cooper McKenna had stopped both Leann and Rory from leaving.

Almost back to the ranch, he saw the school bus stop to let Holly Jo out. As the bus went on down the road, he pulled up and opened his passenger-side door. "Wanna ride?"

She climbed in without a word, hoisting her backpack in ahead of her.

"How are you doing?" he asked, really wanting to know. He hated that she might be getting lost in the shuffle with his dad involved in ranch business and trying to buy the Turner place and the rest of the family just as busy.

"Okay." She didn't look at him when she answered. Bare-limbed cottonwood trees blurred past on both sides of the pickup as he drove. Snow from the last storm was thick under the trees. The only bare spots were on the south-facing slopes. Sunlight poured in through the windshield, making the cab almost too warm.

"You can tell me." For a few minutes he thought she wouldn't.

"There's this boy at school."

"I see." He thought she might, but he wanted to be sure as he turned down the lane to the ranch. "You like him?"

She turned to him with a look of horror. "*Gus?* I can't stand him. He teases me all the time. I want to punch him in the face."

Duffy realized he was out of his league. He knew nothing about kids. But he did know about boys. "Is Gus cute?"

Again, she gave him a stricken look. "No, he is not cute. He's…" She mugged a face and then sighed as if there was no describing this boy.

"Have you asked him to stop?" He read her look just fine. "But he won't, right? Okay. Do you want me to go to school and beat him up?"

She stared at him a moment to see if he was being serious, then slowly shook her head. "You'd make it worse."

"Maybe he's got a crush on you and he doesn't know

how to express his feelings," he said as he pulled into the ranch yard and parked.

"That is the dumbest thing I've ever heard." With another look that said she wouldn't be talking to him about it again, she was out of the pickup and headed for the house.

Duffy watched her go, wondering if he should mention this to his father. He really doubted Holden would have handled it better. But he did consider stopping by the school one of these days and having a little talk with this Gus kid.

PICKETT LEFT HIS pickup at the airport in Billings and flew to New York. There was a car waiting for him at the airport. He climbed into the back of the town car and closed his eyes. The entire flight he'd tried to tell himself that nothing could change his mind about this life he'd made for himself.

He knew it wasn't just being a ranch hand, though he really did enjoy the work. It was being a part of the McKenna Ranch, being a part of a real family. But if he was being honest with himself, it was Oakley.

There would be only one thing that could get him to leave the ranch and the life he'd made for himself. If Oakley chose another man—especially Duffy instead of him, he'd have no choice but to leave. He couldn't bear the thought of staying and watching her make a life with another man.

She was the reason he was going to New York to see his father, he told himself as the car slowed and turned. He had to deal with his past if he hoped for the future he wanted on McKenna Ranch.

He opened his eyes. Tall trees—both taller and thicker than he remembered—hid the house. At the electronic gate, the driver touched the pad but before he could speak into the intercom, the gate opened. He pulled through, the gate closing behind them. Of course, Sarah knew exactly when he would be arriving. A plane ticket had been waiting for him at the airport in Billings.

Pickett had seen that it was round trip or he would have purchased his own. He didn't mind having a little more room for his legs in first class. It had been years since he'd been on a plane, not since he was a boy traveling with his father. The planes and first class had gotten smaller, the seating more compact—at least on the flights out of Montana.

The road twisted and turned through the dense trees until the house came into view. It seemed larger than he remembered with all its impressive towering stone walls and winged wooden gables, but maybe it was because he'd been living in a tiny cabin off the bunkhouse for so long.

That he'd grown up here, once lived in this massive place, surprised him. He now felt more at home on the ranch than here. Holden had added the small cabin for Pickett some years ago. It was all he needed, all he wanted. Except for Oakley.

Just the thought of her made him realize how little he had to offer her. He'd saved his money religiously since being hired on at the McKenna Ranch. He'd picked up enough about investing from his father growing up that he'd turned his meager wage into a nice nest egg.

He reined in the thought, realizing with a start how

far ahead he'd let his mind wander. He hadn't even asked Oakley for a date, and he already had them married and him building a house for them on a piece of land he would buy. No wonder Sarah—and no doubt his father—thought him a fool. Maybe he was. He was back here, wasn't he?

The driver pulled into the circular drive and stopped at the front entry. Pickett opened his door before the driver could and got out, pulling his duffel bag with him. He'd packed just what he needed for a short visit. Not that he owned a suitcase. He'd left home all those years ago with far less.

He had dressed in his Montana formal attire: a pair of newer jeans, a Western snap shirt and a denim jacket. He was wearing his best boots and his Stetson.

He turned to offer the driver a tip, but the man said he'd already been paid and wished him a nice day. He watched the town car pull away before he turned to take it all in. He resented that he'd been forced into coming here and was equally ashamed of himself that he had to be forced to see his dying father. Coercion and blackmail were his father's weapons of choice, but that wasn't the kind of man Pickett wanted to be.

He thought of Holden McKenna, the generous, caring, forgiving man he was. Pickett wanted to be more like him as he slowly started up the stone steps to the huge front door.

THE SHERIFF HADN'T seen Abigail Creed since he'd gone to dinner at her place and woke up alone the next morning after being drugged. It had been a drug that didn't stay in a man's system long, fortunately. Unfortunately, he now knew that if anyone knew how to knock a man out, it was Nurse Creed.

"Got a minute?" Abigail asked shyly. She didn't wait for an answer, stepping into his office and closing the door quietly behind her. "I just wanted to apologize," she said when she finally turned to face him again.

As badly as he wanted to confront her, he asked, "For what?" He was curious to see if the truth would come out of her mouth.

"I was in a rush the other morning. Got called in to the hospital. I should have at least left you a note."

So that was how they were still going to play it? "I'm the one who feels bad. Falling asleep on your couch the way I did."

"All is forgiven, then." Hardly, he thought as she gave him that nothing-here-to-worry-about smile. "I thought you and I might…" Her gaze met his. Did she really think that look would still work on him?

He blamed himself for letting it go this far. Hadn't he suspected something wasn't on the up and up the moment he met her? He'd thought he was just being cynical, thinking there had to be something wrong with a woman who was sweet as pie and liked him. Apparently, he'd been right on both counts.

When he said nothing, she spelled it out. "I was wondering if you wanted to get together later? I find myself free."

He shook his head as if disappointed. In truth, he was. A full confession would have gone a long way with him. "Wish I could, but I'm tied up tonight."

"Really?" she said, her smile teasing. "Tied up. That sounds interesting."

He rose from his chair. "Thanks for stopping by. Maybe some other time."

She nodded, looking disappointed, and he couldn't help but wonder what she'd had planned for this evening. He hated to think as she opened his office door and left.

As she did, he knew he couldn't leave it like this. He would have to confront her and find out why she was so interested in Leann Hayes's death. Why was he putting it off? Unless he was afraid of what she might tell him. Like Cooper, Abigail might be looking for the truth about Leann's death. She might even know who was responsible for it.

Isn't that what he was really afraid of?

OAKLEY HAD SLEPT at the ranch last night. She'd managed to avoid both her mother and CJ by coming in late through the private entrance. She had never been in the habit of locking her bedroom door, but she did last night. Logic assured her that CJ wouldn't get up the stairs. But common sense warned her not to trust logic any more than she did her brother.

Early this morning she heard her mother leave. She watched from her bedroom window, anxious to know if she was leaving alone. Apparently, she was, since she took her SUV. The van equipped to load CJ and his wheelchair was still parked outside.

She felt a chill at being alone in the house with him. The staff had their own wing. Her mother was so hard to work for that there was a constant turnover. Oakley wasn't even sure how many were still employed.

Even though she tried to assure herself that as long as CJ couldn't walk, she had the advantage. But if he could... She wasn't entirely convinced that he wasn't more capable than he wanted anyone to know. Unless, of course, their mother was in on the charade in the hope the chair would keep him out of jail.

Oakley was about to turn from the window when a large black SUV drove slowly up the road toward the house. She got the feeling that whoever was driving had been waiting for their mother to leave. Stepping back from sight, she watched as the SUV stopped and two large men climbed out.

She felt a tremor of fear. Were these the two thugs they'd heard about that the gas company had hired to stop the vandalizing? She held her breath as they reached the front door and waited for the sound of the doorbell.

When she didn't hear it, she cautiously eased out of her bedroom and padded quietly on bare feet down the hall to where she could watch from the landing at the top of the stairs. The two men were now standing in the living room, looking around as if taking in the place. To rob them? They hadn't rung the doorbell or knocked that she'd heard.

At the creak of her brother's wheelchair coming down the hall from the guest room, she started to call out a warning. The only thing that stopped her was seeing CJ's expression. He knew the men. He'd known they were coming out to the ranch.

She knew he'd been expecting them, even though

he greeted them with, "I told you not to come out here, Frankie."

"Don't worry. We waited until the head warden left," the smaller of the two said.

"As always, Norman, you've missed the point. The warden, as you call my mother, could come back at any time. I don't want her to find you here." CJ sounded upset but Oakley could see that he was more scared than angry.

Frankie and Norman. The Lees brothers whom they'd heard about at Dirty Business. So these really were the gas company thugs that had been hired. But what were they doing here?

"Don't talk to my brother that way," Frankie said as he advanced on CJ.

To her brother's credit, he held his ground. "The point is you're not supposed to be here."

Frankie grabbed the arms of the wheelchair and leaned down to whisper in CJ's ear. She watched her brother's face and, while she couldn't hear what Frankie was saying, she could tell by CJ's expression that the man was threatening him.

"I told you," CJ said, his voice breaking.

"I know what you told us, but we haven't seen you," Norman said as if trying to ease the tension that had filled the room.

Frankie shoved the wheelchair back a few feet before turning his back on CJ. "It crossed my mind that you might be thinking of making a deal with the law to save yourself from doing time." He turned quickly and glared at her brother. "That would be a big mistake on your part. Trust me when I tell you that I can get to you here or in jail. Not even your mother will be able to protect you if you narc on me, let alone double cross me."

"I'm sure CJ wouldn't—" Norman started to say.

Frankie cut him off when he moved swiftly to CJ, grabbing his right arm. Oakley heard her brother let out a gasp, then a cry of pain. She took a step, ready to go to his defense before Frankie stepped back again—and she came to her senses.

"Tell me that we understand each other," Frankie said.

CJ acknowledged with a pained nod.

"Good. I'll be waiting to hear from you, then. Don't make me wait too long." With that, Frankie headed for the door, his brother behind him.

Oakley stood, trying to make sense out of what she'd heard. What were the brothers the gas company had hired to protect their equipment and catch vandals doing here threatening CJ?

Clearly, they knew him, seemed to have dealings with him. It made no sense. She listened as the men left before she came the rest of the way down the stairs.

CJ looked up and tried to hide his surprise and fear at seeing her. He'd been rubbing his arm and the angry bright red spot on it. Now he covered it with his sleeve. "I didn't know you were home." He made it sound like an accusation. He looked both angry and at the same time embarrassed, afraid he'd been caught?

"Perhaps you forgot that I live here," she said.

In answer, he started to turn his wheelchair back toward the hallway to the guest room.

"Before you go, how about you tell me why those two men were threatening you."

"It's none of your business." He wheeled toward the hall.

"Bet Mom would like to hear about it."

He stopped and turned slowly to face her. She remembered her earlier feeling of fear being in the house alone with him. She told herself that he couldn't stand, let alone walk. If he could, wouldn't he have risen from the chair to confront the men? Or was he pretending to be helpless so they wouldn't hurt him any worse?

"You know what your problem is, Oakley?" he said, wheeling toward her. "You don't know how to keep your nose out of other people's business." She didn't move, even when his chair stopped dangerously close to her bare feet. "You haven't figured out that it is bad for your health. I guess being shot and almost dying didn't teach you anything."

"You're wrong," she said, sounding more confident than she felt with him so close and fury darkening his narrowed eyes. "I've learned a whole lot. Especially about you, CJ. I knew this wasn't about me being on McKenna land. You are up to your neck in whatever it is I saw that day and it's bad or those two thugs wouldn't be here threatening you. It sounds a lot more dangerous for you than for me."

She started to turn when he grabbed her arm, his fingers digging maliciously into her flesh. "Tell Mother or anyone else and you're dead." He let go of her arm and turned his chair around to leave again.

"So it does have something to do with why you shot me," she said to his retreating back. She pulled her phone from the pocket of her pajama bottoms. Rewound for a few seconds and hit Play.

Tell Mother or anyone else and you're dead.

She snapped it off as he whirled around and started to get out of the chair.

AT THE MANSION'S front door, Pickett rang the bell and waited. He knew he was expected since someone had let the town car in through the gate so quickly. He figured Sarah since she was the one who set everything up as she'd done for years for his father. For that reason, he wasn't surprised that she was the one who answered the door.

She was dressed much as she'd been when he'd last seen her, this time in a gray suit with a freshly laundered crisp white blouse and low heels as if trapped in a role she'd had to play, one that required hiding her true feelings. That stern, hard look was still in her blue eyes, but he noticed a weakness in her usually rigid frame. She wasn't as strong as she wanted him to believe.

"Your father is waiting," she said and turned toward the elevator that would take them up to the master suite.

He followed, willing himself to be as strong as Sarah pretended to be. He didn't want to see his bigger-than-life father frail and dying. He wanted to remember him as an angry giant of a man who used his power and money to force people to be what he demanded. To find his father otherwise would make it harder to hold on to the revulsion he'd had for the man.

Sarah said nothing as the elevator car took them to the top floor. As the car stopped and the door began to open, she said, "Archibald—"

"It's Pickett."

She nodded, meeting his gaze, and said the one thing he didn't want to hear right now. "He isn't the man you remember."

OAKLEY LEAPED BACK as CJ shot out of the chair and lunged for her throat.

At first, she thought the scream that filled the room was her own as her brother grabbed for her, taking them both to the floor. His hands were around her throat. She fought to push him away as the scream grew louder. Stronger than she was, CJ gripped her neck even harder, cutting off her air. She clawed at his fingers. This time, he was going to kill her.

"Stop!" her mother screamed as she grabbed her son's arm, breaking the hold he had on Oakley's throat. He rolled to his side as she gasped for air, their mother standing over them. She looked horrified before she screamed, "What have you done to my son? CJ, are you hurt?"

Oakley rolled away from the two of them as their mother dropped to her knees beside her son. She caught his smug expression before he turned to their mother and said, "It's not her fault. We were arguing. I forgot I can't…" He awkwardly pushed himself into a sitting position, then, using his arms, dragged his lower body over to the chair. Locking the wheels in place, he tried to pull himself back up into the chair.

Their mother hurried to help him as Oakley sat on the floor rubbing her neck and watching his performance. Had she not been struggling to breathe, she might have clapped.

"What did she do to your arm?" her mother cried,

spotting where Frankie Lees had dug into CJ's flesh. "What on earth were you thinking?" she demanded as she strode over to glare down at her daughter. "You could have hurt him worse."

Oakley could feel CJ watching her, waiting to see what she was going to say. "I thought I heard you leave for town."

"I got down the road and realized that I'd forgotten my purse. Good thing I came back when I did."

She said nothing as she got to her bare feet, realizing that she was still wearing her pajama bottoms and a large T-shirt and little else. She shot a look at her brother. He had on his innocent face, but the look in his eyes was pure hatred.

Her mother was breathing hard, scared and furious. What good would it do to tell her anything that had to do with CJ? She would just say that Oakley had provoked him, which was true.

As she turned to head upstairs, she heard her mother ask her son if he was all right. She couldn't hear CJ's answer. At the top of the second-floor landing, she stopped to look back down. Her mother was smoothing CJ's hair back from his face and looking worried.

As Oakley headed for her room, she started to call Pickett, but remembered he had gone back east. She called Duffy. When he answered, she felt the pain in her throat, though it was nothing compared to the pain in her heart.

"Hey, Oak, you better not be calling to cancel tonight."

She swiped at the hot tears that ran down her cheeks. She needed Pickett. He'd know what to say to her right now. He'd listen. He'd know that she was scared. "I for-got Pickett's back east." The words came out because she was thinking them. She heard the disappointment in her voice and hoped he hadn't. She shouldn't have called Duffy.

"Means it will just be you and me," he said. "I'll have you all to myself."

She closed her eyes. What would she do if Pickett didn't come back? "I have news, but I'll tell you when I see you."

PICKETT HAD EXPECTED to see his father lying in bed. As he stepped into the semidarkness of the master suite, his gaze went to the bed first, then slowly moved around the enormous room.

For a moment he felt duped. If his father really was so ill that he was dying, wouldn't he be in bed, possibly hooked up to all kinds of medical devices with a nurse at his bedside? He started to turn, angry that he'd been sent on a wild goose chase, when something moved in a chair by the window.

Pickett must have made a shocked sound as the frail figure in the chair took shape in the dim light that stole in through the gauzy curtains at the window.

"Archibald?" The name came out on a hoarse, grav-elly whisper. "I'm sorry. Pickett."

In that little light stealing in, he got his first look at his father, Archibald the third. The face appeared skel-etal, as did the rest of the diminished body. As Pickett stepped closer, he could see his father's claw-like hand on the arm of the chair.

His first thought was that the man wouldn't want him

seeing him like this. His next was that the only reason his father would allow it was that he had very little time left and was desperate. To his surprise, Pickett felt his heart go out to the man he hadn't spoken to in years.

Swallowing the lump in his throat, he braced himself for what he was about to see and moved closer. He recognized little about the wasted figure in the chair. He would never have known it was his father except for the rheumy blue eyes sunken in the colorless skin stretched over his skull.

Pickett was hit with the thought that if he had delayed his trip even hours, he might not have made it here before his father passed.

His father motioned for him to pull up a chair. He did and sat down, his Stetson in his hand, as he searched for words. But there were none. He'd left here having said everything he'd felt all those years ago.

"You came," his father rasped, his head bobbing slightly as his thin lips grimaced into a macabre smile. "Thank you, son."

He reached out and placed a hand over his father's. It felt like bird wings or dried fall leaves. He feared he might break the brittle bones. His father's eyes filled as Pickett felt his own vision blur.

CHAPTER FOURTEEN

Duffy felt even more unsettled after the phone call with Oakley. He'd heard something in her voice and now wished he'd asked her about her news. She'd almost sounded…scared. Oakley was always so strong, so fearless, he couldn't imagine what might have scared her.

Had to be her family. He hoped that what he'd heard in her voice had more to do with that, than her missing Pickett. It couldn't be easy to be around a brother who had shot her. Charlotte wasn't a warm, nurturing mother by a long shot, but when it came to CJ and even her other boys, she at least was kind. He told himself not to worry about what he thought he'd heard in Oakley's voice.

Instead, he concentrated on tonight. After what he'd thought he'd seen between her and Pickett, he couldn't wait any longer. He would finally move his relationship with Oakley from friend to hopefully lover.

He'd had so few friend relationships with women that he didn't really know how to approach this, though. The one time he'd called Oakley suggesting they go to Billings to a movie, she'd called Pickett and asked him along as if the three of them were inseparable.

Duffy had figured she just wasn't ready yet. His way had always been direct, believing that was what women liked. At least it had worked on the women he'd known. But Oakley was different, he reminded himself. Then again, he suspected Pickett had somehow moved from friend to something else with her.

But Pickett wasn't here tonight.

Duffy would show her exactly how he felt. He wasn't too worried since few women had ever turned him down. He knew that Oakley liked him. She'd even said that she loved him—and Pickett—a few times. Even though he'd known she meant as friends. He told himself that he wasn't worried about Pickett and didn't see him as real competition, even though he was his best friend.

Putting the thought of Oakley aside, he realized he still had time before he met her at their spot. At the back of his mind was concern for Cooper. Leann Hayes's death and the discovery of Rory Eastwood's pickup in that reservoir kept niggling at him. Had the sheriff discovered a link between the two? Again, he wondered if he should warn his brother about this latest development.

But he realized as he grabbed his Stetson and headed for the door, that he shouldn't call his brother until he had more facts.

THE SHERIFF HAD so much on his mind that he didn't hear the tap at his door. The one thing he didn't need was more trouble.

"Got a minute?"

He looked up to see Duffy McKenna standing there, his hat in his hand. Without waiting for an answer, the cowboy came on in, closing the door behind him.

From the look on Duffy's face, Stuart could tell he probably didn't want to hear this. He wasn't sure he was up to more problems at the moment, but he waved him into a chair and waited. As Cooper's kid brother, Duffy had been a pain in the butt growing up. Stuart and Cooper used to ditch him when they were all younger. Two years younger than Coop, Duffy had been a snot-nosed kid they hadn't wanted tagging along.

Stuart studied him now, realizing it had been a long while since Duffy had followed them around, no longer interested in what his older brother and best friend were up to. Duffy had grown into a good-looking son of a wealthy rancher. If the rumors were true, he had a way with women. He was actually better looking than his brother Cooper, which was saying a lot.

The sheriff felt envy raise its ugly head. Not only did the McKenna boys have everything their hearts desired, but they also had the looks. Growing up as the son of the local sheriff, Stu had often wondered why he couldn't have been born into a ranch family like his best friend. *Just bad luck,* he thought.

"What can I do for you, Duffy?"

"That private investigator who's in town?"

"Jason Murdock?"

Duffy nodded. "He thinks there was a man Leann Hayes was planning to run away with and it was Rory Eastwood."

Stu leaned back in his chair. "And you care about what some PI thinks because…"

"If it's true, then it could put Cooper in jeopardy again."

He studied the cowboy, a little surprised that he was

concerning himself with this. Talk around the area was that this McKenna wanted nothing to do with ranching, that there wasn't a serious bone in his body, that all he cared about was dating his way through the female population of the county.

But apparently, he cared about Cooper.

What surprised Stu even more was that Duffy had connected all the dots and come up with the same conclusion the PI had. "We don't even know there was a man."

"Did you find anything in his pickup to connect him with Leann?"

Duffy had apparently given this some thought. "The state forensic team will be going over the pickup looking for any evidence once they get here. All I can tell you is that Rory Eastwood appeared to be leaving town since his belongings were in the truck." He only told him that because he was sure that news had already circulated through the entire river basin.

"Where's his body?"

Stu shook his head, thinking of the deputies who would be continuing looking for the remains in the morning out on the ranch near the reservoir. "We don't even know that he's dead. He could have ditched the truck wanting to make it look like he was dead."

"Why would he do that? He told people at the bar that he had a woman in his life."

"People say all kinds of things, especially when they are trying to cover up what is really going on," the sheriff said. "I especially wouldn't believe everything the PI had to say. Maybe Rory had planned to run away with some mystery woman, but when it came down to it, didn't have the guts to go through with it. Or maybe he made the story up."

"And then drove his pickup into a reservoir?"

Stu shrugged. "Could have thought the truck would be found sooner and the woman would think he was dead—if there was a woman." He could see that Duffy was having trouble with that explanation. "Or maybe she picked him up and they left in her rig and for whatever reason, he didn't want to leave a trail. Who knows what demons might have been chasing him? According to CH4 records of employment, he hadn't been in the area long."

"If he left with her, then you're assuming the mystery woman wasn't Leann, then?"

"Murdock is the only one who thinks Leann Hayes was the woman. Who the hell knows if there even was one? Rory could have been lying." People lied for a variety of reasons. Stu knew that better than anyone.

Duffy seemed to give that some thought. "What if Leann's case is reopened?"

He knew what the young McKenna was asking. "I wouldn't think it would be the best thing for your brother. Right now Leann's case is closed. She committed suicide."

"You really think Rory Eastwood is alive."

"I hope we find him alive because he'll have to pay the county for the costs to search the reservoir for his body, not to mention the cost of dragging the truck from the water and storing it after forensics is through." He rose from his chair.

"Unless his body turns up," Duffy said, not taking the hint.

"I'm glad you stopped by. I've been wanting to ask you about the vandalisms of gas company equipment. You wouldn't know anything about that, would you?"

Duffy shook his head and rose but made no move toward the door. "So Cooper doesn't have anything to worry about."

"I wouldn't say that. He's been pretty insistent about reopening Leann's case. Once he hears the rumors circulating about Rory Eastwood and his pickup being found in the reservoir... Best thing he could do is let it go. Maybe you'll have more luck convincing him of that than I have."

Duffy put on his Stetson and opened the office door. He turned back before stepping out. "I would think you wouldn't want that case reopened, either, since you had been involved with Leann, too." With that, he left, leaving Stu to curse himself for ever getting involved with the woman—and worse, believing he loved her before losing her to his best friend.

CHARLOTTE HAD JUST helped CJ into his bed to rest when she got the call. He swore that his fight with Oakley hadn't injured him more. But she could see a change in him that worried her. He was so angry, so frustrated by everything that had happened. She felt it as well as she closed his door, afraid he'd hurt himself worse and cursing Oakley for picking yet another fight with her brother. "Hello?"

"Mrs. Stafford?" She recognized the voice at once.

"Bob." She knew Bob Turner would be calling. "Is Inez...?"

"She died in her sleep last night."

Last night? And he was just now calling? That definitely didn't bode well. "Just say it," she snapped, no longer having the patience to play this game with him. "But if you tell me that you sold the ranch to Holden—"

"I followed my mother's wishes. The ranch has been put into a conservation easement. It was Mother's desire to protect the land she loved. She wanted to preserve it for future generations by protecting the agricultural and forestry elements as well as the water quality. That is one reason she would have never sold it to you."

"When did she decide this?" Charlotte demanded.

"After you tried so hard to buy the ranch," her son said, an edge to his voice. "She didn't want to see coalbed methane wells on her land. In order to prevent you from ever getting your hands on the property, she did what she thought was best."

Charlotte laughed. "Clearly, she didn't care about you and your family. I suspect you could have used the money from the sale."

"She thought some things were more important than money." He disconnected before she could tell him what she thought of that.

With a curse, she reminded herself that at least Holden hadn't gotten it. They had both needed that land; Holden for the water, she for spite and other personal reasons. They'd both lost.

But her loss could be worse, she reminded herself. She cursed Bob Turner. He'd left her with few options now. As long as Inez had been alive, Charlotte hadn't worried about the ranch since no one was working it. Now, though, she couldn't trust who might be able to gain access to the place—and what they might discover if they looked hard enough.

DUFFY WAS WAITING for Oakley behind an old barn on one of the abandoned homesteads. The land had been bought by an out-of-state conglomerate as a tax write-off. As far as he knew, no one had ever even seen the place in person. It made for a good meeting spot, away from town in the foothills of the mountains. From here he could see the river that wound through the basin.

As far as rivers went, the Powder wasn't much to look at. The shallow water meandered 375 miles from northeastern Wyoming through southeastern Montana to dump into the Yellowstone. Many claimed that the Powder River was a mile wide, an inch deep and ran uphill.

The running joke was that the water in the river was too thick to drink and too thin to plow. Captain Clark of the Lewis and Clark Expedition had named it Redstone River. But the Native Americans called it Powder River because the black shores reminded them of gunpowder and that name had stuck.

For Duffy, the river and this basin was what kept his family here in this isolated place. As he looked up at the endless sky overhead and felt the last of the sun's rays on his face, he yearned to leave and see what was out there beyond the Powder River Basin.

It wasn't a love for the land or his roots holding him back. He honestly didn't know what he wanted to do with his life. Here on the ranch, he didn't have to worry about it. He was Holden McKenna's son. That was all he had to be. Deacon Yates, the ranch manager, oversaw the running of the place. The ranch hands did the work. Duffy helped when he had to or when he wanted to spend more time with Pickett.

So what was keeping him here? he asked himself. His best friend and Oakley Stafford. He might not love the land like the rest of his family seemed to, but Pickett was his best friend and he'd grown attached to the girl next door. If they would have gone with him, he would have left years ago.

Pickett was now back east. Who knew if he'd even come back to the ranch? It made Duffy want to leave, too. But he couldn't imagine leaving without Oakley.

Unfortunately, he feared she might not see him as any more than a friend. He'd been afraid to find out. But he was tired of playing it safe, he thought as he saw her pickup headed his way.

Tonight, without Pickett here, he planned to find out. Her truck slowed. He stayed where he was leaning on his truck, waiting. She parked and looked over at him. He motioned for her to get out.

He could tell that she was all business, as she usually was on the nights Dirty Business met. The woman was driven. He knew that she seldom dated. He had the feeling that she was waiting for something. Or was it someone? When not on the ranch or stirring up trouble elsewhere, she spent her time with him and Pickett. Because they were safe?

Thinking of what he'd seen between her and Pickett the other night, he feared that had changed.

She climbed out of her truck and walked toward him, hands on her hips. "What's up?" Normally, whoever was driving would be waiting in the truck ready to go. "I don't want to be late for the meeting."

He pushed himself off the side of his pickup and moved to her, taking hold of her shoulders and backing her up against the side of her pickup. "There's something I've been wanting to do." He pressed a palm on each side of her, trapping her against the side of the cab as he moved closer.

"Duffy? What are you doing? I need to tell you something on the way to the meeting. We should get going." She'd gone from possibly amused to annoyed.

"I've been thinking about this for a very long time."

She cocked her head at him, waiting impatiently.

He grinned. "Don't pretend you didn't know."

"Duffy!" She tried to step under his arm, but he blocked her.

He leaned closer. "You're going to break my heart, aren't you?" But he didn't give her a chance to answer as he kissed her. It was just as he knew it would be; her lips full, her taste sweet. But after a moment, he realized that she wasn't kissing him back.

He broke off the kiss to look at her and saw from her expression that she hadn't felt it. Not only that, but also she seemed to think he was joking around. "I can do better," he said.

She shook her head as she put both hands on his chest and pushed him back. "If you're through fooling around, we need to get going."

"Thought I'd give it a try," he said, pretending he really had only been joking as he tried to swallow the lump in his throat. "Most women swoon at one of my kisses."

Oakley laughed. "You sure that's what they're doing?" she said as she pushed past him to head for his truck. "Come on. We're going to be late."

OAKLEY HAD TROUBLE concentrating during the meeting. She'd been convinced earlier that Duffy had been only kidding around as usual. But on the ride to the meeting, he wasn't himself. She'd planned to tell him about the Lees brothers threatening CJ, but he'd seemed distracted, even distant.

He hadn't been serious, had he? She recalled his words. "You're going to break my heart, aren't you?" What if he wasn't joking?

She felt awful at the thought that she'd hurt him. He was her friend. She touched her tongue to her upper lip, thinking about the kiss. Had there been something there? She'd always loved Duffy. There had even been a time when she thought he might become more. But did she still feel that way?

Her thoughts swiftly turned to Pickett. She had wanted him the other night, wanted him to touch her, to kiss her, to hold her. She feared she might have misread the look in his eyes. She felt confused. If only the meeting hadn't broken up when it did. She ached to know what he was going to say to her, what he might have done if they hadn't been interrupted.

And now Pickett was gone. He had family! Maybe he would have to stay out there with them. She couldn't bear the thought that he might not come back.

The meeting broke up and she and Duffy headed for his pickup. In all these years, she'd never felt uncomfortable around him. Being his friend had been so easy.

But as they climbed into his truck, she knew she had to do something to break the silence. It felt as if there was now a wall between them.

She'd never wanted to be another one of his women and had always been relieved when he hadn't made a pass at her. Now that he had, she didn't want to lose him as a friend. But she was at a loss as to what she could say that wouldn't make things worse. The last thing she wanted to do was talk about what had happened earlier. If she was being honest, she had feelings for Pickett. But she also felt something for Duffy. She told herself that she couldn't deal with this right now.

"I need to tell you about Frankie and Norman Lees," she said as he got the truck moving. "They came to the ranch earlier."

That got his attention. "To see you?"

"No, CJ. He acted as if he'd been expecting them. He definitely had some business with them. They were worried he'd try to make a deal with the sheriff by ratting them out. They threatened him if he did."

"Ratting them out about what?" Duffy asked, sounding like his old self.

Oakley shook her head. "That I don't know. But they scared him. The thing is how does he even know them? I thought they just came to town to try to stop the vandalism of the gas equipment."

"If they are involved with your brother, then they've been here before." He glanced over at her. "Knowing you, you tried to get him to tell you."

She chuckled, but it held no humor. "It didn't go well." She told him about CJ rising from the chair, lunging at her.

"Are you saying he can stand?"

Had he stood up or had he only thrown himself from the chair? She couldn't be sure because it had happened so quickly. If her mother hadn't forgotten her purse and come back...

"I think he would have choked me to death if Mother hadn't come in when she did."

They had reached her pickup. He parked and quickly turned to her. "Why didn't you tell me this? Are you all right?" He seemed to remember why she hadn't told him earlier and dropped his gaze as if embarrassed.

"I feel like things are escalating," she said quickly, hoping to cover the awkwardness she knew they both felt.

"You need to be careful. You aren't going to stay in that house, are you?"

"Don't worry. Tilly and I have the apartment in town. I'll make sure I'm never at the ranch when Mother isn't there." She hesitated. "You haven't heard from Pickett, have you?"

From his expression, it was the wrong thing to ask. "No. I'm not sure he'll even come back."

She shook her head. "It's Pickett. Of course he'll come back," she said, hoping it was true as she opened her door. "He'd never abandoned us. We're a team." Duffy said nothing, but she saw the muscles in his jaw tighten. "Thanks for the ride. Let me know if you hear anything about the next meeting or the Lees brothers."

"Or Pickett," he said, nodding, but he grinned when he said it. "See you."

She closed the pickup's door and walked to her own rig. She thought he might not wait for her to leave like he and Pickett always did. But as she started her truck, she saw him sitting there, his engine idling, waiting. She was so thankful for his friendship and felt such love for him.

Could one kiss ruin everything? She loved both him and Pickett and that was the problem.

What about the feelings she had for Pickett? What if they weren't reciprocated? What if they were? Even if she kissed Duffy again and felt something more, how would this end? She feared that if she fell for either of them, it would destroy the trio of friends.

CHAPTER FIFTEEN

OAKLEY REALIZED THAT she wasn't up to returning to the ranch. It would be just like her mother to be waiting for her return. She didn't want to get into an argument with her, not tonight. Everything that had happened today had her head spinning as it was.

Getting the apartment had been a great idea, she thought as she opened the door to find her sister hard at work on her wedding planning.

"Am I glad to see you," she said to Tilly and threw herself down on the couch.

"I know that look." Her sister chuckled as she joined her at the opposite end. "I've just never seen it on you before. Who is he?"

Oakley hated to tell her. Tilly knew about Dirty Business and about her spending time with Pickett and Duffy. But like her, her sister had assumed they were just good friends.

"Duffy kissed me tonight," she blurted out, not ready to tell her about what hadn't happened with Pickett— had almost happened maybe.

Tilly's eyes widened. "You and Duffy McKenna? Don't tell me you—"

"We didn't. *I* didn't," Oakley said quickly. "I mean, I

didn't even kiss him back, it happened so fast. I always wondered what it would be like to kiss him, though."

Her sister was shaking her head. "Is this about you and Duffy? Or you and Mother?"

"What?" she demanded. This is not the way she thought the conversation would go, considering that she'd listened to Tilly ad nauseam for years about her dates. "It has nothing to do with Mother."

Tilly raised a brow. "Are you sure?"

Her sister was starting to irritate her. "I never thought for a minute that you seeing Cooper was about Mother so why would you ask *me* that?"

"Are you telling me you haven't had a run-in either with Mother or CJ or both?"

Oakley groaned. "It was just a kiss. But how can you judge me when you're *marrying* a McKenna?"

"I'm not judging you. Cooper and I have been in love for a long time. Clearly, it isn't about getting back at Mother. She just disowned me, threw me off the ranch, but I'm still marrying Cooper. Why do you suddenly think that you're falling for Duffy?"

Oakley let out a laugh. "I said he kissed me. That's all it was." But it wasn't, she knew. Tilly was eyeing her like a big bossy sister. "I love him but I'm not sure I love him like that."

Her sister seemed to breathe a sigh of relief. "I think you need to kiss a few more cowboys before you let one of them rein you in, little sis."

She blurted it out. "I'm interested in Pickett."

"You hardly know him."

Oakley scoffed. "I've known him almost my whole life."

Tilly raised a brow. "Did you know he had family back east? Exactly. I always wondered about the three of you, thick as thieves. I knew you'd end up in a love triangle feeling like you had to choose one of them. Both of them act like they've been in love with you for years. You really haven't noticed?"

"They joke around all the time but—"

"So how serious is this with Pickett? I assume you've kissed, but—"

"Not yet."

Tilly shook her head as if there was no reasoning with her little sister. "You haven't even kissed?" Getting up from the couch, she headed back to the kitchen table. "I need to get back to my wedding planning."

"What if Pickett doesn't want to kiss me?"

Her sister rolled her eyes. "Clearly, you aren't ready for a long-term relationship. You've only had a couple of boyfriends and neither lasted long. You need to sow more wild oats. In my opinion, neither Duffy nor Pickett is right for you. Duffy has no interest in ranching. Who knows with Pickett? I'm betting he doesn't talk about the future or what he wants. Maybe he wants the rancher's daughter. But don't worry. When you kiss the right one, you'll know."

Oakley had her doubts since she'd kissed quite a few, but she could only hope that about at least this her sister might be right.

"There are also a lot more options than what we have here in this river bottom," Tilly said as she returned to the table and her wedding planning.

"Is that why Cooper left? He wanted to see what was out there?"

"Maybe," Tilly admitted. "He had some things to work out. But he came back. That's really what matters."

Would Pickett come back? Oakley had no idea.

"You scared me there for a moment," her sister was saying as she began to check off items from the list she'd made. "If you had told me that you were in love with Duffy—"

"You're marrying his brother Cooper."

"Exactly," Tilly said with a laugh. "I can't imagine how Mother would have taken another daughter marrying into the McKenna family. It might have pushed her over the edge." When Oakley didn't say anything, her sister turned to look at her. "What?"

Oakley threw herself back on the couch with a groan. "What would Mother say about Pickett?"

"I thought you said you hadn't even kissed him."

"I haven't yet. But I think we almost did." Her sister groaned. "I know what you're going to say."

Tilly shook her head. "I doubt you do. Oakley, let's consider what we know about Pickett Hanson. You've known him since you were fourteen, right?"

Her sister rushed on before she could answer. "And yet he never mentioned his family? Cooper said his father doesn't even know anything about Pickett. He just showed up one day and Holden felt sorry for him and hired him, even though he clearly knew nothing about being a ranch hand. He'd never ridden a horse. He was green as spring grass, Cooper told me."

"Well, he obviously learned to ride and to ranch," she said.

"Doesn't it make you wonder why he's never mentioned his family in all that time?" Tilly demanded. "Doesn't that seem a little odd to you?"

"I'm sure he'll tell me when he's ready," she said, not sure about that, either. And that was if he even came back to the ranch.

Her sister turned in her chair to face the couch. "Let's say it's true love, that Pickett Hanson is the man for you. How would you two live? I mean, doesn't he stay in part of the bunkhouse on the ranch?"

Oakley sat up, wishing she hadn't brought any of this up. She needed her sister on her side, but from the look on her face, that wasn't the case. "I didn't say I was *marrying* him. I haven't even… He hasn't even…" She stood. "I don't know what we would do, but I bet we'd figure it out. I'm going to bed."

"YOU'RE LATE," HOLLY JO SAID, hands on her slim hips, as Duffy joined her in the stable the next morning. He'd had a restless night with little sleep and hadn't awoken in the best mood. He'd been helping the teenager with her horseback riding lessons out of the goodness of his heart.

He started to point that out but stopped himself. Just because he was in a bad mood, he didn't need to take it out on her. "Sorry," he said.

"Rough night?" she asked, cocking a brow at him.

He couldn't help smiling at the girl. Smart and sassy, she had a lot of fire in her. He still wondered how she had come to live at the ranch or what his father's connection had been to the girl's mother. Apparently, it hadn't been romantic. Holden had gone away one day and come back with the girl and no real explanation why.

"Feeling guilty for breaking another girl's heart?" she teased.

He shook his head, seeing that she was trying to get a rise out of him. "What makes you think that she didn't break mine?"

"Because you've never been that serious about any of them, except…maybe this one," she said, narrowing her eyes at him.

The kid was tall for her age and also insightful, he'd found. He'd liked Holly Jo the first time he'd met her, accepting her like the older brother he'd instantly become, something she hadn't done with Treyton, who never had two words to say to her.

"How about we just go for a ride today?" he asked her. She'd been working with both Pickett and Cooper, along with Tilly, on her horseback riding tricks.

She had some fool idea of being the best in the world. Duffy had never wanted to be the best at anything. He found her drive remarkable and wished he had more of his own.

"All right," she said, obviously disappointed. "But only if you tell me about your date."

"Yeah, hold your breath on that," he said as they saddled their horses. He listened to Holly Jo's chatter with only one ear and mulled over last night with Oakley. Maybe he shouldn't have kissed her. He didn't want to lose her as a friend and now he worried that he might have.

"Is she the one you think is so wonderful?" Holly Jo asked, making a face.

"Sorry?"

"The one you were out with last night. I saw the way

you kept looking in the mirror before you left for your date." She laughed and brushed her hair back, mocking him as she pretended to primp in front of a mirror.

He couldn't help but laugh. "One of these days you're going to meet a boy and then you'll know what I'm going through."

"Boys are awful," she said as they led their horses outside. "I want nothing to do with any of them."

"Keep that attitude as long as you can," he said as they saddled up and rode toward the mountains. "How's things going with that boy that was bothering you. Gus?"

Holly Jo shook her head. "I can handle him."

"If you need my help—"

"You have enough trouble of your own," she said. "So about the date. Maybe she's just playing hard to get."

Duffy ignored her chatter as they rode. There were still patches of snow on the north side of the mountains, but the valley was mostly bare. That wasn't a good sign with the drought they'd been having for several years now. He often wondered why his father kept ranching with so many odds against him.

Next to him, Holly Jo had fallen silent, her face turned up to the sun, as she absently patted her horse's neck as she rode. Her look was one of absolute contentment. Duffy couldn't help feeling jealous. Had he ever felt that way? Would he have felt that way if things had gone differently last night? Or had he wanted Oakley even more after seeing the way she had been looking at Pickett?

"When is Pickett coming back?" Holly Jo asked.

Her question made him groan. What was it about Pickett? "I don't know."

"I miss him. It's not the same without Pickett here."

Duffy had a feeling that Oakley felt the same way.

PICKETT WOKE IN a strange bed, in a room that was too large and at the same time, too familiar. At first, he wasn't sure what had awakened him. Then he heard a tap at the door. He started to get up and dress, but lay back as the door opened. One of the staff entered with a tray, an older woman who greeted him with "Good morning, sir."

"Good morning. You can set that down anywhere you like." He smelled coffee and what might have been blueberry coffee cake. "Thank you."

"You are most welcome," she said and exited as quickly as she'd come in.

He rose as she closed the door and reached for the coffee. That was when he saw a white envelope next to a plate of perfectly sliced coffee cake and a rosebud in the small vase beside it.

Bracing himself, he took a drink of coffee before he picked up the envelope and opened it, already dreading what he was about to read. He'd been raised in this house, in this family, so he knew that bad news was usually made official in writing rather than broken face-to-face.

He took out the sheet of expensive paper, unfolded it and read, "I'm sorry to inform you that your father passed away in the night. He held on as long as he could, determined to see his son. We need to talk before you leave, Sarah." He balled up the paper, throwing it across the room.

Emotions blindsided him for a moment. He didn't know how to feel, only that he hurt. He couldn't help the regret. How many times had he wished that things had been different between him and his father?

He dressed and went downstairs, knowing that Sarah would be waiting. She would know he would be anxious to leave. There wouldn't be a funeral or even a service—his father's instructions, which of course Sarah would follow to the letter. His father would be cremated, his remains going into the mausoleum with the rest of his ancestors.

Pickett had grown up with all the photographs of the Westmoreland men before him. He'd always found it interesting that no women had ever hung there. Nor had they ever held office in any of his father's holdings. It didn't surprise him that his own mother had escaped this house shortly after he was born. Not that he probably would have seen much of her since children in families like his were raised by nannies, attended boarding school, seeing little of their parents except on a holiday here and there.

Just as he'd expected, Sarah was waiting in the sitting room near the front door. She'd been looking at her phone, but now put it away and turned her attention on him.

"Please close the door," she said and motioned him into a nearby chair.

He told himself that his last requirement in this house was to listen to what she had to say before he left. He did wonder what her pitch would be. He half expected her to pull out a spreadsheet as he took a seat.

"Thank you for coming to see your father," Sarah began. "I know how much it meant to him. He was able to die in peace."

He didn't acknowledge her words. He and his father had said what they had to say to each other last night. They both had regrets, but neither's mind had changed. Pickett could walk away now without any doubts about being gone for all these years.

She hesitated for a moment before she said, "You are aware that your father is worth a large amount of money." That was putting it mildly, he thought. "I'm sure the two of you discussed—"

"No, we didn't talk about money."

She looked up in surprise for a moment, then nodded as if she should have known. "He has made some large bequeaths, but there are still decisions that need to be made about the remainder of his wealth as well as this house and his other properties and businesses. As his only living heir—"

Pickett rose and picked up his Stetson he'd had resting on his knee. "As I told him years ago, I'm not interested." He started for the door, but her words stopped him.

"What about the staff employed in this house, the staff employed in your father's businesses? What about your adopted family? It's one thing for you to act superior when it comes to money, but not everyone can be that callous. Are you aware that the McKenna Ranch is in financial trouble?"

He turned slowly. As he started to say, "That's not

true," she pulled out spreadsheets—just not the ones he'd expected. "Your girlfriend's ranch isn't doing that much better either. I understand it's because of the years of drought, cattle sales down, the lack of fresh well water. Maybe you've heard the expression land poor? It means—"

"I know what it means." Lots of land, not a lot of money. Pickett opened his mouth again to say he didn't have a girlfriend, but the look on Sarah's face told him to save his breath.

"I understand that you want nothing to do with your father's businesses or this house," she continued. "They can all be sold off, the money given to the charities of your choice, severance pay for the employees. Your father has already made large bequeaths for long-time employees, myself included. But with the money your father put away for your 'personal' needs you could make a huge difference in both ranch family's lives." An eyebrow rose as she studied him. "But then you would have to admit that you have never been just a ranch hand, wouldn't you?" She slapped down the spreadsheets. "I suspect you would prefer to keep your pride and let your new family struggle on rather than admit the truth, but I need to know what you want done and I need to know now."

OAKLEY WOKE TO screaming as the nightmare chased her from sleep. She felt someone shaking her and calling her name. A lamp came on next to her bed, blinding her. She looked around the unfamiliar room, terrified from the nightmare, from the feeling that she didn't know what was happening.

"You're all right," Tilly said, sounding close to tears as she hugged her. "It was just a bad dream. You're all right."

She didn't feel all right even as she recognized where she was. Tilly was here. She was in their apartment. But there was something to be afraid of, something to be very afraid of. "I saw...something."

"It was just a dream," her sister said, drawing back to look at her.

Oakley shook her head. "Women, there were a half dozen of them running away." She frowned, the memory trying to pull away, to disappear back into the fog that was her memory. "Some of them ran toward a small airplane, but were shooed away from it. The men forced all of them at gunpoint into the back of a stock trailer." She met Tilly's eyes. "It wasn't a dream. It was real. I saw them. I know now why CJ didn't want me to remember." She sat up, pressing her back against the headboard, refusing to let this memory go. "The meth lab. The women must have been working in it."

She glanced around for her cell phone. Finding it on the bedside table, she tapped on the screen.

"Oakley, what are you doing? It's not quite daylight."

"I have to call the sheriff. I know why CJ tried to kill me. I know what he is hiding. I know why those men are afraid he is going to talk." She started to hit 911, but Tilly took the phone from her hand.

"Don't call 911. I have Stuart's home phone number, but are you sure this can't wait until morning?" Tilly asked.

"It can't wait. The sheriff has to know why CJ has been so afraid I would remember what I saw the day he shot me. I know now. They had women working in the meth lab. Not employed there. I think CJ and the other men were dealing in human trafficking, working them in the meth lab and then taking them somewhere else in the back of a stock trailer. There was a plane, but the men wouldn't let the women board. When someone spotted me, the women all ran." She took a breath. "CJ was there. When he saw me…" She swallowed, hugging herself against the cold hatred she'd seen in his eyes too many times. "He came after me. He meant to kill me so I could never tell."

"You're sure about this?"

"My memory has been coming back, but only in bits and pieces, but tonight I… I saw it. I remembered. I remember CJ chasing me. I knew he was going to kill me if he caught up to me."

"Okay, but is this going to be enough for the sheriff to arrest CJ?" Tilly asked. "Otherwise, what do you expect Stuart to do? Just question CJ? You know what our brother is going to say and since you haven't been able to remember for months…"

Oakley froze, realizing what her sister was saying was true. "My memory will be questionable. The sheriff needs solid evidence before he can arrest CJ." Tilly handed back the phone and sat down on the edge of the bed, her face pale. "If what you saw is true… It's much worse than we thought. I put Stu's cell phone number in your phone, but I wouldn't call until you're sure. You've been saying for months that you knew there was more to the shooting."

Nodding, she told Tilly about the two men who had come to the ranch and threatened CJ. "I don't know if they triggered the memory or if it was my fight with CJ yesterday when he tried to strangle me and would have if not for Mother."

"CJ tried to strangle you? How is that even possible unless... He can walk?"

"I don't know if he can or not. He lunged at me from the wheelchair, knocked me down and... I couldn't breathe. I couldn't get him off me. I thought for sure..." She shook her head. "I know now why he hasn't wanted me to remember. It had to be more than the meth lab although I think we all knew that he had to be involved with it. But it's so much more."

"You realize what this means," Tilly said after a moment. "You can't tell anyone that you remember. Not the sheriff, not CJ, especially not Mother. She's depending on you keeping CJ out of jail. This could send him to prison for a very long time."

Oakley caught her breath. She hadn't thought that far ahead. So like Tilly to think things through first. "I don't care what Mother does and it's not my fault what happens to CJ. The truth needs to come out."

"She'll kick you off the ranch like she did me or worse."

"It was going to happen anyway," Oakley said as she pulled the blanket up around her, the room suddenly feeling colder. "But first, I plan to stop her from drilling on our land."

"It won't be our land anymore, Oakley," her sister said quietly. "They're going to be able to do whatever they want once we're completely gone from the ranch."

She stared at Tilly, stubbornness digging its heels in until she finally said, "You're right. The sheriff can't do anything without proof. This is why the Lees brothers were threatening CJ. They're afraid he'll try to make a deal by throwing them under the bus."

"What is this about someone threatening CJ?"

She quickly told Tilly everything that she missed.

"This is serious. Maybe you should go to the sheriff."

"But what if he talks to CJ? CJ will know that I remembered. There's no way Stuart will ever be able to get proof then."

Tilly agreed reluctantly.

"From the conversation I overheard, CJ plans to get back into business with the Lees brothers. We need that to happen so the sheriff can get proof to put them all away. Maybe especially our brother."

"I'm so sorry," her sister said and hugged her. "But now I'm afraid for you. Oakley, please don't go back out to the ranch. I really wanted to believe that CJ shot you accidentally. He's so much more dangerous than I thought."

"I'll be all right." She sighed. "At least now I know the truth. I have to go back. How else will I know that he and the Lees brothers are back in business—and where? I'll just make sure I'm not alone with CJ again."

But if she was right and he could walk, how could she be sure that he would stay away from her? She would start by installing a dead bolt on her bedroom door at the ranch.

CHARLOTTE FOUND HER son waiting for her the moment she came downstairs for breakfast. "What's wrong?" She'd always been able to tell when CJ was upset, even when he tried to hide it from her.

"Oakley," he said.

This again already this morning? "You can't keep fighting with her," she said, instantly irritated with him. "You know how important it is that she keep her story straight with the lawyer. You want to go to prison?"

She hadn't meant to get angry with him, but her horseback ride this morning hadn't calmed her like it usually did. There was too much going on, things she couldn't manage that now felt out of control. She worried that her whole world could come crashing down around her because of past mistakes.

This morning as she went out riding, she'd seen her ranch manager watching from the shadow of the barn. She could see Boyle smirking as if he knew something she didn't before he turned away. Her stomach had begun to roil. He was always watching her, his interest in her nerve-racking as well as creepy. If he didn't know so much about this family, she would send him packing.

"You have no idea what Oakley will say to the lawyer," CJ snapped. "She's up to something. You can't trust her."

Charlotte sighed and sat down across from his wheelchair. She didn't have time to deal with what felt like an old childhood rivalry. She had hoped Oakley and CJ would both outgrow it. They hadn't. "She'll do what I tell her."

He laughed. The sound sharp as a serrated knife. "You really don't know her, do you? She and her delinquent friends were the ones who vandalized the drilling equipment and set the project back more than six weeks last year."

"You don't know that for a fact."

"She belongs to that group of troublemakers, Dirty Business. She is determined to stop the methane gas drilling in this basin."

"I'm well aware that she is opposed to it, but my drilling on this ranch is none of her business," Charlotte snapped. "She wouldn't be fool enough to try to stop the next well."

"I moved the drilling up," he said. "They should be bringing in the equipment today." He hurried on, no doubt worried she wouldn't like him doing that. "We need the money and you've been busy, so I handled it. Brand and Ryder just got back from taking our cattle to market. The prices are down. We're losing money by ranching this property."

She'd heard this all before and while she couldn't argue the point, she was concerned about the talk circling the basin and had been having second thoughts. Abandoned wells from when the original drilling started were said to be leaking into the river. Look what their well had done to the McKenna's land. She hadn't purposely put in her gas well close to Holden's property in the hopes that something like that would happen. She'd left the location up to the gas company surveyors. But that well had destroyed the McKenna Ranch's artesian water well.

Charlotte was sure that Holden believed she'd done it on purpose to get back at him. What would another well do not just to her neighboring rancher's property but also to her own? "I'm not sure about this, CJ."

"I can't believe that you're waffling on this," CJ said angrily. "You should just let me handle all of it from now on."

She looked up at her son, seeing how badly he wanted to be in charge. Maybe she should just let him take over more of the running of the ranch, especially now that he was tied to that chair. He must be feeling inadequate, the last thing she wanted for her firstborn. Had she ever denied him anything he wanted?

"All right," she said, still uncomfortable with both the well going in so soon and letting go of the control over the ranch. "But I want to know in advance from here on out."

"Sure," he said, dismissing her.

She told herself that she would have to turn the ranch over to him someday anyway, wouldn't she? She worried, though, how Oakley was going to take it. She just hoped her daughter spoke to the lawyer about CJ before she heard about the well. It made her question her son's impulsiveness.

CJ started to roll toward his room, but then turned unexpectedly. "Thanks, Mother," he said, smiling. He looked happy for the first time in a very long time. "I'll take care of everything, especially if Oakley tries to stop the drilling again."

"CJ…" she said, but he was already wheeling down the hallway toward his room again. He'd always loved making the decisions. As she watched him go, she hoped that she hadn't created a monster.

CHAPTER SIXTEEN

PICKETT DROVE STRAIGHT to the McKenna Ranch upon his return. He just wanted to get back to his job, to the life he loved, to his best friends, Duffy and Oakley. His greatest hope was that nothing would have changed by his leaving. Or was it that no one would notice the change in him?

"Pickett!"

As he exited his pickup, he turned to see Holden standing in the doorway of the main house. The rancher waved him over. "When did you get back?"

"Just now," he said. "Thanks again for giving me the time off. I really appreciate it."

"Not a problem. Your father?"

"I got to see him before he passed." He nodded, surprised at the emotion he felt. "It was good to spend time with him." He could tell that Holden was waiting for more. All these years, he hadn't left the ranch, not once, had never mentioned family, had kept his life before the McKenna Ranch a secret. As far as he was concerned, he wanted to keep it that way.

"If there is anything you need…" The rancher was studying him, clearly waiting. For the truth?

"Thanks, but I'm good. Just anxious to get back to work."

Holden nodded. "Well, glad you're back. I'm always here if...if you ever want...anything."

"I appreciate that more than you can know." He tipped his hat and headed for the bunkhouse. The sooner he was back on a horse, the sooner he could get back to what he now considered normal.

But even as he thought it, he knew things had changed. He felt it in the way Holden had been studying him. He couldn't help thinking of Sarah's parting words. *I know you don't want my advice, but you need to come clean with those people you care so much about. Why keep hiding who you really are?*

You have no idea who I really am. I hardly do myself.

His cell phone rang as he was entering his cabin next to the empty bunkhouse. Everyone was out working. He saw it was Oakley calling and felt that welcome nudge against his heart. He was smiling as he answered.

"Are you back?"

"I am." She sounded excited. She sounded good. He couldn't wait to see her.

"I need to see you." He told himself that everything was going to work out. "Duffy, too," she added. His heart had begun to lift as if filled with helium until she said that. "Can you come to the apartment in town?"

"I'll find Duffy and we'll be right there," he said, hiding his disappointment. "Are you okay?"

"I'll tell you all about it when I see you. I'm so glad you're back."

His smile widened as he said, "Me, too. Can't wait to see you." On the way back home, all he'd thought about was Oakley. Maybe Sarah was right. Maybe it was time to at least tell her how he felt. But he knew he couldn't do that without confessing the secret he'd kept from her and the rest of the McKenna family.

OVER THE PAST few days, Holden had debated what to do. He'd done what Elaine had suggested and did a background check on Pickett. It was something he knew he should have done all those years ago—or at least should have asked him questions about himself.

He'd gotten the impression that the teenager had been running from something. He'd wanted to help. Montana had long been a place that outlaws came to hide out, start a new life, make their fortune, put their past behind them. While it was no longer the Wild West, it still wasn't like any other place.

His great-grandfather had been part of a cattle drive up from Texas all those years ago. He'd heard stories about the man and could safely assume he'd been running from something when he'd left Texas because he'd never gone back.

Pickett had been the same way—until recently. Holden liked the young man. Did it matter that Pickett Hanson hadn't been his birth name? Or that he had a family back east he'd never mentioned—or had ever visited in all these years?

"You look troubled," Elaine said as she joined him at the window.

There was little he couldn't talk to her about, but this was something he wanted to keep to himself. At least for now.

"Just gathering wool, as they used to say." He smiled at her, thankful every day to have her in his life. But this wasn't something he was ready to talk about. He needed to talk to Pickett first.

"I'm sorry about the Turner Ranch. I heard Inez put it in a conservation easement. I know how badly you'd hoped to buy the place."

He shook his head. "Buying it for what it's worth would have stretched things a little too tight. It wasn't meant to be. I think Inez did the right thing."

She smiled. "That's what I love about you. You always see the bright side of things."

"Not always." His cell phone rang. He glanced at the screen and frowned. It was the ranch lawyer calling. That couldn't be good. "If you'll excuse me." Once in his den with the door closed, he picked up, bracing himself for the worst.

CJ MADE THE CALL. He needed to calm everyone down. The best way to do that was to get back into business. But he knew he'd have to sell them on the idea. Frankie was jumpy and suspicious. "It's time to get going again." Silence. "Come on, Frankie, I told you, I'm solid. You can trust me. But I can't just sit here doing nothing. I talked my mother into drilling more wells. That way you and Norman can come and go here on the ranch without anyone questioning it."

"You think that's a good idea? What if your sister sees us and remembers something?"

"She isn't going to be a problem because when she tries to vandalize the equipment here on the ranch before the drilling begins tomorrow, you're going to catch her and make sure she never remembers anything ever again."

"Seriously? You realize that wasn't part of the deal. It will cost you."

"That's why we need to get back into business. I already have a place lined up. See, I have too much to lose to make any deals with the law. This time we won't get caught because the operation will be on private land. Satisfied?"

"I hope you know what you're doing."

"Trust me, I do." He didn't mention his concern about Oakley and the sinking feeling that she really was starting to remember. No reason to worry Frankie. No reason to tell him how relentless Oakley can be. Better to have him feeling comfortable so there were no more misunderstandings between them.

He tried to tell himself that even if she did remember, she had no proof. She'd spent months with memory loss. Any memory now wouldn't be credible, not without evidence. The original meth lab had been destroyed before the sheriff could investigate. Nothing could tie them to the place.

But he couldn't take the chance that if she remembered, the sheriff and the feds would be watching him and his friends too closely. His friends were skittish enough already.

"I told you I'd make up for the mistake I made," he told Frankie now. "I'm doing it. Let's get the word out about the new well going in on the Stafford Ranch. The equipment is coming in today. Drilling starts tomorrow. I know Oakley. She'll take the bait."

The sooner the gas company brought in the equipment, the sooner CJ's problems would be over.

OAKLEY HAD FEARED that things would be awkward with Duffy and Pickett. But when they arrived at the apartment, she was relieved that it felt like old times. They were her best friends. She never wanted that to change.

They both looked worried as they came in the door, so she didn't hold them in suspense any longer. "I remember what I saw the day CJ shot me. I know now why he did it."

She offered them seats and coffee, carrying her mug over to the couch and pulling her feet up under her as she first updated Pickett on what he'd missed with CJ and the Lees brothers, and her fight with her brother making her question even more whether or not he can walk. Then she told them about the women she remembered seeing the day she was shot.

"Human trafficking?" Duffy asked. "In the Powder River Basin?" She could tell that he didn't want to believe it any more than she did.

"It makes sense. They needed people to work the meth lab," Pickett said. "I don't know why we didn't think of that before."

"I guess because we thought it was a small operation," Oakley said. "They burned it all down before the sheriff could investigate so we had no idea how many people were working there or how big their operation was. There was an airstrip. I remember seeing a small plane sitting there."

"Big enough to fly the women in and out?" Duffy asked.

She shook her head, remembering what she'd been told. Cooper McKenna had been driving toward his ranch as she'd come flying out of the woods on her horse and landed on the road. He'd called 911 and saved her life.

"I don't know if it was the plane that Cooper said flew over while he was waiting for the ambulance the day I was shot. Tilly told me that she and Cooper tracked it down. It was flown by Howie Gunderson, an employee of CH4. Another gas company employee was in the plane that day. Tick Whitaker, a geologist who works for the CH4."

Pickett met her gaze. "You realize what you're saying? If it was the same plane, then the gas company employees knew about the meth lab and the human trafficking—and were more than likely involved."

"But they weren't the only ones there that day. I saw CJ and he saw me. That's when he jumped on his horse and came after me."

"What made you even know to go back through that ravine over the mountain to the old Smith homestead that day?" Duffy asked.

"That I can't remember," she admitted. "Maybe I followed CJ." She shook her head. "I've always been suspicious of why he seemed to have more money than the rest of us. I just assumed he was getting it from Mother."

"Have you told the sheriff?" Pickett asked.

"I can't yet. Once I do, it will be my word against CJ's. With my earlier memory loss, it wouldn't hold up as evidence. The sheriff wouldn't even be able to prove that CJ had a connection to the meth lab operation. I saw him there, but that's not enough. Maybe worse, my mother will kick me off the ranch and I need to be able to come and go there as long as I can. After hearing CJ with the Lees brothers, I think he is getting back into business with them at a new location. I need to find it, to have evidence to finally put them all out of business. Meanwhile, I need to make sure CJ doesn't drill on the ranch."

"That's an awful lot to put on yourself," Pickett said. "It sounds way too dangerous and if you're convinced CJ is lying about his ability to walk, you're really not safe out there on the ranch."

"CJ's in this up to his neck," she said. "I can't leave the ranch until I get proof. CJ can't keep up this pretense much longer."

Pickett swore and Duffy said, "Pickett's right. You can't stay on that ranch. It's too dangerous."

"CJ shot you. He could have killed you. If you're right, he was trying to," Pickett said. "Those bruises on your neck should convince you that your brother isn't going to stop."

Oakley touched her neck before she pulled her sweater collar up. Of course Pickett would have noticed them. "I was trying to push him so he told me the truth about that day. But now that I've remembered, I won't confront him again."

Pickett shook his head. "I'm not sure that's a good idea."

"What?" Duffy asked.

"If she backs off, he might get suspicious that she's remembered, which she has," the ranch hand continued. "She needs to be less confrontational, that's for sure. But if she is going to keep going out to the ranch, then she has to make him believe that she hasn't remembered." He met her gaze. "Can you do that?"

She smiled, glad at least Pickett understood that she couldn't stop now. She had to remain on the ranch.

"Tell us what we can do," Pickett said.

"I need your help to find the location of the new meth lab," she said. "If they haven't got it going yet, they will soon. We need proof. We also need to make sure that CJ and his buddies can't hurt anyone else."

"Are you sure you shouldn't go to the sheriff, let him handle this?" Duffy said.

"I can't let CJ know that I've remembered," she said. "If Stuart starts questioning him…"

"She's right," Pickett said. "Let me try to find where they might be setting up again and then we'll go to the sheriff and let him take it from there."

Oakley smiled over at him. Pickett, while clearly concerned, seemed to know that she was going ahead with her plan—with or without them.

Duffy swore. "I don't like it. What the hell is wrong with your brother?"

She'd often asked herself the same thing. She shook her head. "I don't know but he's always been…different than the rest of us. He's my mother's favorite. Needless to say, she's spoiled him rotten."

"Any ideas how to find a meth lab that we aren't sure even exists yet?" Duffy asked. "No offense, but it sounds like they aren't even back in business yet."

"The men who paid your brother a visit could be waiting to make sure he doesn't turn on them before they resume," Pickett said. "But I'd bet they have a place already in mind—even if they haven't moved the business there yet."

"Another abandoned ranch?" Duffy asked.

Pickett shook his head. "Isn't that what the sheriff and the FBI are expecting? I would think that an operation like this could afford to buy a piece of land using a front man."

"Or CJ's own mother," Duffy said. "If you're right and CJ is scared of the Lees brothers, then one way he could convince them that he isn't going to turn on them, would be to buy property for the new operation."

Pickett slapped Duffy on the back. "The perfect front. I think you might have something there."

Oakley grinned. "I don't know what I would do without you two. My mother was planning to buy the Turner Ranch. It might be easy for CJ to suggest some other property for her to buy, especially if he hinted that Holden McKenna was looking at the land."

Her cell phone began to ring. "I need to take this," she said to Duffy and Pickett. "It should only take a minute. It's my mother."

"You need to talk to CJ's lawyer," Charlotte said without preamble the moment Oakley picked up. "You need to assure him that it was an accident, that you're fine, that your brother isn't a threat."

She almost laughed. CJ not a threat? She reminded herself that she had to play along, at least until she found the proof she needed.

"I told you I would," she said, as hard as it was. She had no choice but to lie. CJ needed to feel that he was safe, that he had gotten away with everything. That way he and his cohorts wouldn't worry about getting back to their criminal behavior. Meanwhile, Oakley would do her part while Duffy and Pickett tracked down any recently purchased property.

She disconnected. "We need to stop CJ and soon," she told her friends.

PICKETT WAS ABOUT to leave Oakley's apartment when Duffy got a phone call and stepped out in the hall to take it, leaving him alone with Oakley.

She looked as uncomfortable as he felt, both of them knowing that Duffy could return at any moment.

He turned the brim of his Stetson in his hands, still shaken by what had happened in his absence with Oakley remembering the day she was shot and her run-in with CJ. He was also rattled by the tension he felt between his best friend and Oakley. Duffy wasn't his usual self. Also, Pickett had seen the two share looks a couple of times as if more had happened while he was gone.

Duffy came back in. "That was Ralph Jones on the phone. The barn we used at the last Dirty Business meeting burnt down last night. Ralph said it was arson. He's out there now. I want to go out and talk to him."

"Let's go," Pickett said, still holding his hat. He settled the Stetson on his head and looked at Oakley.

"I'm coming with you," she said and met his gaze as if she thought he might object. He merely gave her a nod. She held his look a little longer. He tried to read it, but didn't get the chance as Duffy said, "Of course you're going."

Duffy smiled at her, but he didn't put his arm around her as they left. He seemed to be giving her some distance. But was it for Pickett's benefit or hers?

Pickett hated this feeling that he'd missed something important that had happened between the two of them. He was scared for Oakley and wanted to protect her but didn't know how it would be possible—even if she would allow it. She was a Stafford; he worked for a

McKenna. If he was even caught on the Stafford Ranch, he could be shot. Duffy was no better off when it came to keeping her safe, he told himself.

He hated feeling helpless, especially since he had the feeling something had changed while he was gone. He wanted to believe it was just him imagining it because he'd missed so much.

But he knew better. Oakley and Duffy weren't themselves. Something had happened between them; he saw it in their too-polite exchanges. He should have known Duffy would take advantage of his being away. It was his own fault, he told himself.

Now more than ever he knew that if he was serious about Oakley, he needed to act. But what had always held him back was the truth. He still didn't want to share it with her. Not until the time was right.

But he had to show her how he felt about her. He had to know if he stood a chance with her. Oakley and the McKenna ranch hand. He told himself that it would never happen. But he had to know if she cared about him more than just as a friend.

They all climbed into Oakley's pickup for the ride out to the barn. Duffy stopped as they were loading up to fiddle with his boot, allowing Pickett to slide into the seat next to her. He noticed that his friend couldn't meet his gaze as he climbed in next to him, confirming what Pickett suspected. Something had definitely happened between Duffy and Oakley.

They didn't talk on the way out to the smoldering remains of the barn. Ralph Jones was waiting for them. "Let me talk to him for a minute," Duffy said as he jumped out, closing the door behind him.

"How was your trip?" Oakley asked nervously, as if the cab and just the two of them felt too intimate. Pickett had slid over a little but not gotten out. "I hadn't realized that you had family back east."

"My father. He passed while I was there."

"I'm sorry. He was your only family?"

Pickett nodded. "I'll tell you all about it one day," he said as Duffy came back to the truck, opened the door and stuck his head in to say he was going to get a ride with Ralph. "You should go on back. One of the sheriff's deputies is on his way."

Oakley didn't hesitate. She turned the truck around and headed for Powder Crossing.

She was almost to town when Pickett cleared his voice and said, "I need to ask you something. You and Duffy…" He looked over at her, his gaze never leaving hers.

PICKETT'S QUESTION TOOK Oakley by surprise. She didn't know how to answer it even though she knew exactly what he was asking. She swallowed before she dragged her gaze away, found a wide spot and pulled off the road.

She looked over at him and blurted it out, relieved the minute the words left her lips. "We kissed. While you were gone. It just…happened."

Pickett nodded. "I know how these things happen."

His look took her breath away as waves of electricity arced between them. He'd been a friend for years. But friendship was the last thing she was feeling as she stared at this cowboy sitting only inches from her.

Had he ever looked at her like this? Yes, the other

night in the hallway right before he started to reach for her. Right before she thought he was going to kiss her. She told herself to breathe, but her body's reaction to this Pickett had her heart beating like a jackhammer, so hard that she had trouble taking a breath.

"I know you're thinking about kissing me." Her thoughts were coming out of her mouth as if she had no control over them. "Do you have to think that hard about it?"

He smiled, that reckless, amused smile she'd always loved even as it sent a shiver through her. "If you know what I'm thinking then kissing you is the least of it."

Oakley felt heat rush up her chest and neck to make her cheeks flame. Tilly was right. She had little experience other than short-term relationships. Often, she found herself being her crush's best friend rather than his lover. With Pickett she felt as if she was entering uncharted territory.

"I really don't have much experience at any of this."

He chuckled. "Not to worry. I know what to do."

She tried to swallow as he reached for her, wrapping one warm callused hand around the side of her neck. She leaned into his strong touch as his thumb caressed the tender flesh and his fingers worked their way into the hair at her nape.

Her body trembled as her eyes locked with his. She felt her lips part and the word, "Please," escape.

Pickett's dark blue eyes widened along with his smile as he leaned toward her until his lips brushed over hers. She moaned, closing her eyes as he drew her closer until she could feel the solid hardness of his chest against her breasts. He dragged her over onto his lap. She straddled

him; her arms encircled his neck, wanting more, needing more. Her already hard nipples ached as he deepened the kiss.

She could feel his need. It matched her own. Duffy's
kiss had been nice enough, but Pickett's kiss was a
whole different rodeo. She wanted to ride this out no
matter what happened. She'd never been reckless with
her heart or her body, but Pickett made her want to
throw caution to the wind. He thumbed the side of her
breast, making her nipple pucker. Her heart thundering
in her ears, her blood running hot as molten lava raced
to her aching center.

He drew back, making her groan. "That's just in
case you don't know how I feel about you," he said. "I
want you, Oakley. But I want all of you. For the long
haul. You let me know. I'll give you some time to think
about it."

She stared at him as he lifted her off his lap and back
onto the seat. He motioned toward the rearview mirror.
A vehicle was coming.

Her hands were shaking as she got her truck going.
All she could think about was what Pickett had said.
She didn't have to think long about it, she told herself.
She'd known the moment he'd kissed her. She wanted
more and yet he'd said he wanted all of her. The thought
had her shiver with desire. For the long haul?

They said nothing on the ride into town as if both
lost in thought. Or was he reconsidering? Once there,
she parked in front of her apartment.

"Also," he said as if their conversation had continued
all the way to town, "please don't do anything about

the new methane well drilling without me. I'm in this with you."

She nodded, not wanting to do *anything* without him. As Pickett started to get out of the pickup, she grabbed his arm. "I've thought about it."

His gaze locked with hers as she leaned toward him and cupped his strong jaw to kiss him.

CHAPTER SEVENTEEN

"I DON'T UNDERSTAND," Holden said into the phone not for the first time.

"It appears to be some kind of endowment," his attorney said. "I wouldn't look a gift horse in the mouth, especially one offering this kind of money. With the interest on this alone, it would keep your ranch going for years. Or you could buy up the whole Powder River Basin."

"And you have no idea where it came from or why I was chosen to receive it," Holden said.

"Just what I've told you. You want me to dig deeper? Or just accept it and be grateful?"

From his den window, he watched Duffy and Pickett drive up. Earlier, they'd taken off together to go into town. It had seemed strange that Pickett was leaving already, since the ranch hand had seemed so anxious to get back to work.

"Accept it," his attorney said. "You'd be a fool not to. There are no strings attached. I've checked it out."

He did want to know where the money came from— and why now. He might have had the attorney hire someone to dig deeper if he hadn't heard about Pickett visiting the hotel recently. Someone had seen him coming out of room 403. At first, he'd thought the ranch hand had a lady friend.

But then he'd found out that the woman in 403, Sarah Johansen, was too old for Pickett. Also, her address had been New York City—the same place the ranch hand had left for, saying his father was dying.

And now a huge endowment for the ranch? Of course he was suspicious and yet he still didn't know how to broach the subject with Pickett. But he would talk to him, he told himself.

He turned at the sound of footfalls and saw his daughter, Bailey, heading for the door. "Bailey," he called. "A minute of your time?"

She looked as if she was trying to come up with an excuse to keep going, but changed her mind and stepped in.

"I have hardly seen you lately," Holden said. "What have you been up to?"

"Why would you think I've been up to something?" she asked.

He studied his beautiful daughter. Her long, dark hair was wavy more like her mother's than his own. Her eyes were definitely his shade of blue, though, and he recognized himself in the wild, free-spirit streak she kept well hidden.

She'd been so secretive lately, always on her phone, coming and going without any explanation. He'd always known that she would be impossible to control. He'd had a few wild horses like her.

Now he told himself he should just be glad that she'd come home from the university after six years and a degree in English. She seemed content enough staying in the Powder River Basin, though he worried about what she did all day.

"Is there someone in your life?" he had to ask. Someone she didn't want him knowing about was what he was really asking.

She frowned. "Are you asking if there is a lover in my life? Really, Dad?" She laughed and turned toward the door to leave again. "There are some things you are better off not knowing."

With that, she was gone, leaving him thinking she was probably right.

He wondered if that could also be true of this large amount of money the ranch had suddenly come into.

COOPER HAD DROPPED Tilly off at her apartment after lunch and was headed for the ranch. He'd had enough wedding planning talk for a while. He was tired after making a quick trip out to Oregon to pick up the bull. He couldn't wait for this damned wedding and would have gladly eloped. Not that he could deny his bride-to-be anything, even a wedding that he feared was more about her mother than the two of them.

His cell phone rang. "How was Oregon?"

Cooper heard something in his friend's voice. "A long quick trip. What's going on?"

"Something happened while you were gone," the sheriff said. "A pickup was found in a reservoir on one of the ranches. It belongs to Rory Eastwood. That name mean anything to you?"

"No, should it?"

"You never met the man?"

Cooper pulled over to the side of the road. "Am I

being interrogated right now? Who the hell is Rory Eastwood?"

"A former gas company employee and possibly the mystery man Leann Hayes planned to run away with."

"Why would you think that?"

"Supposedly, he'd mentioned at the bar that he was leaving town with a woman he'd fallen in love with. It was all hush-hush because she had a boyfriend."

"I wasn't her boyfriend."

"Right. But you had been sleeping with her."

Cooper groaned. "He never said he was leaving with Leann?"

"No, but he was never seen again after that night. His pickup was full of his belongings."

"Was his body…?"

"No, he's missing. That PI who's been in town trying to find Charlotte's husband, Dixon Malone, has become interested in Rory's disappearance and Leann's suicide case."

"Why are you telling me this?" Cooper said, running a hand through his hair. He didn't need this. He really wanted to get back to the ranch and crash for a while.

"Because you need to leave Leann's death alone. This would only make it look worse for you if you insisted that her case be reopened."

"I told you from her notes that I found that she was leaving town with a man she said I wouldn't approve of," Cooper said. "That's why I wanted her case reopened. This only makes me more convinced I was right and that she didn't kill herself. She was *murdered*."

"Who had a motive, besides you?" the sheriff demanded. "Until you know that, I'd suggest you leave it alone. Otherwise, you won't make it to the altar with your lovely bride. Let me handle this. I have to go."

Cooper swore. His first instinct was to go to the prosecutor—the one who'd been convinced he had killed Leann. But Stu was right. Unless he knew who had motive to kill Leann and her lover and dump his body who knew where, and his pickup in a reservoir, then he'd just be putting a noose around his neck.

He lay back, staring out at the snowy road, the bare cottonwoods dark against the white. He couldn't let this go. He knew in his heart that Leann hadn't killed herself. How could he live with himself if he didn't find out who had? They'd been friends. Didn't he owe her that?

But Stu was right. Until he had a suspect, he couldn't go to the prosecutor. First, he had to be sure that Rory Eastwood was the man she was planning to leave town with. If so, then hopefully it would lead him to the person who'd killed not only Leann but also her mystery lover.

In the meantime, he reminded himself, he was hiring contractors to build his new home with Tilly—and getting ready for a wedding where he was the groom. He called the sheriff back.

"What?" Stu demanded. "I don't have time to argue this."

"Just wanted to ask you if you'll be my best man." It had been on Tilly's list, something else he hadn't gotten around to doing.

"I'd be honored." His friend actually sounded touched.

"I trust you to find Leann's killer." Silence. "You still there?"

"Yeah. It's just that you were even suspicious of *me* not all that long ago."

Cooper sighed. "You're the sheriff and my best friend. You'll find her killer." He disconnected.

THE SHERIFF DISCONNECTED feeling good, definitely better about things than he had in a long time. Cooper trusted him to find Leann's killer—if she'd been murdered. That his friend had taken his advice was shock enough. Cooper putting his faith in him meant everything. It wasn't that long ago that his friend was insinuating that Stuart had reason to want to cover up Leann's death.

He actually felt a lump in his throat and that made him more determined to prove himself by finding out the truth. It wasn't like he didn't know where to start. A name came to mind immediately. Abigail Creed, his friendly nurse, whom he now knew was looking into Leann's death. Wasn't it time to find out why?

He'd run a check on Abigail but had come up with nothing criminal in her background other than a couple of speeding tickets. As for her connection with Leann, he'd found nothing.

If Abigail came here looking for answers, Stuart thought, she hadn't found them. He'd investigated Leann's death more than two years ago and agreed with the coroner that she'd committed suicide. Maybe Abigail had realized the same thing and was now ready to let it go.

Or not, he thought as his cell phone rang and he saw that it was her and felt a strange chill as he picked up. "Sheriff Layton." He really hoped she wasn't calling about dinner at her place again. He wasn't that naive.

"I think you owe me a burger."

"Is that right?" That she wasn't giving up made him wonder what she planned to do this time. He was certain lovemaking wasn't on the agenda and never had been. But what the hell did she want from him?

"I've heard that they make amazing burgers at a place in Baker," Abigail was saying. "Any chance I can tempt you into taking me after work?"

Stuart questioned why she'd want to get him out of town even as he realized this might be the perfect opportunity to get her alone and away from Powder Crossing and find out exactly what she was up to and why. "I could use a burger."

"Great." She sounded a little too enthusiastic about the date—even for her.

"I'll pick you up. Five?"

She was driving. Maybe even better. He wouldn't be at a disadvantage behind the wheel in case she decided to—to what? "Sounds perfect. I'll be ready."

He disconnected, fighting that gnawing feeling in his gut that reminded him that this woman could be dangerous. She'd already drugged him. Who knew what she might do on a two-lane stretch of highway with little to no traffic late this afternoon?

CHAPTER EIGHTEEN

CHARLOTTE BREATHED A sigh of relief as she hung up from speaking with her lawyer. She'd been worried sick about what Oakley would tell him. Her daughter had been so furious with CJ that she could have said just about anything—not that she could blame her. What CJ had done was unforgiveable. What had he been thinking taking a potshot at her like that? He could have killed her and then nothing Charlotte could do would have saved him from prison.

As she'd disconnected, she'd felt her son watching her, waiting, and now turned to look at him. She hadn't heard him come down the hall. He looked tense until she said, "Oakley said exactly what I told her to say."

"You're sure?" he asked, even as he looked as relieved as she felt.

"I just spoke to our lawyer." Charlotte had hoped Oakley would obey her, something she seldom did. Although it did surprise her. She thought about that awful fight Oakley had with CJ. She could have disabled him for life or worse. Whatever had made her come to her senses, Charlotte wasn't going to question it.

She was more worried about CJ. "We need to take you to Billings for your next checkup," she said.

"I don't need my mother to take me."

"You're not driving yourself all the way to Billings."

"Then call and move my checkup. I'm doing well. I want a little more time to heal. I don't want to be poked and prodded right now."

She looked at him with concern. "Are you sure Oakley didn't injure you worse?"

"Yes, I'm fine, all right? Set it up for a few months from now. Being here on the ranch is the best medicine I could ask for."

Charlotte smiled, loving to hear that. She hated arguing with him. But she also worried about him.

"Anyway, I know all these doctor bills, even with insurance, are costing you a fortune. That's why I'm glad the new methane well is going in tomorrow. We should be getting a check from CH4. There are several sites they found last time that they believe are viable. I was thinking, since we didn't get the Turner Ranch, I'm looking at some other property I'd like to personally invest in. I know you don't like drilling on the ranch. We could drill on that land and use the extra money for this ranch."

It thrilled her, this interest CJ was taking in the ranch. Her first husband had taught her that a ranch needed to keep growing to survive. "I love that idea."

"It's the smart thing to do," he said, nodding. "I'll take care of all the arrangements and dealing with the gas company and the workers. It's the least I can do since I can't do anything else from this chair. It might make me feel like I'm not completely worthless."

Charlotte's heart went out to her son. She told herself that giving him more control over decisions had definitely been the right thing to do. Although she hated to drill on the ranch, buying property away from the ranch to drill on sounded like a good investment in their future.

CJ asked for so little and clearly, he needed this. And he was right; they certainly could use the cash flow. Cattle prices were down. So much of her worth was tied up in land. She would have had to risk some of it to buy the Turner place—but that was behind her now.

"Fine, you take care of that," she told her son. "I'm going to have Boyle get the cattle shipped. There's no reason to wait any longer."

CJ didn't show any interest in the cattle side of the ranch. He didn't respond as he wheeled down the hall toward his room. She heard him making a call and decided to go out to the stables in the hopes of catching her ranch manager around. Otherwise, maybe she would go for a ride.

She almost called down the hall to ask CJ if he would be all right alone. But stopped herself. There was always staff if he needed someone and she was only a phone call away. She headed for the stables almost hoping she didn't see Boyle Wilson before her ride.

She figured Boyle had heard about the PI being in town asking about Dixon Malone, the man she was still married to but hadn't seen for years. Boyle had always hinted that he knew what had happened to Dixon, but she'd ignored him.

In no mood for his veiled threats, she entered the stables, glad not to cross paths with him today. She reminded herself that with Oakley's testimony, CJ probably wouldn't spend any time in jail—let alone go to prison. She couldn't let CJ go to prison any more than she could let Boyle Wilson hold his suspicions over her.

But as she started to saddle up, she realized that there was something she'd forgotten to take care of back at the house.

WITH TIME BEFORE he met Abigail for a burger, the sheriff decided to find out what he could about Rory Eastwood. Duffy's visit this morning had him wondering. Someone had to know who Rory was planning to leave town with, he thought as he drove out to the airfield. The closest airport with a paved landing strip was in Miles City. The local airport had a windsock and a grass landing strip. CH4 had even built themselves a hangar for their plane. Unpaved, the strip was used by crop dusters and more recently, by gas company pilots who flew employees into the area.

If he wanted to find out what he could about Rory Eastwood, it was the place to start since Rory had worked for the gas company—up until the night he allegedly left town with a mystery woman.

Stu was hoping to catch one of the company's pilots, Howie Gunderson, and lucked out. Gunderson's pickup was parked next to the CH4 hangar. As he pulled in, he saw the hangar door was open, a small plane inside. Not Gunderson's. His was sitting a short distance away.

The pilot was in conversation with a man wearing a suit, no small occurrence this far from Billings. He parked and climbed out. The two men looked up, breaking off their conversation as he approached. "Afternoon," he said. "Howie." He looked to the other man. "I believe we've already met."

"This is Douglas Burton," Howie said nervously. "He's the CEO of CH4."

"That's what he told me when he came by my office," the sheriff said and turned to the CEO. "I thought you would have left the area by now."

"I was just getting ready to fly him to Billings," Howie said before his boss could respond.

Stuart kept his attention on Burton. "I'm glad to catch you, then. I wanted to ask about a former employee of yours. Rory Eastwood." He saw the CEO recognize the name even as the man shook his head. "His pickup was recently found in a reservoir."

"Do you have any idea how many employees CH4 has around the world, Sheriff? You expect me to know all of them? Why the interest?" Burton asked.

"I suspect foul play. But you probably wouldn't know anything about that," Stuart said.

"I'm afraid not," the CEO said. "We really need to get going."

Stuart looked at Howie but knew the pilot wasn't going to be forthcoming in front of his boss. "Well, thanks for your time." He turned and walked away, feeling the two men watching him.

The sheriff realized that the man he needed to talk to might be at the hotel bar by this time of day. Sure enough, once he reached town, he saw the Texan's pickup parked out front. He found the geologist for CH4 at the bar.

Alfred "Tick" Whitaker was busy entertaining a couple of regulars. The Texan was a big man in his midfifties who had the gift of gab, Stuart's father would have said. Tick also liked the ladies according to the local scuttlebutt. Apparently full of stories, abundant charm and plenty of spending money, Tick also liked to drink.

The sheriff let him finish his story before he asked the man to join him at a table. "What are you drinking?" He told the bartender and motioned to a table away from the bar. "Need to ask you a few questions."

"What can I do for you, Sheriff?" Tick asked as he pulled out a chair and sat down.

"Tell me about Rory Eastwood."

Tick didn't even pretend not to know the man. "Wasn't that something about his pickup being pulled out of a reservoir?" He shook his head. "I thought for sure you'd find his body behind the wheel. Only been a couple of years. Wouldn't have decayed all that much that they wouldn't have found something when they dragged the reservoir."

Clearly, he was fairly well informed. Stuart pretended to take a sip of his beer and watched Tick take a large gulp of his. "What was Rory like?"

"Seemed like a fine enough guy, kind of full of it, you know?" He did know. He thought Tick was full of it, too.

"Had a way with the ladies, did he?"

The geologist laughed. "I wouldn't say that. He was kind of shy around women. Hadn't worked for the company long. That's why I was surprised when he quit. It's a good job that pays well."

"Heard he was telling people he'd fallen in love and was leaving town with her," Stuart said and raised his beer to his lips, watching Tick over the bottle.

"Why are you asking about Rory?"

"It must be boring as hell being stuck in this tiny

town in the middle of nowhere. I figured if anyone might have known Rory, it would be you since I heard that you both frequented this hotel bar." Tick finished his drink and the sheriff motioned to the bartender for another one for him. "Also, you're the kind of man that someone shy might confide in—especially when it comes to women. Bet he told you about her."

The bartender brought over the beer and took Tick's empty glass before the Texan answered. "Not that I can recall."

"Guess you two weren't as close as I thought." He took a sip of beer. He wanted to be completely sober when Abigail picked him up later.

Tick picked up his drink and took a gulp. "He didn't want anyone to know."

"Why was that?" he asked.

"She kind of had a boyfriend and she hadn't told him yet."

"Or she hadn't made up her mind yet?"

"No, she was going with Rory. He quit his job and they were leaving town that night."

"So you saw him the night he was leaving."

Tick took another gulp. "Look, I don't want any trouble. I've been advised not to talk about it. CH4 is worried that it will somehow come back on the company. The bigwig is in town…"

"I've met him. This is just between you and me. Was it Leann Hayes?" He saw the answer in the Texan's eyes and nodded. "I'm pretty sure you know I dated her some and so did my best friend. I need to know if she was leaving with Rory because she and I were friends. It wasn't serious. But I did worry about her. She seemed to have a knack for picking the wrong men."

The Texan rubbed a hand over the back of his neck. The two regulars he'd been entertaining had left. The bar was empty except for the two of them and the bartender, who was fiddling with the television as he apparently tried to find a ballgame on it.

"It was Leann, wasn't it?" the sheriff said.

Tick looked pained. "He never said exactly, but I suspected it was. Saw him with her once."

"What do you think happened that night?" Tick shrugged. "Was Eastwood the kind of man who would kill her and then take his own life?" He wasn't surprised when Tick shook his head. "Then who wanted them both dead?"

The Texan met his gaze. "There was someone else. Someone before she came to Powder Crossing. Someone she was trying to get away from."

That stopped Stuart cold. "Any idea who they were?"

He shook his head. "Some past relationship that had gone sour, that's all Rory knew. That night Rory was worried that she wasn't completely over it. He was afraid that now that he'd quit his job and packed up to leave, she might change her mind. She sounded flaky to me. I figured he was probably making a mistake. I never dreamed someone would kill him.

"If you ask me—" he leaned in and lowered his voice "—I think Leann killed him, ditched his truck, his body and then realizing what she'd done, killed herself. Or, maybe the person from this former relationship killed them both."

That definitely added a new dimension if Tick knew what he was talking about.

The geologist seemed to remember his beer, drained it as he got to his feet. "Thanks for the brews. I'd appreciate it if you left this just between the two of us. Wouldn't want to lose my job."

Stuart nodded as he felt a familiar roiling in his stomach. Someone before him, before Cooper. He and Cooper could have been on a long list of lovers Leann had left. That certainly put her death in a new light.

CJ CHECKED TO make sure there was no one outside the guest room before he made the call. "Tell me that we're all set," he said the moment his party answered.

"I did my part if that's what you're asking. You have the money?"

He could hear the recrimination in Treyton McKenna's voice. He tried to tamp down his anger. "I have it covered. After all, I saved you from a Lees brothers visit. You should be thanking me. Not giving me—"

"Thanking you? This is your mess, not mine. Just like another time as I recall."

"Old history. This is *now*. You're the one who came to me wanting to be cut in," CJ snapped back. "Don't bite the hand that feeds you."

Treyton swore. "Think much of yourself? Let's not forget what I brought to the table or what I know about you."

"Okay, we're business partners. I have enough problems without fighting about this with you," CJ said. When Treyton said nothing, he asked, "You want out?

I'll have the Lees brothers stop over and give you what you have coming."

"Don't threaten me, Stafford. None of this would have been a problem if you had been more careful."

"You know my sister, but I'm having it taken care of."

"What does that mean?"

"You don't want to know," CJ said. "I've talked to our suppliers. They're ready to get back into business. Isn't that what we both want?" Silence, only this time he took it for agreement. "Get ready. You'll have company soon."

As he disconnected, he thought about the circumstances that made strange bed partners. Now he and Treyton McKenna were in bed together again, so to speak. He could hear his grandmother say, "You've made your bed, now lie in it."

CJ had never really understood the expression, until now. It basically meant he was screwed if things went south. His bond with Treyton had always been risky. But McKenna or not, Treyton was as hungry as he was for power and money. CJ would just have to never turn his back on the man. But if this paid off the way he planned, he would run this river basin.

He rose, walked over to the small refrigerator his mother had put in the guest room for him. After opening the door, he pulled out a can of cold beer. "Thanks, Mom," he said sarcastically and then heard someone coming down the hall. He realized that he hadn't locked the bedroom door. At least this time he had remembered to close the curtains.

He'd barely gotten into his wheelchair when the door opened.

CHAPTER NINETEEN

THE SHERIFF HAD planned to stop by Abigail's small house she rented behind the hospital, but to his surprise she was waiting for him on the front steps of the sheriff's department building when he returned. "You really are excited about going to get a burger," he said.

She smiled her come-hither smile. "Maybe I'm excited about seeing you."

Maybe, but he doubted it.

"My car," she said, pointing to her SUV parked on the street. "My treat today."

He felt something cold creep up his spine, but nodded, even more curious. What was she up to? This wasn't about a burger. He was an officer of the law. He was armed. And he wasn't going to eat or drink anything she'd had a chance to doctor.

Stuart told himself that he should be fine. They would be eating in a café. He would watch her like a hawk. But as he thought it, he was reminded of the empty miles to Baker with few ranches, even fewer other vehicles on the road this time of year.

It struck him that today he might actually find out just how dangerous this woman was. He knew she was looking into Leann Hayes's death. She'd drugged an officer of the law to go through Leann's files and search his house. She'd taken one hell of a chance so whatever she was looking for, she was fairly desperate to find it.

But what was it she suspected and, more important, how far would she go to get it?

He slid into the passenger seat and buckled up. Out of the corner of his eye, he watched Abigail take the wheel. Was it just his imagination that she was nervous, as if readying herself for what she was about to do?

What the hell was she about to do?

"WHAT DO YOU WANT?" CJ snapped as his mother stuck her head in the guest room door. He'd thought she was going for a horseback ride. He'd heard her leave. But for some reason she'd come back. To spy on him?

She seemed surprised at his sudden rage. "I realized that you hadn't had lunch." Her gaze went to the can of beer in his hand. He fought the urge to hide it even though he was a grown man and she'd had the small refrigerator put in his room. What did she think he was going to stock in there, fruit juice?

"How about a little privacy?" he demanded.

For a moment she looked as if she was going to lecture him on his rudeness, but good sense must have prevailed. "Sorry to bother you. I'll have the cook put your lunch in the refrigerator until you're ready for it." She closed the door.

He sat, heart thundering in his chest. She'd gotten so much worse since his accident. There was one way to get her to quit babying him. Tell her the truth. But he couldn't. Not yet. He had to use this to his advantage. Even she would agree.

But he hated it. He hated the van. He hated the wheelchair. He hated that he was trapped here in this room even temporarily. Worse, he felt like everyone was watching him; not just Oakley and his mother but the entire staff. Not to mention his...associates. He had no choice. He had to keep pretending he couldn't walk. But this couldn't be over soon enough.

First, though, he had to set things up for Oakley. Once she heard about the new well being drilled on the ranch, she would walk right into the trap. Maybe she'd even bring a couple of her cohorts. Did she think he didn't know how close she'd gotten to Duffy McKenna? He wasn't worried about Pickett Hanson, who was just a ranch hand over on the McKenna place. But wouldn't it be great if Duffy and Oakley could be lured out to the site where the Lees brothers would be waiting? Accidents happened around drilling rigs all the time.

He thought about Dixon Malone and now Rory Eastwood. People tended to disappear in this part of Montana and not even that PI could find them. If Duffy and Oakley disappeared it would cause much more of a stir, though. Better to have them injured while trying to vandalize the equipment.

CJ rolled over to the door, opened it and checked to make sure his mother wasn't standing just outside in the hallway. All was clear. He closed the door, locked it and, moving to the window, placed the call. "Make it look like an accident," he told Frankie after telling him that their business venture was moving forward. "With Oakley gone, we'll be home free. She'll come to the new drilling site at midnight—just like the other times she and her partners in crime vandalized the rigs. She might come alone this close to the house, but do what you have to do if she brings her friends."

He disconnected. With luck, Oakley would be history soon, maybe Duffy and Pickett, too, if they got in the way. Their deaths should scare off other vandals.

It was a win-win situation and CJ would never have to worry about Oakley again. Not to mention that the tragedy would give his mother something else to obsess over other than him. He could see her at the funeral, him next to her in his wheelchair, the perfect son.

Of course she would blame the McKennas—this time Duffy and his hired man, Pickett. It would keep the feud between the families alive, which was exactly what he and Treyton wanted. Neither of them could bear the thought that Charlotte and Holden might find their way back together. That wasn't part of the plan.

CHARLOTTE HATED FEELING this anxious as she looked down the hallway toward the guest room before moving out of sight. Sometimes, her oldest son scared her. He had reason to be angry, she tried to tell herself. But in truth, CJ had always had a bad disposition, especially when he didn't get his way as a child, as a teen and now as an adult. She blamed herself for spoiling him more than the others. He'd been her firstborn. But he'd also always worked at being her favorite.

Her other children had picked up on her shortage of maternal instincts and her lack of interest in raising them. In those days she'd been happiest on a horse, riding through the vast land that had become her ranch. Marrying her first husband after Holden had broken her heart had also saved her—and made her a wealthy, powerful woman.

She'd been in her late teens when she'd married Rake Stafford. Rake had been seventeen years older. He'd brought order to her life along with money that he used to build the Stafford Ranch. Before that, it had been the Carson Ranch, small because that was all her parents, John and Ruth Carson, could afford.

With Rake, the now Stafford Ranch had flourished and grown. Together, they'd had five children in the eight years before Rake died. Oakley was just a baby when he passed and left Charlotte a widow.

She'd felt safe married to Rake and then he was gone. Holden had lost his wife as well just months before. That she'd even let herself think he might finally come back to her made her despise herself. When she'd heard that he'd remarried so quickly—and who he'd married— she'd been beyond devastated and furious. Lulabelle Braden?

The only satisfaction she got was that the loud, obnoxious redhead had made Holden's life miserable the few months they were married. Still, Charlotte blamed him for making her feel she had to rush into a marriage with Dixon Malone, the second biggest mistake of her life. The first had been falling in love with Holden and letting him break her heart.

Dixon had been a mistake in so many ways. Her children had been so young, and she'd been so miserable. But being married to him had been pure hell. He was lazy, spent too much of her money and thought he would boss her around.

CJ was twelve when Dixon disappeared. She often

wondered how much he remembered of the almost year that she spent with Dixon before one day he was just gone. CJ had never asked what happened to him. Brand and Ryder had been told that their stepfather had left. The girls were so young, she doubted they'd noticed he was gone except for the lack of fighting in the house. None of them was sad to see Dixon go.

So she thought as she went to the kitchen to tell the cook what to do with CJ's lunch, she knew she had only herself to blame. She had made CJ the way he was. Was it any wonder that he resented her the way he did?

She swallowed the bitter taste in her mouth as she headed for her office, no longer interested in a horse-back ride. She already missed Tilly, who'd been helping her with the paperwork involved in running a ranch. But she couldn't forgive her daughter. How could she marry a McKenna knowing how her mother felt about it?

Oakley was another story. She'd made this mess. What had she been doing on the McKenna Ranch to start with? She just needed Oakley to stand by her brother until this all blew over. The problem was that she wasn't sure she could trust Oakley right now. Her daughter was a hothead, stubborn and determined in what she believed. Charlotte couldn't remember ever being that headstrong. But she'd certainly raised two daughters who were.

She thought about Tilly's upcoming wedding that everyone was talking about in town. That Tilly had sent her an invitation showed how out of touch with reality she was. Charlotte's heart held no place for forgiveness. Once someone turned on her, she wrote them out of her life. It was the only way she could survive, she told herself.

Now, as she glanced toward the hallway to the guest room, she tried not to think about CJ. She couldn't imagine how she would feel if she ever found out that she couldn't trust him or worse, that he'd already turned on her as well.

THE SHERIFF WATCHED Abigail out of the corner of his eye as she drove. What was he doing with this woman? It felt like a game of Russian roulette. How long was he going to keep playing? It worried him that he was playing at all.

Maybe it was time to make a change in his life. He'd never been cut out to be a sheriff. He'd thought about leaving Powder Crossing, but there was nowhere he wanted to go, nothing he'd always wanted to do. So what did that leave?

Stuart chuckled to himself. He wanted to be Cooper McKenna. No, he amended that. If he was being truly honest, he only wanted what his best friend had—what came with being Holden McKenna's son. A ranch, roots, a family and now a bride.

Had it really not been all that long ago that Stuart had wanted Tilly? Not because he loved her, but because he'd known she'd always been Cooper's from the time they were kids.

That he was that small, that damaged, that begrudging, made him feel even worse about himself.

He looked over at Abigail. What the hell was he doing? She drove as carefully as someone who knew they were drunk. Maybe she was doing her own soul searching. No, he thought, she appeared to be debating something. The bad feeling that filled him earlier confirmed that this trip wasn't about a burger.

As if making up her mind, she slowed and pulled off onto a dirt road into a grove of trees next to the river. Without leaves, the stark-limbed cottonwoods looked like fingers clawing at the cloudy Montana sky.

He noticed for the first time that a storm was coming in from the west. Snow? It wouldn't be that unusual this time of year. But it always seemed to happen just when the land had been bearing off and the temperatures had been rising, giving everyone a break from winter.

But he doubted that was why he felt a chill as Abigail pulled over to the side of the road and cut the engine.

"I thought this was about a burger," he said, hoping his tone didn't reveal just how anxious he was. She wasn't looking at him. Red flag alert! All his instincts were telling him he should never have gotten into this car. His hand was already resting on the gun at his hip, hoping he could pull it quickly enough if he had to in this small SUV.

"I haven't been honest with you," she said, turning a little in her seat to look at him. He was watching her hands that now worked nervously in her lap. "I didn't come to Powder Crossing because of the job at the hospital or my photography."

"I know," he said.

Her eyes widened. "You do?"

"You came to town because of Leann Hayes."

All the air seemed to rush from her as she leaned her head back. She looked as if a huge weight had been lifted from her shoulders. "How long have you known?"

"I was suspicious from the start, but I didn't know until you drugged me and searched my office files and my home."

She froze for a moment before she licked her lips and sighed. "So you know. You didn't say anything so I thought…"

She'd thought that she'd gotten away with it. Maybe he wasn't as lousy a sheriff as she thought he was. "What is your connection to her?"

"She was my friend," Abigail said. "We were like sisters."

"Had you been in touch with her since she came to Powder Crossing?"

"Of course, I just told you. We were like sisters."

That bad feeling he'd had earlier now settled in his gut. "Then you knew about her relationship before she came to Powder Crossing, before she met me." He was watching her closely. "Did she tell you about me? About Cooper?"

He still had his hand on his gun when she reached with her left hand into the driver's side door cubby. He'd been ready but all she pulled out was a tissue. She blew her nose, dropping the tissue back into the door's side pocket.

"She didn't love you," Abigail said. Her gaze when she turned it on him was brittle and bright. Her words came out fast and hard. "She was trying to get away from you. She said you were obsessed with her. That you used to follow her. She was terrified that you would kill her if she didn't go back to you."

"That's not true," he said, even as he groaned inwardly, knowing it could have been true. He'd tried to hang on to her. He had been obsessed. He'd followed her a few times, furious when he'd heard that she'd hooked up with his best friend. It had been a bad time in so many ways. He wasn't that man anymore. He'd promised himself he would never be that man again.

"She'd broken things off with me. She'd moved on. She was with Cooper McKenna." Why were they arguing about this? "Abigail, Leann was leaving town with some man she'd fallen in love with. It wasn't me and it wasn't Cooper."

"No," she cried. "That's a lie. We'd been saving our money to get a house together in Billings. I was going to work at the hospital there and she was going to open her own photography studio. She was a much better photographer than I am. She was teaching me."

He saw it now. The only personal thing in her house, a photograph taken by a friend. "Leann took that photo in your house," he said.

But she wasn't listening; her expression went dark again. "She didn't want any of you, especially Rory Eastwood. But like most men, he wouldn't leave her alone." He felt his pulse jump. "She said she had to leave the state to get away. She was trying to get away from all of you, but especially *you*." There was spittle on her lips, her eyes wild and leaking angry tears.

He felt his chest tighten as he began to make sense of her words. This wasn't about him, no matter what she said. "You knew about Rory and Leann?" he said, heart in his throat. Clearly, Abigail knew more than he did. "You saw her that night," he said quietly and saw that it was true. "You were her friend. You were trying to help her."

"I *loved* her. We were like sisters." Her voice broke. "We had plans. She'd promised." Her expression hardened. He felt the tension in the car spike. "I came to save her from you, from Rory, from all the men who'd hurt her, deserted her, confused her. She said she was sick of all of you. Sick of the life she'd been living. She'd promised she would change. That it would just be the two of us."

He saw it as clear as if he'd been in Leann's apartment that night. Friends, like sisters, she'd said. Leann going from man to man, searching for something elusive while she made promises she never meant to keep. "You tried to stop her from making a mistake."

Abigail made a swipe at her tears. She looked so young, so heartbroken. The woman she'd loved like a sister had been about to abandon her, probably not for the first time. "I couldn't let her leave with that man. She knew it was a mistake, but he'd promised her a new life far away."

Stuart suspected she was right, given that Leann's alleged suicide note had made it sound as if she was questioning what she was about to do. That was why it had been ruled a suicide. Had she left the note because she knew Abigail was coming to Powder Crossing? Had she thought she and Rory would be gone before her needy, clingy friend arrived?

Abigail's voice dropped to almost a whisper. "She was changing her mind about leaving, but then…"

"Rory showed up," he guessed.

Her face went blank, her eyes unfocused as if lost in the past. "I told him to leave but he wouldn't. He was going to make her go with him, saying that he was protecting her from me." She looked over at him, frowning as if confused by that.

"What happened then?" he asked, but suspected he already knew.

Her gaze, steady, tear-free, met his. "Leann walked him out to his truck. When he climbed behind the wheel, I killed him to save her. But then she said you would come after us. You were obsessed with her. That you would find out what I'd done. That she could never be free because you were smart and would figure it out. And you would lock me up."

That was why Abigail had searched the file and his house. She thought he was coming after her.

Her voice broke as she said, "She said that we were never getting that little house. We couldn't be sisters anymore." Tears welled in her eyes. "We couldn't even be friends because of what I'd done. But I did it to save her. We could have run away like she was planning to do with Rory, but she said no. She was going to call you. *You.* I couldn't let her do that."

"Abigail," he said, his heart hurting for this misguided, trusting woman who'd been through too much disappointment. "You made it look like she'd committed suicide. It worked. It was over. I wouldn't have come after you."

Tears cascaded down her cheeks even as she smiled. "I know. You really thought she'd killed herself." Her voice dropped to a scary, paper-thin level. "But then you found his truck." She wiped at her cheek and reached into the side pocket of the door again, only this time, she didn't come out with a tissue.

The blade of the knife caught the dull light before the

storm. Before he could react, she struck out with it and suddenly she was screaming at the top of her lungs, her eyes wide. He got his arm up, saw the blood before he felt the pain as the blade sliced his arm open.

"Stop!" he yelled, the word lost in her screams as she slashed at him again and again in the close confines of the car, driving the blade into him as he tried to grab her wrist. But she was too quick, too abnormally strong, in her frenzy. He tried to fight her off as he fumbled for his weapon.

The sound of the gunshot seemed to surprise them both.

She swung the knife in an arc, but slower, less in control. He was able to grab her wrist with his free hand and wrenched the knife from her bloody fingers. He realized he was holding his gun in his other hand. He had no memory of pulling it from his holster, let alone firing it.

She stared at him with unseeing eyes for a moment before she slumped over onto the steering wheel. He jumped as the horn began to sound and quickly pulled her away from it. She collapsed back into the seat. Like everything around them, she was covered with splattered blood, now not all his. As he stared at her, still in shock, her blood stopped leaking out of the hole in her chest and she fell to the side, her cheek against the driver's side window.

Stuart felt in shock, almost unaware of how badly he was injured. He still had his gun in his hand, the knife in the other. He dropped both to the floor, fumbled to open his door, his hand slick with blood, and stepped out.

The sky had darkened over the bare limbs of the cottonwoods. He could feel the cold as the snowstorm blew out of the mountains, the temperature dropping. He reached for his phone with fingers still dripping with blood. He was shaking so hard he could barely make the call. As he did, he stumbled off the roadbed, dropping down into the snowy barrow pit and into the trees. The ground was soft from layers of dried leaves and piles of snow that had blown in against the large trunks, too deep to have melted even during this warm spell.

What had he done? "You reap what you sow," he heard his grandmother say in his ear as he fell face-first into the decaying leaves and dirty snow.

CHAPTER TWENTY

CHARLOTTE RODE HER horse into the meadow. It had been unusually warm lately but there was still snow banked against the north side of the trees and the creek. Elaine was already there, standing next to the creek where water burbled under a thick layer of ice. The smell of snow was in the air and Charlotte could feel the temperate dropping. A snowstorm was blowing in.

She crossed the creek and dismounted, walking over to join her friend, who appeared lost in thought. Charlotte still marveled that she and Elaine were friends at all. Elaine was a fixture at the McKenna Ranch and had been for years. She'd become good friends with Holden's first wife, Margaret "Margie" Smith—just as Charlotte had been at one time. Then Margie had married Holden, crushing Charlotte's dreams.

It had been Margie's idea for Elaine to reach out to her, to broker peace between the families. Even when Margie was dying of cancer, she'd kept trying to get Charlotte to forgive Holden through Elaine.

Elaine would ride over, and they would meet secretly. At first, Charlotte had wanted nothing to do with either Elaine or Margie. Yet, she'd agreed to the meetings after a while. For Charlotte, it had been a tenuous connection to the man she'd loved, one she'd guiltily indulged in.

Over the years, she and Elaine had become good friends, cloak-and-dagger friends. It was her only way to know what was going on over at the McKenna Ranch. It was also Elaine's way of still trying all these years later to get her to forgive Holden and bringing peace between the families.

"I'm sorry about the Turner place," Elaine said, knowing how much her friend had needed that ranch. Charlotte nodded. "At least this way, the ranch will stay as it is. How is CJ?"

She shook her head. "I'm worried about him."

"Of course you are. He's not any better?"

"No. You know about Tilly and Cooper?" Of course Elaine did. She would have known even before Charlotte herself.

"They're in love." Charlotte made a rude noise, making Elaine laugh. "Don't you want to be part of that love? Part of their lives? Do you really not want to know your own grandchildren?"

"Is she pregnant already?" she asked, afraid of how little she knew.

"No." Elaine laughed again. "She's too busy planning the wedding." Elaine reached for her hand. "It's time to let the past go and look to the future. You aren't going to want to miss this next part. You've been angry long enough." She squeezed her hand. "Let it go. Come to Tilly's wedding. It's just that easy."

"She doesn't want me there."

"Charlotte, you know better than that. Just one small step. That's all it will take."

"Holden will be there."

"Of course he will," her friend said, releasing her

hand. "And you'll be all dressed up with a whole new attitude."

She laughed. "You really are a dreamer." For a moment she studied Elaine's pretty face. "Why have you never married?"

"Really?" She chuckled. "My life has always been so full at the ranch. I've never considered leaving."

"You're in love with Holden," Charlotte said, voicing something she'd known in her heart for years.

"Isn't everyone?" Elaine said, smiling. "But he's in love with you and always has been."

She huffed. "That's why he keeps marrying someone else. Can you believe he married Lulabelle Braden?"

"That was definitely a mistake, but he was young and foolish, making one mistake on top of another. He'd never make that mistake again and hasn't. I think he's realized that he'd rather be alone than be with the wrong woman."

"He was happy with Margie."

Elaine nodded. "But Margie knew that she wasn't his first choice. She did her best to make him happy. The woman was a saint," she added with a laugh.

"Don't I know it and I'm nothing like her." When her friend said nothing, she added, "You could argue the point."

"When we both know it's true?"

They laughed, then stood in companionable silence, the approaching snowstorm darkening the sky over the bare-limbed cottonwoods to throw shadows over them.

"Was there a reason you needed to see me?" Elaine asked. "Other than for me to try to talk sense into you?"

Charlotte smiled in spite of herself. "It's always good

to see you. I feel as if I have alienated everyone, especially my family, and been an example to CJ of how to act badly. Now he blames me for the way he is and he's probably right."

"CJ is a grown man. It's his choice how he lives his life."

She studied Elaine again, hearing something in her tone. "What? Have you heard something?"

"Nothing specific. Those two men the gas company hired for security were seen coming from your ranch recently."

"That's because CJ hired CH4 to drill another well."

"And they sent their security men out first? Have you seen them? They're trouble, Charlotte. I just worry about Oakley after what happened to her before."

On the ride back, she felt a wave of shame wash over her at the memory of her argument with her daughter. She had blamed Oakley for the shooting because she'd been so afraid CJ would go to prison. A part of her knew he wouldn't survive in that kind of setting. Or maybe he would thrive, she thought, remembering her recent concerns about him.

She felt a chill that had nothing to do with the approaching storm.

THE SHERIFF OPENED his eyes to find two state police standing over him. Through the fog of both sleep and drugs, he told himself that he'd never seen either of them before. He had no idea what they were even doing here.

Here, though, he realized, was a hospital room. He glanced down, seeing bandages on his arms, shoulders and chest. Everything came back at rocket speed. He tried to sit up.

"Let me help you with that," the larger of the two police officers said, moving to the end of the bed to crank up the top portion so Stuart was in a sitting position.

He hurt all over. The movement of simply sitting up made him hurt worse. "How did I get here?"

"You called for help." The two cops introduced themselves. All he caught was Officer Forester for the larger of the two. Andrews for the other one. "Do you remember what happened?"

His last memory was lying in dead leaves and snow, bleeding badly. Before that... Abigail. His heart began to pound. "Is she..."

"Dead," Forester said.

Stuart closed his eyes, trying to blot out the memory of all the blood, of the wild, inhuman look on her face, the frantic screams as she attacked him. All he'd ever seen was the capable, accomplished, calculating woman who'd drugged him. But like him, there'd been that lonely, lost part of her that she'd thought she could fill with Leann's love.

He opened his eyes again as he heard one of the officers pull up a chair next to the bed. The other had turned on a video recorder. "We need to know what happened," Forester said. "Can you start at the beginning?"

The beginning. How could he possibly explain why he had gotten into a car with Abigail Creed, when he knew he shouldn't have?

NEWS OF WHAT had happened to Sheriff Layton spread like wildfire across the Powder River Basin. CJ couldn't believe his good luck. With life-threatening stab wounds, the sheriff had been airlifted out to Billings. The state police had been called in to investigate the nurse's death.

Which meant that until it was finished, there would be no law in Powder Crossing or the surrounding area. It felt like a gift from heaven. Now was the time to move on everything.

"I need that drilling rig on the Stafford Ranch asap," CJ told Frankie. "We need to move while the sheriff is in the hospital."

"The snowstorm held it up. Everything's ready. You sure about this?"

He didn't have to ask what Frankie was referring to. Few people could understand a person who could kill his own kin and yet it happened every day. When your own blood turned against you, you did what had to be done.

"I'll make sure my sister and her cohorts show up. You make sure we put them out of business. Otherwise—"

"I got it."

"Also, let's find out where Dirty Business is meeting. I'm in the mood to burn a few more barns and community centers, aren't you?"

Frankie chuckled. "You're making this into a war zone. You do realize that, right?"

"Barns and community centers catch on fire all the time. I just want the message sent to those people that we aren't playing around anymore."

STUART TOLD THE state police about meeting Abigail while investigating Oakley Stafford's shooting and how the nurse had brought him dinner when she saw him working late.

"Were you sleeping with her?" Forester asked.

"No." He'd already warned himself to be careful about what he told the officers. Which meant he couldn't mention her drugging him. Any law officer with a brain would have brought her in. The problem was that most of the drug had already left his system by the time he realized what she'd done.

But after that, a law officer without a death wish wouldn't have gotten into the car with her and let her take him out into the country and try to kill him.

Nor could he tell them that the first time she'd stopped by his office with dinner for the two of them, red flares had gone off. He hadn't trusted her. But then again, he trusted few women, given his history with them.

"We were just friends. At least that's what I thought. She had me over to dinner recently. When she stopped by saying she wanted to go to Baker for a burger, I didn't feel I could say no. I wasn't planning to see her after that. She seemed lonely. I never really understood what she was doing in Powder Crossing."

He saw the two cops exchange a look. *Oh damn,* he thought as his heart dropped. What did they know that he didn't?

The sheriff waited, aware that guilty people tended to talk too much when being interrogated. He didn't want to be one of them, but he couldn't help the feeling that the two officers knew something that might land him in trouble.

While he waited, he tried to think of what he would

say when they asked him why Abigail had tried to kill him. He had no choice but to tell the truth—up to a point. Otherwise, it might look as if he had tried to attack her, and she'd merely fought back.

Forester cleared his throat. "Please tell us what happened on the way to get a burger."

He took his time. "Abigail wanted to drive. I didn't realize anything was wrong until she pulled off the highway in an isolated spot. She'd mentioned having sex before, but I'd never taken her up on it and I wasn't going to then."

"But that wasn't what she was after?" Forester said.

Stu shook his head. "I told you that I wondered what she was doing in Powder Crossing. She finally told me the truth. She was a close friend of a woman I had dated for a short period of time. A woman who later committed suicide, but by then the woman was with someone else."

"Leann Hayes," Andrews said, verifying what Stuart had feared. The state cops had somehow found the connection between Abigail and Leann, a connection he himself hadn't been able to find. "Can you tell us why the victim was interested in an old case of yours? A suicide?"

"She was only interested in how much I knew about Leann's death," he said. "I quickly realized that two years ago she came to Powder Crossing to stop her friend from running off with Rory Eastwood. Abigail thought she was saving her friend when Rory showed up, an argument ensued and she killed Rory.

"When Leann told her that I would know what she'd done and come after her, that all of Abigail's dreams of she and Leann getting a place together, being like sisters, was ruined because I would find her and put her behind bars, she and Leann fought and she killed Leann, making it look like a suicide."

"So she feared you were coming after her even though the death had been ruled a suicide?" Forester said.

"Apparently so. I think that Abigail couldn't get over what she'd done and at some point she blamed me, but I'm no psychiatrist. All I know is that she tried to kill me."

"Almost did," the cop said.

CJ STAFFORD WAS thinking about burning his bridges as well as barns when his phone rang again. "You said to call if I had something for you," Rusty Malone said without preamble.

He sighed. "This had better be good. What have you got?"

"You still paying for information?"

"Depends on the information." CJ found it ironic that his former stepfather, Dixon Malone, was somehow related to a ranch hand on the McKenna Ranch.

"Oh, this is good," Rusty assured him, keeping his voice down. CJ hoped the fool wasn't at the bar in town where someone could overhear him. "You know your sister Oakley is tight with Pickett Hanson and Duffy McKenna, right?"

"That's not news." As much as it ticked CJ off, the three had hung out since they were kids.

"What if I told you that some fancy-dressed woman

came looking for Pickett. She stayed at the hotel in town. Pickett met her there."

"I'm really not interested in Pickett's love life," he snapped.

"It wasn't like that. The woman, Sarah Johansen, was old enough to be his mother. The thing is I heard her making arrangements for a plane ticket for him to fly to New York City. Word was that his father was dying."

"I heard all that. So what? The old man must have kicked off because I heard Pickett is back."

"The plane ticket was in the name Archibald Vanderlin Westmoreland."

Now Rusty had his attention. "Who the hell is that?"

"Exactly. Clearly not some ranch hand named Pickett Hanson."

Clearly, CJ thought. "Nice work," he said, promising to pay Rusty for the information as he hurriedly disconnected and went online to find out who the hell the McKenna ranch hand really was—other than his sister Oakley's BFF.

THE SHERIFF COULD feel every stab wound as he closed his eyes. Abigail had almost killed him. He opened his eyes slowly, desperately wanting to keep them closed as exhaustion washed over him. The weight of the drugs and his injuries and the accusations dragged him down even further.

"Can you tell us about your relationship with Leann Hayes?" Forester asked.

"It was a long time ago. We dated. She moved on."

"To Cooper McKenna—your best friend, right?" he

asked. "Didn't you originally arrest him for Leann's murder?"

"That was the county prosecutor's doing. Not mine. Those charges were dropped."

"For lack of evidence," Andrews said.

Stuart wasn't up to this; his patience was running thin because of the pain and the need to close his eyes and let the drugs take him back to that dark, near-dead peace. "Do you want to retry that case or do you want to know what happened with Abigail?"

Forester nodded. "Why after all this time?"

"Rory's pickup. She heard it had been pulled from the reservoir. I guess she thought I'd put two and two together."

"You weren't aware that she'd brought a weapon?"

He scoffed. "Clearly not. She was upset. I thought she was reaching for a tissue in the side pocket of her door. Instead, she pulled a knife. It happened so fast. She was screaming. I tried to take the knife from her, but she kept stabbing me. Blood was flying everywhere. I was fumbling for my gun, but I was bleeding so badly, and she was stabbing me again and again. I pulled the trigger. By then I was barely able to stay conscious. I somehow managed to get out of her SUV. Apparently, I called for help. That's the last I remember until I woke up in this bed."

"You had no idea that she planned to kill you when she invited you out for a burger?" Forester asked.

"Seriously? You think I would have gotten into the car with her?" He saw the change in the two men. The interrogation was over. They'd done what they'd come to do. They seemed satisfied with his answers.

"So you weren't aware that she had other weapons in her car?" Andrews asked. "A stun gun and what appears to be a variety of drugs as well as rope and duct tape."

Shock shot through him, rattling him to his bones. Who knew what she had planned to do to him? Torture him? He shuddered at the thought, remembering her frenzied slashing of him. It had been so fast, so furious, so out of control, that he'd been taken off guard, unable to react quickly enough.

He never should have gotten into the car with her. What had he been thinking? "I should have known," he said with a curse.

"You can't always tell when someone is that… unbalanced," Andrews said as he turned off the video recorder.

"Still, I'm the sheriff," he said. "I should have…" He shook his head. He *had* known and still he'd gotten into the car with her. He just hadn't thought she would go that far. But the truth was he'd wanted to see how far she would go. What the hell was wrong with him? She could have killed him. Almost had.

Andrews was saying something. All he caught were the last few words. "…it's too bad you didn't know. Abigail Creed and Leann Hayes met at a private mental hospital out in Washington. Leann was a patient. Abigail worked there, but not for long. She hasn't stayed at any job long. She was let go from her last nursing position because of a behavioral issue."

You attract unstable women. The thought cut to the center of him, sharper than Abigail's knife blade. *You're the one who's messed up. You got into that car with her.*

Do you have a death wish? Or were you so arrogant that you thought you could handle her?

"You'll have time to heal since you're off duty until the investigation is complete," Forester said. Both state cops were looking at him with sympathy now. "You got lucky."

"Yeah," he said. Lucky didn't even come close.

CHAPTER TWENTY-ONE

THE SHERIFF LOOKED up to see Tilly and Cooper come into his hospital room. He saw her look of horror at all his injuries. She quickly hid it as she stepped to his bedside. "How are you?" Her voice broke and he saw tears spring to her eyes. He was touched that she cared. As a friend, he reminded himself.

"Damn," Cooper said, taking his free hand.

Stuart could tell that his friend had been about to make a joke about bringing a knife to a gunfight and was glad he hadn't. Like him, Cooper didn't know what to say in a situation like this.

"Why would Abigail Creed do this to you?" Tilly demanded.

"She was afraid that I'd find out the truth about Leann's death," he said. "Once Rory Eastwood's pickup was found in the reservoir, she feared it was only a matter of time before I put it together. She was...sick. Unfortunately, she died before I found out what she'd done with Rory Eastwood's body."

He saw Tilly look at Cooper, her eyes wide with fear. "I doubt she would have come after Cooper next." But he wasn't sure about that. Abigail had been a whole lot more unstable than he'd realized—even after she'd drugged him.

"Still, she could have killed you," Cooper said.

"She certainly was trying." He had a flashback of her lunging at him with that blade. "But it was my own fault. I foolishly got in the car with her. I'm the sheriff. I should have known better."

"Are you going to be all right?" Tilly asked.

"The knife wounds will heal. I'll have scars." He smiled. "Nothing wrong with scars. Kind of manly, don't you think?"

"This isn't funny," Cooper said. "We could have lost you. You aren't going to be charged for anything, are you?"

He shook his head. "Self-defense. She assaulted an officer of the law. I was fighting for my life."

"How long are you going to be here?" his friend asked, looking concerned.

He shrugged. "It's going to give me time to think. I'm not sure I should be sheriff."

"You've had a scare. Anyone would be questioning a job like yours after what you have been through," Cooper said.

"It's not fear. I got in that car with her even though I already suspected she was up to no good. Who does that?"

"Suspected her? But you couldn't know that she would try to kill you," Tilly said.

He could feel Cooper's gaze on him. "If you thought she might try, why would you get in that car with her?"

Stuart chuckled. "That's a good question. I keep asking myself that same thing."

"Maybe you should talk to someone, you know? A trauma like this…" Tilly offered.

He suspected that they both knew he was struggling long before Abigail Creed tried to kill him. "Maybe I will…talk to someone."

An aide came in with his dinner tray and they left him alone. He wasn't hungry. He was still in a lot of pain that not even the drugs seemed able to knock it down.

His door opened again. He looked up to see Bailey McKenna step in. "Up for a visitor?" she asked as she came over to his bed. "Might help that hideous food go down better."

He smiled through his pain at just the sight of her. Her wild, dark mane was pulled up in a ponytail, making her look like a teenager. Her blue eyes sparkled as usual with mischief.

"You just missed your brother and Tilly," he said.

"I was waiting for them to leave," she said as she sat down on the edge of his bed, forcing him to move over a little. He hardly felt the pain. "So tell me. Why do women want to kill you?"

OAKLEY AND PICKETT had gone back to her apartment after returning to town and her telling him she didn't need to think about what she wanted. She wanted him. The moment she closed the apartment door, Pickett said, "There's something I need to tell you. I'm not who you think I am."

She put a finger to his lips and shook her head. "You're exactly who I think you are," she said and kissed him.

He let out a moan, circling her waist with his hands and dragging her to him as the kiss deepened. He knew he should break off the kiss, tell her everything, but he'd wanted this for so long...

They moved together, lips locked, toward her bedroom. She shrugged off her jacket but quickly stepped back into his arms. That she wanted this as much as he did had his blood rushing hot through him. He'd dreamed of holding her, kissing her, making love to her, but it had only been a dream.

Until now.

She pulled off his jacket and tossed it aside, then jerked his Western shirt snaps open. Easy, he wanted to say, but he couldn't slow this down. He fumbled at the buttons on her blouse. She laughed and pushed his hands away to quickly free the buttons and toss off her blouse.

"Oakley." He said it on a sigh, the sight of her standing there in nothing but a bra and jeans was his undoing. He could see her erect nipples pushing against the thin fabric of her bra. He pulled her to him, releasing the bra and bowing his head to nip and suck and tongue the hard tips of her breasts.

She arced against his mouth, her hands moving over his shoulders, his back, his chest. He swung her up into his arms and carried her to the bed. He lowered her slowly, his gaze locking with hers.

The stark need so like his own made his heart beat faster. She grabbed the waist of his jeans and drew him closer. He watched as she unbuttoned his jeans and dragged them down. Kicking off his pants he reached for her jeans. She had them almost down to her ankles. He laughed and tossed them in the pile with his own and took her in his arms again, their kisses fevered, their desire like a runaway horse they both knew how to ride.

This was not the way he'd seen their first time. But he should have known this was how it would be with Oakley. She had a passion for everything. He shouldn't have been surprised that they would make love with wild abandon.

LATER, THEY LAY breathing hard, both spent, wrapped in each other's arms. They might have stayed like that the rest of the night if Tilly hadn't returned home.

"I should go," he whispered.

Oakley hesitated as if like him, not wanting to let go before she heard her sister calling her name from the living room and nodded. "Be out in a minute," she called back.

He dressed quickly as she pulled on panties, a large T-shirt and socks.

She stood on tiptoe to kiss him. "Can we do this again soon?"

Pickett chuckled. "Very soon." He opened her bedroom door, picked up his jacket from the floor where it had been discarded, then his Stetson. Tilly watched him, arms crossed, doing her best to look stern like the big sister she was.

He tipped his hat as he left and smiled, getting a half grin out of her before she closed and locked the door. He heard her call her sister's name as he started down the stairs.

"TURNS OUT PICKETT did want to kiss me," Oakley said as she stepped from the bedroom. Tilly shook her head.

"Save the lecture. It won't do any good anyway." She curled up on the couch to look at her sister. "I knew the moment he kissed me."

Tilly groaned as she took the other end of the couch. "You look...happy."

She grinned. "I am."

"I hope you'll be this happy tomorrow," her sister said, true to form.

"I will be," she said, hugging herself as she remembered their frantic lovemaking. At least the first time. "I just feel like it was a long time coming and yet I wasn't really ready until now. I've never felt like this before."

"I can see that." Tilly reached across the couch to take her sister's hand and squeeze it. "I hope it works out."

"It will," Oakley said confidently. She knew Pickett and he knew her. No man had ever known her as well. She and Pickett were friends as well as lovers now. He'd seen her at her worst. He knew that she fought for what she believed in. He also knew that she would probably never tread lightly.

She smiled to herself and saw that her sister had a faraway look in her eyes. "Where have you been?"

"Haven't you heard? Stuart's in the hospital in Billings. Cooper and I went to see him. That nurse, Abigail Creed? She tried to kill him."

"How is he?" she asked, shocked.

"He'll survive, but that woman almost killed him. How do you get over something like that?" Tilly shook her head and rose from the couch. "I'm tired. I'm going to bed." She turned back to Oakley. "Are you all right?"

"Great," she said, savoring the earlier lovemaking.

She realized that she couldn't remember the last time she'd been this happy and content.

"Pickett appears to be good for you," her sister said, smiling as she went into her room. "He'd better be, if he knows what's good for him," she said before closing the door.

PICKETT KNEW HE wasn't going to be able to sleep. He lay in his bunk thinking about Oakley. They'd made love. He hadn't planned on doing that until he told her the truth about who he had been. But he couldn't regret it. She now knew how he felt about her—and he had a pretty good idea of how she felt about him.

Before he'd left New York and that life his father had planned for him, he'd often wondered how he could trust anything, especially friendships. He saw the way people treated his father because of his money. He hated questioning if people really cared about him. If they would still like him if he had nothing.

Oakley cared about him as the ranch hand she'd known since they were teenagers. He'd never questioned her friendship or Duffy's, either. He didn't want that to change. He would tell her the truth next time he saw her.

He couldn't wait to see her again. She'd left an ache at heart level that could only be soothed by being with her. *You know you could ask her out on a real date at least.*

He thought a real date might be awkward, but he knew his heart was right. He placed the call. Oakley answered on the third ring. He hadn't realized how late it was. "I hope I didn't wake you."

She chuckled. "Can't sleep, huh?"

"No, how about you?"

"Nope." Silence filled the line for a few moments.

"I was lying here thinking about you," he said.

"Funny, I was doing the same thing."

He smiled in the darkness. "I like the sound of that. What are you doing Saturday night?"

That was still three days away. "Pickett Hanson, are you asking me on a date?"

"I am. Want to hear what I was thinking we could do?"

She laughed. "No, surprise me."

He chuckled. He loved what the late night did to her voice. He could imagine her curled up in her bed, comfortable, her guard down—like she had been earlier. "It could be weird going on a real date even after all these years being around each other."

"I suspect it will be. At least at first."

"Guess we'll have to make a point of getting to know the people we are now," he said.

"I like the sound of that. Who are you, Pickett Hanson?" His pulse jumped. "I don't even know your favorite color or if you even have one."

"I have one. The green of your eyes," he said, realizing it was true. "What about you?"

"I've never thought about it, but I'd have to say… that faded blue like worn denim and the way it looks on you."

"Favorite food?"

"Beef!" they said in unison and laughed.

"Favorite season?"

She chuckled. "You know the answer. It's the same as yours. Spring when the grasses are that blinding green and the air smells of pine and fresh mountain air and all anyone can see is blue sky."

Oakley did know him. "Smells like new beginnings," he agreed.

They fell silent and he thought she might have fallen asleep.

"Would you have asked me out if Duffy hadn't kissed me?"

"I was headed there," he said quietly, and heard what sounded like a pleased sigh. "I've been wanting to for a long time. I wasn't sure you were ready."

"I wasn't. But I am now. You should pick me up at the apartment on Saturday."

"Good idea." He had a thought. "Where are you now?"

"At the ranch. After you left, I couldn't sleep so I drove out to the ranch. With the sheriff in the hospital, I'm thinking CJ might take advantage of no law enforcement being around. Don't worry, I'm treading lightly."

He laughed at that, not believing her and filling himself with worry. He didn't want to think about CJ or how dangerous it was for Oakley to get out there. But he'd learned a long time ago that she was her own woman. He wasn't about to mess with that.

"Six o'clock okay Saturday?" he asked, getting back to their date. He wanted it to be special. He was going to tell her everything. "I plan to feed you someplace other than the café in town if you don't mind leaving Powder Crossing on this date."

"Like I said, surprise me."

"I'll do my best. Get some sleep. If I don't see you

sooner, see you Saturday night. And Oakley? Be careful. If you need me, call and I'll be there."

He found himself grinning like a fool as he disconnected, but it felt good. He'd put this off for too long. Maybe it was seeing his father or maybe it was just time. All he knew was that he was ready to get on with his life. He hoped Oakley was, too.

He wished she wasn't out at the ranch, though. Worse, she was keeping an eye on CJ and planning to try to keep CH4 from drilling out there. He might be able to distract her for a while with a date, but he didn't know how to stop her from getting herself hurt or worse, killed.

CHAPTER TWENTY-TWO

PICKETT HANSON WOKE, heart pounding. He'd had the nightmare again. He climbed out of his bed and went outside to stand under the stars and breathe in the freezing night air. The snowstorm had passed, leaving behind a good half foot of fresh powder. He'd learned that fresh snow absorbed sound, lowering ambient noise over a landscape because the trapped air between snowflakes attenuated vibration. And that was why it got so quiet when it snowed.

He'd never heard so much silence in winter or seen so many stars when the night was clear before he ended up here. Every day he was grateful for that, even though he'd been living a lie all these years.

He felt the chill begin to sink in, but at least it held the horror of the nightmare at bay. It always started the same way, racing through the snow toward the creek, terrified of what he would find beneath the ice. Shuddering at the memory, he moved back inside the small cabin where he'd been living since he was a teenager. The weathered log walls, the plank flooring, the single bed, his stack of books next to it. Everything he needed.

Climbing back into bed, he shivered under the covers for a few minutes. The cold that left goose bumps on his skin gave him the comfort of knowing it had only been a nightmare. A recurring nightmare since before she'd gotten shot.

The dream made little sense on the surface, but the feeling he woke with was that he'd let Oakley down. He'd failed her when she'd needed him the most.

He'd never paid much attention to his dreams. But this one scared him. This one felt like an omen.

Even now, wide-awake, he couldn't throw off the image of Oakley lying on the ground, those beautiful green eyes lifeless. It was always the same. Always the face of Oakley Stafford, the woman he wanted with all his heart, but feared he could never have because he wasn't the man she thought he was.

The only thing that was real was his love for her. He'd do anything to protect her—even from himself. But as he closed his eyes, his greatest fear was that he would be running through the snow looking for her only to find her too late, only to fail her when she needed him the most.

HER MOTHER WAS waiting for her when Oakley came downstairs the next morning at the ranch. "I just spoke to the lawyer."

She started toward the kitchen, not in the mood for this. She'd gone to bed thinking about Pickett Hanson and woke up this morning doing the same thing. The sun beaming in her window had made her smile. She'd never gotten silly over a boy or a man in her life, but she now saw how it could happen.

All she wanted to do was keep this warm glow feeling. Talking about CJ's lawyers was the last thing she wanted to do this morning. "I talked to him yesterday, just as you asked."

As she started past, her mother grabbed her arm. "He said he's worried because your so-called testimony sounded rehearsed."

Oakley stopped to look at her mother, dumbstruck. "Of course it was rehearsed. It was exactly what you told me to say."

"It's not good enough. You're going to have to do better. He thinks you want your brother to go to jail or worse, prison."

She stared at her mother. "What? Why would I want there to be consequences for what CJ did? You've spoiled him, letting him get away with everything, always bailing him out. Now he thinks he can get away with even attempted murder."

Her mother let go of her abruptly, her expression livid. "*Attempted murder?* What are you talking about?" She shrieked the words. "That kind of talk will get him sent to prison."

"That's where he belongs, Mother!"

At the creak of his wheelchair, they both turned to see CJ come into the room. Oakley felt his cold stare and had to fight not to shudder. She hadn't meant to say as much as she had.

But she doubted it made a difference. The moment she'd looked into her brother's eyes when he returned to the ranch, she could tell that he feared she would remember. She'd known then that he would be coming for her again.

Even if he was locked up for "accidentally" shooting her, he could still get to her. She'd seen the kind of friends he associated with. She'd believed that CJ couldn't do the job himself. Not if he really was tied to that chair. But after his attacking her the other day and the memory of his hands around her throat, she knew he could kill her himself. And would if she gave him a chance.

"What's going on?" CJ asked as if he didn't know.

Oakley shook her head. "I don't know. I was just on my way into the kitchen to get some breakfast." She stepped away from the two of them, feeling two sets of eyes boring into her back as she went.

She thought about the smirk she'd seen on her brother's face. It was going to be hard to keep her breakfast down.

CHARLOTTE WATCHED HER daughter walk away. She could feel CJ watching her as well. She didn't want to look at him. She didn't want to see the expression on his face.

Her cell phone rang, saving her. She turned away from him as she pulled it out and was surprised but at the same time concerned. "I need to take this," she said, her back still to her son as she walked into her office and closed the door.

"Is something wrong?" she asked, moving to sit behind her desk. She told herself to be careful as to what she said. CJ could be just outside the door. For that matter, he might have the whole house bugged. That thought sent her pulse into overdrive. It would be just like something he might do. "Can we meet? I can't talk here. Great." She disconnected and moved quickly to the door.

With relief she saw that there was no sign of CJ, but

that only made the thought of bugging devices more plausible. "I'm going riding," she called and hurried to her room to change. Twenty minutes later she walked into the stables after calling Boyle and asking him to saddle her a horse.

Her horse was saddled. Boyle handed her the reins and she led her mare outside. She shuddered, feeling his gaze on her.

"Sure you don't want company?" he asked.

"Positive." She checked to make sure her horse was properly saddled. She didn't have to look in his direction to know that her lack of trust would anger him. Better he know that she didn't trust him, she thought as she swung up into the saddle and spurred the mare as she rode toward the creek where she and Holden used to make love.

The creek pooled there among the rocks, deep enough to swim. There'd been a time that the two of them had skinny-dipped there, then lay naked on the large boulders to dry. It was still her favorite spot.

It was also the place she went when she was upset. It was also the place where Holden knew he could find her.

OAKLEY WAS JUST finishing her breakfast when she heard the creak of the wheelchair behind her. She braced herself as her brother stopped on the opposite side of the table, facing her.

"You're looking…different today," CJ said. "Almost… happy. What's that about?"

"None of your business."

His eyebrow arched up. "A friend of mine saw you

and Pickett go into your apartment in town yesterday. It was hours later that Pickett came back out. He had that same look on his face that you do this morning."

She pushed her plate away. "You disgust me." She shoved back her chair and rose. "Stop spying on me."

"He's lying to you," CJ said. "Didn't you wonder when he left to go back east to see his dying father? He ever mention his family before? Did you ever question a name like Pickett Hanson?"

She stopped and turned slowly to face him, amazed at how low he would stoop. "You don't know what you're talking about."

"Don't I?" CJ's mouth twisted into a familiar smirk. "His real name is Archibald Vanderlin Westmoreland. He made up the name Pickett Hanson. Got to wonder what else he lied about. Whatever it is, it must be something bad enough that he doesn't want you to know about it."

Oakley wanted to make him take it all back. But hadn't Pickett tried to tell her yesterday before they'd made love that he wasn't who she thought he was?

"He's lied to everyone for years," CJ said. "Especially you."

She didn't want it to be true. She stared at her brother, hating him more this moment than she thought possible. "You really are a miserable human being, you know that?"

He laughed as she turned and left. That laughter followed her all the way to her truck. Her first instinct was to call Pickett, but she didn't want to do this over the phone. They had a date Saturday night.

A sob caught in her throat. She had to know the truth.

Could it wait until then? She'd been so happy. What if she really didn't know the man she'd fallen in love with?

AFTER A DAY of mending fence and rounding up the cattle that had gotten out, Pickett was on his way back to the stables when he got the call. The latest storm had dumped a half foot of snow on the ground. The temperatures were dropping again.

Montana weather was more unpredictable than a woman, ranch manager Deacon Yates liked to say. Pickett didn't care how long it snowed or froze. He'd never felt like this before. He didn't need anyone to tell him that he was in love. He felt it soul deep. His mind had been full of Oakley all day. It was no wonder that he'd forgotten his call to the county office about recent land purchases in the Powder River Basin. If his theory was right, then CJ would figure out how to buy land for more privacy before starting up his business again.

"I have those sales you inquired about," the clerk at the county office said when he answered his phone. "There aren't many." She began to read them off. He was listening for the name CJ Stafford. When she stopped, he realized ruefully that he hadn't heard the one name he'd been expecting.

"None by CJ Stafford or the Stafford Ranch?"

"Sorry."

"Wait, what was that second one?"

"Treyton McKenna. The purchase of a small area east of the river."

Treyton? East of the river in the badlands? Was it possible? Treyton and CJ? Still, he asked, "Can you give me the location?" He put it into his phone, thanked her and hung up. For a moment he merely stared at his phone. If he was right, that area east of the river was not farmable, hardly ranch-able.

Pickett couldn't be thinking what he was thinking, right? Treyton and CJ were rivals. They hated each other, didn't they? But they were also a lot alike, he reminded himself.

Why would Treyton buy badlands unless the area was rich in coalbeds and he planned to drill methane wells. Or hide a meth and human trafficking business?

He'd been wondering if Holden knew about Treyton's purchase and was anxious to see the property. But he'd promised Holly Jo that he'd teach her a few more riding tricks when she got out of school today. There were a couple that he hadn't practiced for a while.

On his way to saddle up a horse, he heard his name being called and turned to find Holden motioning to him. He turned back toward the house, wondering if he should share what he'd discovered. Holden might already know and would take offense that his ranch hand was keeping tabs on his son.

"Big day planned?" the rancher asked.

"Didn't get much done yesterday," he admitted. "I've got a trick riding lesson later with Holly Jo. I was just going to saddle up."

The rancher smiled. "Thank you for doing that. I know how much it means to her. If you have a moment, I'd like to talk to you about something."

Pickett nodded and they headed for the den where Holden had his office. It was a large, well-appointed room with deep leather chairs, a large wood desk and a fireplace and bar. He was curious what his boss wanted, but became more concerned when Holden closed and locked the door behind them.

Holden must have seen his expression because he said, "I just don't want us to be disturbed. In this household, that is always a problem."

Pickett waited as the rancher took one of the leather chairs and motioned that he should join him. He dropped into a chair across from his boss, his heart drumming. He'd never asked for any time off to leave the ranch. Since his return, he hadn't worked much. Was it possible he was being fired? Or was this about Dirty Business? Maybe his boss had found out about him being in the subversive grassroots organization to stop drilling. Or maybe—

"This isn't easy for me," Holden said. "I'm not one to butt into other people's business." He cleared his voice. "Can I get you a drink?"

Pickett shook his head. "You don't need to beat around the bush with me. We've known each other for too long."

The rancher smiled and seemed to relax a little. "After all these years, I think of you as family."

"I'm glad to hear that because that's how I feel about the McKenna Ranch."

Nodding, the older man said, "When you asked for time off because your father was ill, I was worried about you. I was aware that you'd never left the ranch before that I knew of—or mentioned family. It was out of concern that I did some checking on you," he said, rushing on before Pickett could speak. "I apologize for that."

"You found out that I wasn't born Pickett Hanson," he said. Hadn't he always figured that might happen?

"I'm the one who should be apologizing. I didn't mean to keep anything from you. I had my name legally changed."

Holden sat back. "Why did you?" He sounded more curious than upset.

"Because I wanted a new life when I left home. When you hired me on, I thought it would be temporary, but I loved living here, the job suited me and I felt as if I'd come home."

"That's why you insisted on being paid with cash, under the table, so to speak," Holden said.

"I couldn't get my name changed legally until I was twenty-one. I legally became Pickett Hanson. By then, it felt too late to say anything."

"It's none of my business, but I have to ask why you had to do that."

Pickett chuckled, shaking his head. "It wasn't because I was on the run from the law or being mistreated by my family or in any kind of trouble. I'm assuming you found out that my name is Archibald Vanderlin Westmoreland the fourth. That alone should explain why I was anxious to change it—and change the life that had been laid out for me from my birth. I felt I had no choice, as the only heir. Because of that, I was expected to take over my father's holdings. It was the last thing I wanted so I left, escaped. I'm sure you can understand also why I didn't tell anyone out here my real name. I wanted people to like me for who I was, not for my family's money."

Holden nodded slowly. "You've certainly succeeded in doing that. Duffy thinks the sun rises and sets on you. The rest of us are quite enamored as well. But I have to ask..." The rancher's gaze held his. "What happens now that your father is deceased? I hope you're not planning to leave us."

Pickett laughed and shook his head. "Not a chance as long as you're happy with me being here."

"What about your father's...holdings?"

He knew right away what Holden was asking—just as he'd known that the rancher would see through the endowment that he'd had the family lawyer set up.

"I gave almost all of it away except for enough to purchase some land for a house should the day come when I get married, and plenty of savings for retirement when I can't get my foot into a stirrup—though I'll fight that as long as I can."

Pickett could see that his boss was waiting for him to say it. "I never saw my family's wealth as a blessing. To me it was an anchor around my neck. But my father and I talked before he died. He convinced me that it didn't have to be that way. That I could share some of it and still keep the life I love. I hope he was right. Because I'm still Pickett Hanson. Just a ranch hand who loves his job."

Holden studied him for a long moment. "Well, son, you have a place here on the McKenna Ranch for as long as you want. As for that land should you get married, I would be honored to have it be on this ranch. Like my other sons, you have your choice of a spot to build on." With that, he rose and extended his hand. "Thank you. Your secret is safe with me."

Pickett tried to swallow the lump that had formed in his throat. "Thank you," he said as he shook the man's hand. "I can't tell you how much I appreciate that. There is no place I'd rather be than right here."

Now all he had to do was tell Oakley.

As he left, he was glad that Holden hadn't mentioned the endowment. This way they could both pretend that they didn't know where it came from.

OAKLEY WAS ON her way into town, still upset about what CJ had told her about Pickett, when she passed the drilling rigs. She pulled over to let them pass and called Pickett out of habit. Fortunately, his phone went straight to voice mail. She didn't leave a message. She felt confused, angry, hurt and worried. What else didn't she know about the man?

Her phone rang. Pickett? It was Duffy.

"I just saw drilling equipment headed for your ranch," he said without preamble.

"I saw it, too," she said.

"Guess that means we go to work tonight. Midnight again? You know where they're drilling?" he asked, sounding excited.

"Not yet." She was thinking about her date with Pickett Saturday night, hoping she wasn't in jail by then, because she really needed answers. While she didn't trust CJ, she trusted that he hadn't lied.

"You'll let me know as soon as you have a location?" Duffy said.

"Yep." She disconnected, hating that she was lying to her friend. She was doing this alone. The plan had been cooking for a while now. It was dangerous. Another reason she couldn't bear Duffy or Pickett or whatever his name was now getting caught up in it.

Her fingers trembled as she pocketed her phone. Just the thought of Pickett's kisses and lovemaking, not to mention their intimate phone call last night warmed her in a way she didn't think she'd ever felt. Why hadn't he told her last night on the phone that his name wasn't really Pickett Hanson? Was he ever going to tell her now?

She pushed the thought away. She had to stop the drilling on the ranch. She couldn't sit back and let her mother and CJ do this without a fight. Now more than ever she wanted to stop her brother. She headed into town to get the supplies she needed, assuring herself that she could pull this off.

Fortunately, she'd grown up on a ranch so she knew exactly what she needed and how to use it. If she planned this right, she'd get away with it as she had the other times.

And if things didn't go as planned… Well, at least Duffy would know where she'd gone. Except she wouldn't be meeting him at midnight. She planned to hit much earlier. It was a message to CJ and her mother.

But first, she needed to know where the gas company employees were headed with the drilling equipment. CJ would know. He, too, was trying to make a statement, she thought. And that was when she knew. Where was the one spot on the ranch that would make the most impact?

She knew her brother so well that she could predict exactly where the equipment was headed, she realized. A plan materialized as she drove. It was risky, but being in the same house with CJ was already dangerous and she feared it would get worse. She had to take a stand. Stopping the drilling was only the beginning if her mother and CJ didn't get the message.

With the sheriff in the hospital she needed to be extra careful, because she feared her brother would take Stuart's absence as a get-out-of-jail-free card. It was hard to say what he would do if he knew what she was up to. Or worse, that she'd remembered the day he shot her.

That was why she had to hit long before midnight—before CJ expected it. And without Duffy or Pickett. This time she was going it alone.

CHAPTER TWENTY-THREE

PICKETT DROVE TOWARD the small acreage in the badlands that Treyton had purchased. The price for the land had been low because of the mostly unusable property. It was questionable even if the area was viable for methane wells.

So why would Treyton buy it? It made no sense. Or maybe it did. Suspicious, Pickett had put the coordinates into his pickup's navigation system. He hadn't gone far when he'd spotted Treyton driving out of town—not in a McKenna Ranch pickup with the logo on the side—but his own truck. He had no choice but to follow him since he had a feeling they were going to the same place. He became even more convinced when he spotted a tarp covering a load of something in the bed of the pickup.

Tailing someone in this part of the country wasn't easy, though. There was little to no traffic on a normal day on the main two-lane. So Pickett stayed back. He wasn't worried. According to his navigation system, he and Treyton definitely appeared to be headed for the same place. They had gone quite a few miles when in the far distance ahead, he saw Treyton turn off onto a dirt road heading deeper into the badlands.

Pickett backed way off, catching only glimpses of Treyton's truck ahead of him. As suspicious as he was, he felt uncomfortable following the oldest McKenna. Holden wouldn't like it. Worse, Pickett should be at work right now. He'd hardly worked at all since returning from New York.

Worse, he was losing daylight. He caught brake lights flash on the back of Treyton's pickup in the distance. Almost there, he thought as he checked his nav system and Treyton's truck disappeared over a rise.

Pickett slowed. He let the truck coast, the growing darkness forming shadows in the rough terrain. This area was rocky, harsh, but beautiful in its own way.

Before the top of the rise, he rolled to a stop, put the pickup into Park and got out quietly. He wasn't sure how far Treyton had gone past the hill in front of him as he walked toward the crest and peered over.

Treyton had stopped down in the bottom next to a couple of old buildings that looked like mining shacks. He had begun unloading what looked like equipment and supplies into one of the larger shacks. Pickett couldn't tell exactly what the supplies were from this distance. Maybe Treyton was planning to mine. Maybe Pickett was all wrong about what the oldest McKenna was up to.

It was too dark to take a photo with his phone. Not that it mattered. He had a pretty good idea what was going on.

He walked back to his pickup, debating what to do. Calling the sheriff might have been at the top of his list if Stuart wasn't in the hospital in Billings. But there was also the fact that unless the supplies incriminated Treyton, Pickett had no proof of anything. There was also the fact that Treyton was Holden McKenna's son, and

Pickett worked for the family. Until he had proof of his suspicions, he had to keep this under his hat.

Climbing into his truck, he started to call Duffy when he remembered that he'd turned his phone off. He turned it back on. No messages from either Duffy or Oakley. He decided he'd rather tell them in person, especially Oakley since they had several things to talk about.

He pocketed his phone, and backing down to the main road, headed into town, hoping she would be at the apartment.

Duffy had been mentally kicking himself all day. He'd hidden it well from Pickett, but earlier he'd overheard that damned Rusty Malone saying he'd seen Pickett go into Oakley's apartment. He hadn't come out until hours later—in the middle of the night.

Any questions Duffy had about what was going on with his two best friends were quickly answered. He wanted to fire Rusty. Instead, he told him to get his ass out on that fence that needed to be mended. By the time he saw Pickett, he'd calmed down and hadn't said anything.

But it was like a burr under his saddle all day. Pickett and Oakley. It would ruin their friendship. It would leave him out in the cold. He felt betrayed. True, it wasn't like after one kiss he and Oakley... Hell, clearly, the kiss they'd shared hadn't meant anything to her. She'd thought he was just goofing around.

He thought about earlier. Oakley had said she would call as soon as she knew the location of the well to be drilled as early as in the morning. It was starting to get dark. Why hadn't he heard from her? Maybe she didn't know. Maybe she was leaving him out of it. Maybe it was just going to be her and Pickett.

Like hell, he told himself.

He'd find the drilling spot. But he knew he'd better find it before it got too dark. He headed for the stables to saddle up.

Something else was bothering him, he realized as he swung up into the saddle. Earlier at dinner, his father had asked Holly Jo how things were with her. "Everything all right at school?"

She'd looked up as if she, too, had been as deep in thought as he'd been, then quickly dropped her eyes to her plate. "Fine."

Something was wrong, Duffy had thought. He'd promised himself that he'd get her alone and find out if that boy Gus was still bothering her. If so, he'd take care of it.

PICKETT WAS DRIVING through Powder Crossing when he saw Oakley loading something into the back of her pickup. He swung in next to her truck. "Hey," he said as he put down his window.

He couldn't believe how glad he was to see her. Not that this was anything new. She was like sunshine for him, always brightening any day he was around her.

She looked surprised to see him, then her face clouded over as she shut the tailgate on her pickup and walked over to his driver's side window.

"Archibald, right?"

His heart dropped. "Who—"

"CJ with that stupid smirk on his face."

"I tried to tell you last night."

"Not hard enough," she said. "What else haven't you told me?"

"Let me explain—"

She stepped back. "Was this the surprise you had for me Saturday night?"

"No, but I was planning to tell you everything then."

Oakley nodded. He could see how hurt she was and hated himself for not telling her long before this moment. "I thought I knew you."

"You do know me. I'm Pickett Hanson. Nothing has changed." He could see that it had changed for her. "Oakley, please." He started to get out of his truck, but she pushed the door shut, shaking her head.

"Save it for Saturday. Maybe by then I'll want to hear it." With that, she walked away, leaving him desperately wanting to go after her, but she didn't give him a chance as she got into her truck and took off in the direction of the Stafford Ranch.

He slammed his hand down on his steering wheel. He could do nothing but watch her leave. All he could hope was that by Saturday night she'd be willing to listen to what he had to say. If she still wanted to go out with him.

OAKLEY COULDN'T BELIEVE how much time the gas company employees were taking to unload their equipment. She concentrated on that rather than think about the fear she'd seen on Pickett's face. Archibald the fourth's face, she corrected and swore. She would always think of him as Pickett.

It was getting darker. She raised the binoculars to her eyes again. The men were almost finished. Only three men. She didn't see Frankie or his brother Norman. That was a good sign, right?

She felt guilty letting Duffy think they would meet here at midnight. By then, it would be all over. She didn't want him involved, Pickett either. Knowing her brother, the drilling could start as early as tomorrow morning. This was her only chance.

The night was quiet, the last snowfall a cushion for sound. A sliver of moon hung over the tops of the bare cottonwoods. She could see her breath. Another cold night after those days and nights that had teased of spring.

She hadn't realized how much she would miss Duffy and Pickett. It surprised her how a couple of kisses and one big lie could change everything. They'd been a trio, best friends, partners in crime. But now she had fallen for Pickett, hurt Duffy and ruined their friendship and probably ruined Duffy and Pickett's friendship as well, and she wasn't sure how much of it had been a lie.

The worst part was that it had been her brother who told her about Pickett lying to her. CJ had enjoyed telling her too much. Just as he had acted quickly to get this drilling done. Her brother's actions felt desperate. You would think this was his money he was making from the gas company. Maybe it was. Maybe their mother had offered him part of the proceeds for being in charge of this. It wouldn't have surprised Oakley. How could her mother be so blind when it came to him?

Oakley watched from a safe distance as the last of the drilling equipment was locked up and the men finished up. She hadn't been surprised to discover that the well would again be drilled near McKenna Ranch property.

Once she'd thought about what CJ would do to show their mother, she'd known he would put the well close to their mother's favorite spot next to the creek. Oakley had always suspected that this was where Charlotte used to meet her teenage lover, Holden. Surely, she hadn't chosen this spot. This had to be CJ's doing—not her mother's. At least she hoped that was true. Who knew what the well would do to other McKenna Ranch wells, not to mention the creek? Were her mother and CJ that determined to put Holden out of business?

Oakley didn't want to believe it. Her mother was capable of shame. CJ wasn't. When news had gotten out about the last methane well drilled on Stafford Ranch destroying the McKenna's artesian well, there'd been an uproar around the river basin. Her mother hadn't been completely immune to the adverse public opinion.

For a moment Oakley thought about going to her mother and trying to reason with her—rather than taking the drastic step she was about to take. If her mother didn't know what CJ was doing...

The thought swept on past. Her mother would stand with CJ—even if she hadn't known; even if this wasn't what she'd wanted. CJ had been trying to take over the ranch for years. Oakley feared that was exactly what he was doing now from his wheelchair.

She thought about exposing him. But not even that might sway her mother. No, there was only one way to stop this well being drilled, she thought as she watched the gas company employees drive away together in one of the pickups.

Had they really all left? Or was it a trap? She didn't think anyone had seen her back here in the trees. But

CJ would be expecting her to try to stop this once she found out, which meant so would the gas company employees. She hadn't seen the Lees brothers. They were probably coming back when it was full dark. The other vandalisms had happened around midnight. They would be expecting her to hit then, she hoped.

Oakley took a breath and let it out. Was she doing this knowing how dangerous it was? Vandalism hadn't worked. The equipment had been too easily repaired. She knew that it was going to take something dramatic to stop her mother and CJ. She hoped this might also send a message to the gas company and area ranchers.

She was doing this, she told herself as she swung up onto her horse. The sled with her supplies dragged behind her horse as she rode slowly toward the dark outline of the massive drilling rig etched against the deepening darkness.

CHAPTER TWENTY-FOUR

PICKETT NOTICED THAT Oakley's truck wasn't parked outside her apartment. She'd gotten supplies to take to the ranch, he'd assumed. Maybe she wasn't coming back to the apartment. Immediately, he felt his stomach churn at the thought of her being out there with CJ in that house. Pickett would have loved to have gotten his hands on her brother. He feared Oakley probably felt the same way.

He'd tried to call, but her phone had gone straight to voice mail. He was anxious to talk to her. It couldn't wait until Saturday. He had to explain. He just hoped she could forgive him. He also wanted to tell her about what he'd discovered. But more than anything he wanted to make sure she was safe.

He climbed the stairs to the second-floor apartment and knocked. Tilly's pickup had been parked where she usually left it, he thought with a frown. Was Oakley with her sister?

He knocked again. No answer. He tried Oakley's number again. It went straight to voice mail again. He left a message, "At your apartment. Need to see you." He waited. No answer. He knocked one more time.

Back down the stairs, he decided to wait outside for a little longer in case she came home. Pushing open the door, he saw an older waitress he knew taking a smoke break. "Neither of them is home," she said. "Tilly left with her fiancé. Came in late last night after visiting the sheriff at the hospital in Billings but you know all about that since you were here."

"Wait, the sheriff is in the hospital?" he asked in surprise. He hadn't hung around long enough last night to hear anything about this.

"You live under a rock?" She laughed at her own joke and took another drag on her cigarette. "That nurse, Creed, I think her name was. She tried to kill him with a knife. He shot her. She's dead, he was rushed to Billings to the hospital. Last I heard he's going to make it."

"I guess I do live under a rock," Pickett said. "I saw Oakley earlier. She was heading toward the ranch. I was hoping she might have come back?"

"Not that I know of." She finished her cigarette and stubbed it out under her shoe. "Suppose you can't go out to the ranch to see her, huh."

"You are well informed," he noted.

"The girls know I worry about them, so they keep me in the loop. Oakley had been at the general store before that. Looked like she bought a bunch of supplies. Want me to give her a message?"

He shook his head, thinking that when he'd seen Oakley she'd been loading supplies into the back of her truck. He'd assumed they were for the ranch since Tilly used to do a lot of that before she was banned from the ranch. He hoped that was all it was, but even as he thought it, he had his doubts. After what CJ had told her about him…

He walked down to the general store before it closed, unable to shake the bad feeling that had settled in his gut. "I'm just checking to see if I need to pick up more supplies for Oakley Stafford. Did she get everything she needed earlier?"

The man behind the counter replied, "Doubt she'll need more dynamite. She got enough to blow up a half dozen stumps out on the ranch."

Dynamite? She'd been headed for the ranch with a whole lot of dynamite? The one thing she wasn't blowing up was stumps, he thought as he left the store and almost ran into Tick Whitaker as he came out of the hotel bar.

"Just the man I wanted to see," Pickett said, trying to keep the anxiety out of his voice. "Heard your company is doing some drilling out on the Stafford Ranch. They need any extra hands? I could use some extra money, you know…off the books."

Tick grinned and Pickett caught alcohol on the man's breath. "Wish it was my company." He chuckled. "Drilling in the morning out on the Stafford Ranch. Equipment went out today. As for a job, you'd need to talk to Douglas Burton."

"Thanks, I'll do that. You know where they're drilling in the morning on the ranch?" he asked. "Maybe if I just showed up—"

Tick shook his head. "Top secret." He put a finger to his lips. "To keep the damned vandals from causing trouble." He laughed and patted Pickett on the shoulder. "Sorry." With that, the geologist walked toward the café.

Fortunately, Pickett knew who to ask. Unfortunately for CJ Stafford, he planned to do whatever it took to get the information.

DUFFY SAW THAT Pickett was calling and excused himself from the table. "Hey, I was going to call you."

"Have you seen Oakley?" He sounded upset.

"No, but I talked to her. You know about the drilling rigs?"

"That's why I'm on my way out to the Stafford Ranch to see CJ."

"That's a bad idea," Duffy said. "Oakley wants us to meet her at midnight."

"Where?" Pickett demanded impatiently.

"On the creek between the two properties. I'm sure she'll let us know before midnight."

"I'm not so sure about that," Pickett said. "Oakley bought explosives in town earlier." The ranch hand swore, something he seldom did. "I'm afraid she's planning to take things into her own hands. I plan to stop her—if it's not already too late."

Before Duffy could say another word, Pickett disconnected. Duffy felt the weight of his betrayal. He should have called his friend earlier. Not that Oakley had let on as to what she was up to—or where the drilling was happening.

He pocketed his phone and spurred his horse forward toward the boundary between his ranch and Stafford's. Going to the Stafford Ranch to confront CJ was a bad idea. His first instinct was to try to stop Pickett, but he knew his showing up as well would only make things worse.

Instead, he needed to stop Oakley himself. He recalled Treyton saying to their father that there was a spot near the creek just opposite Stafford property that he had wanted to drill.

"It's a large coalbed in there according to the geologist I talked to," Treyton had said. "If we don't drill there, you know your old girlfriend will."

His father had been furious, saying he would never drill there, and neither would Charlotte. It would destroy the creek.

Maybe Charlotte wouldn't, but Duffy bet CJ would.

At least he would check that spot out first. Maybe by then he would hear from Oakley or Pickett if the ranch hand wasn't already behind bars or worse. As he rode, he kept thinking about the worry in Pickett's voice.

Oakley was going rogue? He tried her number. Straight to voice mail. He told himself there was still the chance that she would contact him before midnight, but he feared Pickett might be right. Oakley was planning to do this alone—and not at midnight.

So why hadn't Duffy realized that? Because he'd been too busy worrying about Oakley and Pickett—and feeling left out.

That Pickett seemed to know Oakley better than he did wasn't lost on Duffy as he neared the creek between the two properties.

PICKETT SWUNG HIS pickup into the Stafford Ranch yard and, leaving it running, jumped out. He ran up the ramp to the door and didn't bother knocking. No one locked their doors in this county, especially ranchers who lived a good mile off the county road.

Bursting through the door, he called CJ's name. He was almost all the way through the living room before he saw the little weasel.

"Someone call the sheriff's office," CJ began yell-ing at the top of his lungs. He'd come partway down the hallway, but now was trying to get turned around in his wheelchair as if to make his escape.

Pickett charged down the hall, grabbed the wheelchair handles and spun him around to face him. "Where are they drilling in the morning?"

"None of your damned business," CJ snapped. "You're trespassing. If I could get to my gun—"

"What is going on?" a woman screamed behind him.

He turned to see Charlotte Stafford. "Oakley is in trouble. I need to know where the gas company is drilling on your ranch in the morning. I suspect it's near the creek. I need to know exactly where now."

"Drilling in the morning near the creek?" She shook her head. "You don't know what you're talking about. Now, get out of my house before I call the law and have you arrested."

Pickett heard the creak of the wheelchair and turned to see CJ again taking off down the hall. He went after him, spun the wheelchair around and rolled him back into the living room. "Your son is going to tell me, one way or the other," he said to Charlotte.

"Don't hurt him," she cried. "He's already injured."

"Is he? Why don't we find out?" He started to tilt the wheelchair forward to dump CJ out, but the cowboy hung on. "Because if I have to, I will beat the truth out of him."

She fumbled her phone from her pocket, but Pickett didn't try to stop her from calling for help.

"He lays a hand on me and after he gets out of jail, I'll sue him for every penny he's worth and as it turns out, he's worth a lot, aren't you, ranch hand?" CJ said, baring his teeth.

Pickett moved around to the front and pulled back his fist, ready to knock those teeth down his throat. Charlotte grabbed his arm and CJ tried to get away, as Pickett's cell rang. He shook off Charlotte's grasp and, keeping a hold on the wheelchair, picked up, seeing it was Duffy. "Have you found her?"

"I can see the gas rig in the distance," Duffy said. "It's just as I thought. By the creek where we used to swim with Oakley."

Pickett knew the spot only too well. "I'm on my way," he said. "As soon as I finish up here."

"CJ, tell him where they're drilling," his mother cried.

"Over my dead body," CJ said, daring him to touch him.

Pickett fought the urge to do just that. Instead, he turned to Charlotte. "The drilling rig is at your favorite spot on the creek. Unless I miss my guess, Oakley is there trying to stop the drilling from happening in the morning."

"I would never drill there," Charlotte said. "You're mistaken."

She shot a look at her son. "*You* wouldn't drill there."

"I'll drill anywhere I please on my ranch," her son blustered, but cringed as Pickett made a move toward him.

"I've called the sheriff's department," Charlotte said. "They're on their way."

"Good, tell them to meet us at the drilling site because that was Duffy on the phone. He told me where it was. He said he was looking at the drilling rig sitting right by the creek. If I'm right and Oakley is there, I know what she's about to do." He turned to CJ. "If I find out that you set her up…"

The cowboy came out of the chair and rushed him. Pickett had been expecting it. He caught CJ with a right hook that sent him sprawling onto the floor. But CJ was quickly up again, charging Pickett, who wouldn't have expected anything less.

Unfortunately, he didn't have time to finish this. He had to get to Oakley. He hit him a little harder this time. CJ hit the floor, but Pickett could tell that he wasn't done. "You get up again and it will be your last time. If anything happens to Oakley, I will be back for you and no one will be able to save you. Not even your mother." With that, he stormed out.

CHARLOTTE STUMBLED TO a chair and dropped into it. She was shaking so hard that her teeth clattered. CJ had deceived her. He could walk and yet when she opened her mouth it was to say, "You wouldn't drill there."

CJ didn't meet her gaze. "I do what I think is right for this ranch. We can't afford sentiment. I know what you did at that spot along the river. I know that you met him there, let him use you, let him throw you away. You should be happy that the drilling will destroy it. This should have been done a long time ago." He started to turn to head back to his room.

She was on her feet so quickly that it startled him. She grabbed his arm and spun him toward her. "Make the call."

"I don't know what you're talking about," he said, not quite as cocky as he had been just moments before.

"Call whoever it is." Her throat tasted of bile. "Do it now. If anything happens to Oakley, Pickett Hanson will be the least of your worries."

His jaw set, but he pulled his phone out. For a moment he only looked at it. "Oakley did this," he said. "She gets what she deserves. She wouldn't leave well enough alone. She has only herself to blame."

Through clenched teeth, Charlotte said, "Make the call, CJ, or leave this house right now and never come back."

He looked at her in surprise and must have seen that she was serious. He lifted the phone. Keyed in a number and then held it to his ear. "There's no answer. There's nothing I can do. It's done."

OAKLEY HAD ALMOST finished setting the explosives when she heard the vehicle coming. She only needed a few more minutes. She didn't dare hurry for fear of blowing up not only the drilling rig, but also herself with it.

The sound of the vehicle's engine grew louder and louder as it came closer and closer. There was no doubt it was headed in her direction. She concentrated on the job at hand.

She almost had it finished when headlights washed over her. She heard the vehicle speed up as she began climbing down from where she'd set the charge as a pickup roared up. She saw both doors fly open as she recognized the two men who came rushing toward her.

"Get down from there!" Frankie ordered as the smaller of the two Lees brothers began to climb up the rigging, trying to grab her leg to pull her down.

"I wouldn't do that if I were you," she called down to him as she climbed up out of his reach. "This whole thing is about to blow sky-high."

"She's lying," Frankie said, scoffing. "Bring her down."

Norman began to climb though she could see he was hesitant. She quickly swung around to the other side of the tall drilling framework out of his reach. She had to get off here and quickly. She wasn't lying.

She'd given herself time to get down and ride far enough away before it blew. She hadn't planned on the Lees brothers showing up until later. By then, she'd hoped that all they'd find was twisted metal.

She heard what sounded like banging around in the back of the pickup the men had arrived in. Frankie saw her surprise. "We would have been here sooner, but we ran into a friend of yours, Duffy McKenna. Norman, I hope you did a good job of tying him up. But he can join our girl here as soon as I'm finished with her."

"No," Oakley cried. "We all have to get out of here. You have to take Duffy out of here. This is going to explode and when it does—" She scrambled down, hoping to slip past Norman, who was hanging on for dear life. But just as she reached a spot where she could jump down, she was grabbed from behind. For a few moments she had lost track of Frankie in the darkness beyond the pickup's headlights.

He locked an arm around her throat as he lifted her off the ground and hauled her over to the edge of the creek. She fought, kicking and clawing at him, but he was much larger, much stronger, and she guessed she wasn't the first woman he'd pulled off a gas drilling rig.

"Get down from there, Norman," he called. "I'm going to need your help with this wildcat." At the edge of the creek, he began to stomp on the ice, breaking a path into deeper water as he walked. "You know the thing about cats? I heard they don't like water."

"I wasn't lying about the explosives," she cried. "We need to get out of here before it blows."

He didn't seem to be listening. He was knee-deep in the freezing water. "This should do it," he said and flung her down on the ice. She hit hard, heard the ice crack under her and felt it give. Icy water washed over her as she tried to catch her breath and get to her feet.

Frankie pushed her back down, forcing her under the icy flowing water. She tried to fight him off as he shoved her under, but he grabbed a handful of her hair and pushed her down. The water took her breath away as she was fully submerged. He held her under, but she twisted, coming up to gasp for air before he plunged her deeper, this time pushing her under the ice, farther out into the deepest part of the creek.

She grabbed at the edge of the ice but couldn't hold on as she kicked at Frankie. The freezing water made every movement slower, harder. She could no longer feel her body. Desperate to breathe, she grabbed again for the ice edge above her. A piece of ice broke off in her hand as Frankie shoved her under again.

CHAPTER TWENTY-FIVE

PICKETT SPOTTED THE drilling rig in his pickup's head-lights. He sped up at the sight of a truck engine running, lights on, in front of the rig. But its headlight beams did little to cut through the rising fog moving through the bare limbs of the cottonwoods from the creek.

There was no sign of Oakley as he roared up, grabbed the shotgun from the rack behind the seat and jumped out. As he ran by the pickup parked next to the drilling rig, he heard a noise in the back. He couldn't see any-one in the blackness of the pickup's bed. Past the drill-ing rig, the creek was cloaked in fog. He reached into the back of the truck, shotgun ready and uncovered the body squirming there.

"Duffy?" He jerked the cloth gag from his friend's mouth.

"Frankie and Norman. They have Oakley down by the creek. I could hear the ice breaking."

Pickett felt the impact of his recurring nightmare as he hurriedly pulled out his pocketknife, tossed it to Duffy and headed for the creek. Behind him, Duffy yelled, "Oakley said the drilling rig's going to explode any minute!"

Pickett hadn't gone far when a figure emerged from the darkness near the drilling rig. He caught Norman in the chest with the butt of the shotgun. The man went down hard, gasping for breath.

"Duffy, take care of Norman," he called back, and rushed into the dense fog at the creek. Within a few steps, he spotted a large figure out in the creek bent over pushing something under the ice. As he charged, Frankie was still leaning down, one hand holding a struggling Oakley under the ice, the other lifting a gun to fire in his direction.

Pickett wanted desperately to pull the trigger on the shotgun, but he couldn't chance hitting Oakley. He charged, swinging the rifle, the butt knocking the gun from Frankie's hand, but not before he got a shot off. Pickett felt it whiz past his ear.

He brought the shotgun back across, hitting Frankie in the side of the head. A loud crack filled the air, but the big man was still standing, and past him Oakley was no longer struggling. She lay, her face pressed against the ice, not moving.

Pickett drove the shotgun deep into the man's big belly and pulled the trigger as he shoved him aside and grabbed Oakley.

As Frankie fell back, breaking the ice and falling into the water, Pickett pulled Oakley from the creek and into his arms. Around Frankie, blood stained the ice and darkened the water.

Oakley began shaking, no doubt freezing, and her eyes fluttered as he held her close, giving him hope. She was alive, but had to be suffering from hypothermia. He dropped the shotgun and ran with her, anxious to get her to his pickup where he could get her warm before it was too late.

"Norman just told me that CJ set this all up," Duffy said as Pickett rushed to his truck. Out of the corner of his eye, he saw Norman on the ground. "CJ told them to kill all of us."

"We have to get out of here," Norman said as Duffy bound the man's hands with some of the duct tape that had been used on him and pulled him to his feet. "She said there was explosives. Frankie thought she was lying, but I don't think she was."

"Duffy, take him in their pickup," he called over his shoulder. "He's right. There are explosives. The sheriff's deputies are on their way. You'll meet them on the way."

"I have to get my horse," Duffy said. "I'll be right behind you."

"Hurry." Pickett reached his truck and put Oakley inside, quickly closing the door. He couldn't see Duffy as he climbed in after her. He drove up the road a safe distance in case the dynamite blew. Oakley lay against him, her teeth chattering. He had to get her wet clothing off.

In the warm pickup, he stripped off her freezing clothing, then pulled a bedroll from the back and wrapped her in it, pulling her close to give her some of his warmth as he drove toward town.

He hadn't gone but half a mile when he heard the explosion. It lit the night sky behind him. "Damn it, Duffy," he said under his breath, hoping his friend had gotten out of there.

Next to him, Oakley moaned. He pulled her closer. "It's okay, baby. I'm going to get you somewhere warm." Town was too far.

Ahead was the turnoff to the McKenna Ranch. Oakley was conscious as he pulled into the yard. He saw with relief that Duffy had gotten away. He was dismounting his horse as Pickett pulled in.

"I met some sheriff's deputies on the way into town and dropped off Norman."

"Help me get her into the house," he said to his friend. With Duffy's help they carried her in. She couldn't stand and was shivering badly even in the dry, warm bedroll.

"What's happened?" Holden asked. He'd been standing at the window where the sky glowed bright orange.

"Oakley's suffering from hypothermia," Pickett said. "I need to get her warm."

"Use the guest bedroom down the hall," Holden said without hesitation.

Elaine came in from the kitchen. "Duffy, go make her something hot to drink. I'll get her something warm to wear."

Pickett hurried down the hallway and into the bedroom. Putting Oakley down on the bed, he pulled off the now damp sleeping bag and tossed it away as he carefully slid her under the layers of quilts on the bed. Taking off his own wet outer clothing, he crawled in beside her, drawing her close, his arms around her as he tried to give her all of his heat.

Elaine tapped at the door frame. "I thought you might want these." She brought in two pairs of freshly washed flannel pajamas and picked up the wet items from the floor and left, closing the door behind her.

"Where...am...I?" Oakley asked from between trembling lips.

"You're safe. Let's get you warmed up."

She snuggled against him. "Did…it…blow?"

"It blew."

"Duffy?"

There was another tap at the door. As if she'd made him materialize, Duffy appeared in the doorway with a tray. "Hot apple cider?" He moved to the opposite side of the bed and put down the tray. "Looks like you have this," he said to Pickett and left the room, closing the door again behind him.

"Can you sit up a little?" Pickett asked Oakley. She nodded and he helped her take a few sips of the warm cider. Her color was returning and her skin was warming.

He took the empty cup and she lay back, her gaze locked with his. "You saved my life. How can I ever—"

"You owe me a date."

She smiled. "I do."

"And I owe you the truth about Pickett Hanson."

He curled up next to her until she fell into an exhausted sleep. Still, he monitored her breathing. He was afraid to close his eyes for fear this part was a dream and like in his frighteningly real nightmare, he hadn't reached Oakley in time to save her.

CHARLOTTE STOOD AT the window, staring at the orange ball of fire in the distance.

"That's Oakley's doing," CJ said behind her. "I had nothing to do with it."

She couldn't bear to look at him. "How long have you been able to walk?" she asked without turning around. At first, she didn't think he would answer her.

"I thought it would help my case if I was confined

to a wheelchair—at least temporarily. I was doing it for you as much as for myself."

A bitter laugh escaped her throat as she turned. "All your life I've made excuses for you. I blamed myself for your behavior. I blamed your sisters, your brothers. I blamed everyone but you."

"You're not going to throw me out," he said, some of his old cockiness returning. "You can't run this ranch without me. We can get past this. Oakley did us a favor. The only evidence they will find at the drilling site will be what Oakley put there. It was an accident. Everyone knows she and Duffy McKenna and Pickett Hanson have probably been the ones vandalizing the gas company equipment."

Her cell phone rang. She quickly took the call, her back to her son. "Yes. Yes, I understand. Yes, please." Her voice broke. "Thank you." She slumped against the window for a moment. Hadn't she feared that this day was coming? Had she really thought she could save her son from himself?

"They all got what they had coming," CJ said behind her, no doubt thinking that the deputies had found them all dead because of her reaction to the call. "The only real victims were the gas company's security guards, Frankie and Norman Lees—if they were caught in the explosion. I'm assuming they were."

Still, she said nothing, letting CJ believe they were all dead. Let him find out from the deputies what she'd been told. Norman Lees had survived and had confessed that he was working for her son, who'd said he'd wanted Oakley and anyone else who got in their way killed. "You set up your sister to die tonight."

All he seemed to hear was what he wanted—that Oakley had died tonight. "I wasn't the one who blew up the gas rig," he said. "Oakley's always done whatever she wanted. If anything, I tried to stop her."

The sky over the trees glowed orange as smoke billowed up from her once favorite spot on the river. "Yes, she is a very strong, determined woman."

"If you don't want to drill on the ranch anymore, fine," CJ said. "We don't have to. Like I told you, I'm going to buy some more land. With Tilly and Oakley gone and Brand and Ryder spending most of their time down in the bunkhouse with the ranch hands, we can run this ranch any way we want. No one will get in our way now."

She turned to look at him. He'd gotten by on his good looks and his name and her money. He'd never wanted for anything and yet he'd always wanted more, would always want more, and God help anyone who got in his way.

"That's what you've always wanted, isn't it? This place all to yourself," she said, studying his handsome face, finding no remorse at all. "It's why you've always resented your siblings so much."

He smiled. "Who could blame me? They've always been a pain in my ass. Why do you think Brand and Ryder stay away from me?"

"And if I got in your way? You'd get rid of me as well, wouldn't you?" She stepped to him and slapped him, something she'd never done, something she never thought she would ever do to any of her children, especially to CJ. The sound was like a gunshot in the room.

His head snapped back, his shocked expression priceless.

"I can't stand the sight of you. Get out now while you

can," Charlotte said, the words feeling like daggers in her throat. She'd alienated all but the two sons who took care of the ranch, spending no time at all around her or CJ. She'd taken CJ's side for years, leaning on him, spoiling him, making him into the man standing before her now.

He rubbed his cheek. "You don't mean that. It's always been the two of us. Except for when you married Dixon Malone. But as long as his body never turns up—" He laughed. "I'm not leaving and you're not going to make me leave. You'd have to physically throw me out of the house and we both know you're not going to do that—even if you could."

"You should have gone when you had the chance," she said as headlights flashed on the front living room window. More headlights. A vehicle pulled up out front, followed by another one. Charlotte turned away from him and went to open the door for the sheriff's deputies.

"You called the cops on me?" CJ asked, almost sounding amused. Out of the corner of her eye, she saw him move to his wheelchair and drop into it again. He still thought he could get away with everything he'd done.

"He's in here, Deputies." She let the officers in. "He doesn't need the wheelchair. He can walk perfectly fine."

"I don't know what she's telling you," her son said. "She's not herself right now. You can't believe anything she says."

The deputies headed toward CJ; one of them began reading him his rights. As he was dragged to his feet and cuffed, he told her to call the family lawyer. She ignored him.

"Tell them they're making a mistake," he ordered her as he was being led out. "Mother, tell them." She turned away. "I'll be out before morning. Our lawyer will sue the county and you hick cops. Mother!"

"Goodbye, CJ," she said, unable to look at him.

"You're going to regret this," he yelled back at her before the door closed behind him. "You don't know who you're dealing with."

Except that she finally did.

Charlotte stood listening to the sheriff's deputies drive away with her son before she dropped to her knees and, after years of being unable to shed a tear, sobbed her heart out.

It was still dark out when Pickett woke, a shaft of moonlight splayed across the bed. Even with his eyes open, he wasn't sure where he was or how he'd gotten there for a moment. Then Oakley came into view. She was leaning over him, propped up on one elbow, staring down at him in the semidarkness of the room.

For a startled moment he thought something might be wrong, but she quickly pressed a finger to his lips before removing it and replacing it with her mouth. The kiss was sweet, her tongue teasing, her mouth so tempting.

He could think of a half dozen reasons this was a bad idea. They were in the McKenna house's guest room. Anyone could walk in. Duffy could walk in.

As if seeing his concern, Oakley got out of bed, padded barefoot and stark naked to lock the door. The shaft of moonlight played on her pale skin as she turned to look at him. It glowed on her full breasts, her flat stomach, her long legs, while making her erect nipples darker than the V between her legs.

But it was the look in those green eyes that was his undoing. He would give this woman anything. She moved slowly to him, stealing his breath as she climbed into his side of the bed. Her nipples brushed his bare chest as she bent over him to kiss him again.

"Oakley?" he whispered. Last night he'd gotten up and pulled on the pajama bottoms of the larger of the pairs Elaine had left for them. At that time his only thought was keeping Oakley warm. Now he was having trouble reining in his thoughts as she put a finger to his lips again for a moment before she reached under the covers and pulled off his pajama bottoms, tossing them aside.

He wanted to ask her if she was sure about this. To tell her he didn't have any protection on him. But even a weak attempt to make her stop was met with a shake of her head. He was already hard and throbbing. If she touched him… He had to slow this down. He cupped her slim waist with his hands, lifted her and swung her back over on her side of the bed, pulling the covers over the two of them. Leaning over her, he kissed her, tonguing away her protests when he wouldn't let her touch him.

"PICKETT," SHE WHISPERED, a plea. She needed him inside her. He pulled back, his gaze locking with hers as he gently cupped her breast. His callused thumb brushed over the hard and aching nipple, making her arch against his hand.

Again, she reached for him, but he pushed her hand away, shaking his head, before leaning down to take her nipple into his mouth. He sucked, he nibbled, he pulled, moving to her other breast as she tried not to wake the rest of the household with her stifled moans of pleasure.

"Pickett," she breathed against his mouth again as he kissed her before trailing kisses down between her aching breasts and over her stomach. He gently spread her legs as she cupped his head in her hands and arched against his mouth. His tongue had barely touched her, his lips had only started to suck her, when she had to put her hand over her mouth as she came.

He moved slowly up her body until she thought she might scream. She grabbed for him, drawing him down on her, whispering his name against his warm flesh, against his lips, as he started to lower himself and stopped.

She stared at him, eyes wide in warning. If he didn't want her waking the entire household… She'd never wanted anything more than to feel him inside her. Her need overpowered everything. She saw the question he was asking in his eyes. She nodded and pulled him toward her. Their gazes locked as he entered her. For a moment he didn't move. They were frozen in time, cast in moonlight, as if the two of them were the only two people left in the world.

Then he began to move. She lifted her hips, rocking with him to the age-old rhythm as the pleasure mounted to a breath-stealing crescendo. They shuddered, locked together in the intimate act. He said her name as he collapsed in her arms. She held on to him, arms wrapped tightly around him, never going to let him go.

"You saved my life," she whispered as she remembered being under the freezing water last night. She'd been so sure that she would die there. Her own fault. She'd jeopardized not only her own life but also Pickett's and Duffy's.

She shuddered at the memory of the creek. He pulled her tighter. She'd never imagined it could be like this. She looked into his handsome face, her smile so broad it actually hurt as tears rushed her eyes. Pickett Hanson. Her hero.

"You know I'm headed for jail," she said.

"Not if I have anything to do with it," he said and rolled to his back to pull her over to him.

She rested her head on his chest and closed her eyes as he held her and whispered her name like a promise.

PICKETT COULDN'T BELIEVE that just before daylight they made love again, both of them ending up in the shower together. He'd left Oakley in the shower. When he'd come out of the bathroom, he'd found their clothing from the night before dried and folded neatly on a chair by the bed. *Elaine,* he thought.

He could hear loud voices somewhere beyond the guest room. He dressed quickly, feeling like a teenager. He couldn't get enough of this woman and if he'd waited in the bathroom to help dry her off, they would have ended up making love again in the bed.

"I need to call the sheriff's office," Pickett said, sticking his head into the bathroom. Through the steam he could see her behind the glass. He quickly closed the door and tamped down his desire.

The truth was he had a feeling based on the sound of the loud voices that he wouldn't have to call the sheriff's office. As he walked into the living room, he saw that Holden and Elaine were at the breakfast table, surprised that there were no uniforms.

It was late. Holly Jo would have already left for school. Apparently, Duffy and Treyton either hadn't come down yet or were already gone. He thought about what he'd learned about Treyton yesterday. He hadn't had a chance to tell Duffy.

"Pickett, come join us," Holden called to him.

"Thank you, but I need to call the sheriff's department. I should have done it last night."

"Oakley needed you. That was more important." Holden waved him to a seat at the table. "Please come have some breakfast. You'll see the deputies soon enough. How is she?"

"Good," Pickett said, avoiding his gaze.

"Have some breakfast. Two deputies are waiting outside. Before I let them in, I thought we should talk." Holden passed pancakes, bacon and eggs to him.

The deputies were waiting outside? He started to rise again, but Elaine touched his arm as she poured him a cup of coffee.

"I'm assuming you've never been arrested before," Holden said. "That's what I thought. They're going to run your prints, your DNA…"

Pickett realized what Holden already had. "They're going to find out that I changed my name." He swore under his breath. It would make him look like he had something to hide.

"I'm assuming Oakley knows—" He stopped speaking as she walked into the dining room and there was a loud knock at the door. Holden put down his napkin and rose to get the door. "Have something to eat," he said to Oakley on his way.

"Oakley knows what?" she said as she sat down next to him and took a piece of his bacon.

He was struck again by how beautiful she was. There was a glow to her this morning that melted his heart. "That Pickett Hanson is the name I had changed from my birth name."

Behind them, Holden cleared his voice. "Sorry to interrupt, but these officers are insistent, Pickett. They have questions for both you and Ms. Stafford. My attorney will meet you at the sheriff's office."

CHAPTER TWENTY-SIX

DEPUTY TY DODSON hitched up his jeans, smiling broadly as he looked down at the sheriff in the hospital bed. "Norman Lees spilled his guts. It was something to see, but nothing like when we arrested CJ Stafford. He screamed, he threatened, he demanded and then he cried like a baby." Clearly, the young, green deputy had enjoyed that the most.

Not that Stuart could blame him. The deputy wasn't the only one who would enjoy seeing CJ get what he had coming to him. "Sounds like I missed a lot."

"I called the state boys in like you said. I would imagine Norman will plead out. He has enough on CH4 that he'll get a deal—not to mention what he has on CJ Stafford."

"Make sure all of the documented evidence on your part and the other deputies is on my desk."

Dodson nodded. "Wait until you hear Oakley Stafford's part in all this," the deputy was saying. "She remembered what she'd seen that day her brother shot her." Dodson rocked back on his boot heels, grinning as he hooked his thumbs in his jeans pockets. "They weren't just making meth at that old ranch. They were operating a human trafficking ring, using those women to cook the dope for them, then farming them out to other meth labs."

Stuart rubbed a hand over his neck. He really had to get out of this hospital. "Oakley's sure about that?"

"Norman backed up her story. He and his brothers were working with CJ on the whole deal," the deputy said. "We got Stafford dead to rights and this time his mother won't be getting him out. When her attorney refused to take his case, he had to go with the public defender the county assigned him. That's when he really cried." Dobson laughed, clearly delighted to see the cowboy brought down to size.

"Let's not be too cheerful here, okay? Have you talked to Charlotte Stafford? Is she okay?"

"I didn't speak with her personally, but the state boys told me that the big hotshot from the gas company isn't filing a complaint, even though her daughter blew up his drilling equipment."

"Really?" Charlotte had apparently backed her daughter. That surprised him since Oakley had gone against her mother and brother.

"The state boys talked to her. Doubt she'll be charged for anything since Holden McKenna's attorney was there when they brought her and Pickett Hanson in for questioning. She knew her brother was going to try to kill her. He thought he set her up, but maybe that's what she was doing, blowing up that rig like she did." Dobson shrugged. "You'd think CH4 would come after her. Destroyed one of their drilling rigs along with a lot of other equipment and a large truck. But they aren't."

It sounded as if CH4 wasn't in a strong position to

do much of anything, given that Frankie and Norman were employed by the gas company.

"Pickett Hanson was taken in for killing Frankie Lees, but it was in self-defense. He was released once they sorted out the name problem."

"Name problem?"

"His real name is Archibald Vanderlin Westmoreland the fourth. He changed it to Pickett Hanson. Some fancy lawyer showed up with paperwork that detailed how Pickett had his name changed legally."

Stuart was trying hard to take it all in. Frankie had tried to drown Oakley in the creek. Oakley had blown up the drilling rig and equipment. Pickett—not his birth name—had saved her after killing Frankie. Duffy Mc-Kenna had been duct taped in the back of Frankie's truck, but helped once Pickett tossed him a knife and he cut himself free.

"Oakley and Pickett are the talk of the town. Word is that they stayed in a guest room at the McKenna Ranch. Holden took them in since both were soaking wet and suffering from hypothermia. Bet Charlotte Stafford is losing her mind."

"Just another night in the Powder River Basin," the sheriff said under his breath. "You should get back to Powder Crossing," he told his deputy.

He couldn't take too much of the young deputy. Dodson often jumped to conclusions without the facts, but what bothered the sheriff most was the pleasure the deputy took whenever one of the wealthy ranchers in the basin was brought to his knees.

Dodson needed to learn to hide his feelings better. Like Stuart had had to learn. He hated that he'd felt any pleasure at all in seeing CJ Stafford brought down. It made him feel small because of his resentment of what others had. It made him sick to his stomach because he didn't want to be that man. He didn't want to be an older version of Dodson and yet, he knew he was.

"Don't worry. We've got everything under control," the deputy assured him. "You just get better. Hell of a thing what that woman did to you. Hell of a thing."

The sheriff pushed his call button the moment Dodson left.

He had to get out of there.

"HAVE YOU TALKED to Mother?" Tilly asked after her sister told her about what had happened as the two sat in their apartment. Cooper and Tilly had missed most of the excitement, awakened in his far wing of the McKenna house by the explosion.

Oakley shook her head and curled deeper into the corner of the couch. "I really doubt she wants to talk to me. She did send the family lawyer down to the sheriff's office to make sure I wasn't arrested. But Holden's lawyer was already there."

"That surprises me about Mother sending her lawyer," her sister said.

"You still haven't heard from her?" Oakley guessed. Tilly shook her head.

"I sent her a wedding invitation, but she hasn't responded. I didn't really expect her to."

Oakley heard the catch in her sister's voice and knew she was hurt. It amazed her that she'd want their mother at the wedding, given the way their mother felt about Tilly marrying a McKenna.

"You're still going to be my maid of honor, though, right?"

"Of course." Unless she was in jail. But it didn't look like that was going to happen. Even CH4 wasn't filing charges.

"So you and Pickett, huh?"

She smiled. "He saved my life." Her cell phone rang. "It's the sheriff."

Tilly looked at her wide-eyed. "I thought you said they weren't going to arrest you?"

Oakley shrugged and took the call.

"Your brother is asking to see you," Stuart said. "I understand if you don't want to—"

"Oh, but I do want to see him. I'm in town. I'll be right there." She glanced at her sister as she disconnected. "CJ wants to see me."

"Are you sure this is a good idea?"

"Probably not," she admitted as she put on her jacket. But she was curious why he'd asked to see her. Because he had no one else?

She walked the couple of blocks to the sheriff's department, glad Stuart was back. But she wasn't prepared to see him looking so pale, his arms still covered with bandages. She tapped at his door and he rose to take her down the hall to lockup.

"How are you?" she asked.

"Recovering. I'll be fine."

She wondered about that. After everything she'd been through, almost dying twice, she had changed. Every moment felt precious. Would he be fine after everything he'd gone through?

Stuart studied her for a moment before he opened the door to the cells. "Can I trust you not to try to kill him?"

"No."

"Okay, then you'll just have to see him behind bars," he said. "You sure about this?"

She nodded even as she felt a shiver of anxiety at the thought of seeing CJ—even behind bars—as the sheriff opened the door into lockup. "Last cell at the end. Just push this button when you've had enough," he said and closed the door behind him.

"Well, if it isn't my sister come to visit me," CJ said at the end of the short line of cells. "About time." She couldn't see him until she walked a few steps. He'd been lying on a bunk.

Now that she was here, she couldn't work up the anger she'd felt for so long. In its place was just an empty, sad space. She stared at him. The cell with its bars diminished his size and took away his power.

"You always said I'd end up behind bars," he said as he rose slowly from the cot and ambled over to the bars. "I thought it was just wishful thinking on your part. But…" He held his arms out to encompass his surroundings. "Guess you were right, sis."

"I'm only here because you asked to see me. Why?" she asked.

"Why?" He laughed. "You put me in here. You ruined my life because you couldn't mind your own business. That's why. I wanted you to see what you've done to me."

She shook her head, not surprised that he saw it that way. "Never your fault, huh, CJ? You shot me. You tried to have me killed again. But not your fault."

"I don't know what you're talking about."

"Norman Lees told the cops everything. You won't be able to lie your way out of it. Not even Mother's highly paid attorneys will be able to get you out of here." She saw him wince. "Mother did call her attorneys, didn't she?" The fury in his face told her that she hadn't weakened and sent them. "Seriously? Mommy not coming to rescue you this time? Wow, you really have hit rock bottom."

"Speaking of rock bottom, you and the McKenna's ranch hand? Not Pickett but Archibald Vanderlin Westmoreland. How's that for a mouthful? Everything about him is a lie. Poor, sweet sister, you've been his buddy all this time and you had no idea that he'd been lying to you and everyone else and now you're both going to end up behind bars just like me." He laughed.

"Sorry, but there are no charges against either of us," she said and saw his disappointment.

"Seriously? You blow up a CH4 drilling rig, you get one of their security members killed and they don't do anything to you?"

"So unfair, huh? While innocent you rots in jail." She shook her head.

"I need a good lawyer. That's the least you could do since you put me here."

She stared at him. "You can't really think I'd hire a lawyer to get you out of here."

"You and I can run the ranch. We can—"

"Not happening, CJ. Not ever, even if Mother would let you back on the ranch. You only have yourself to blame for all of this because of your greed. It's never enough, is it?"

He shook his head. "No, it's not." From pleading, he'd quickly turned to fury. "I'm going to get out of here and when I do—"

"Save your threats, CJ. By the time you get out of prison, you'll be too old and frail to do anything. That's if someone doesn't shank you while you're in there."

"I'm going to be running that place and making friends, the kind of friends who'll do anything I ask them to. They'll have friends on the outside who'll do my bidding. You'll never be free of me, and neither will Mother. She, like you, will rue the day she turned on me."

She stared at him, again reminded how dangerous he was.

"I know about the two of you spending the night at McKenna Ranch," he called after her. "Pickett was seen carrying you inside. You didn't come out until morning." He laughed. "I have my sources."

"What you won't have is freedom," she said. "We will all be living our lives, free to do whatever we want. I feel sorry for you, CJ. While you lose your mind plotting revenge against us, we won't be giving you a thought. Goodbye, CJ."

She walked down the hall and pushed the button, not looking back. As the door opened, she stepped out, took a deep breath and let it out as she walked away.

CHAPTER TWENTY-SEVEN

"Can you ever forgive me for not telling you the truth?" Pickett asked. He and Oakley were lying in bed after making love at her apartment. "I've wanted to tell you, but I didn't know how after so long."

"Maybe, someday, I'll find it in my heart to forgive you," she teased as she kissed him. "I still don't really understand."

"Most people wouldn't. They dream of coming from a wealthy family," he said. "From as far back as I can remember I was to take over my father's empire. My life was mapped out for me. It didn't matter what I wanted to do with my life. As the only child of Archibald Vanderlin Westmoreland the third, I had no choice."

"Obviously, you did have a choice, one you made when you showed up at the McKenna Ranch."

"When I left at such a young age, I was running for my life. I told myself that if I failed, I would have to go back, that I really had no other option, then I got on at the ranch. I loved the work. I learned to ride a horse, mend fences, herd cattle, pull calves. I worked with my hands from sunup to sunset. I fell in bed at night, exhausted. I loved it. I needed it."

She could see that it was true. He'd become the man

he wanted to be, and he'd done it on his own. "Your father must have been proud of you."

Pickett nodded. "He was. I'd burned that bridge. I believed there was no going back and yet I'd thrived and done well for myself." He chuckled. "Nothing like my father. I'd started with nothing but a desire to be my own man."

She curled into him, thinking what a man he was. He'd saved her life in so many ways. "Where did you get the name Pickett Hanson?" she asked, leaning back to look into his face.

He grinned. "I saw it on an old gravestone. I liked it. I wanted to be someone else. Once I met you…" His gaze held hers. "You and this life were all I wanted."

"I wish you would have told me," she said.

"Told you that I came from a wealthy family, that I'd walked away from all that to be a ranch hand, that I had no contact with them or that I'd changed my name? That's about all that I could have told you. Would it have made a difference?"

She heard it in his voice. "You wanted me to fall in love with Pickett Hanson—not Archibald the fourth." Everything about this man drew her to him, his blue eyes, his head of thick sun-blonded brown hair, one lock that fell over his forehead, that mouth that kissed like it had been heaven sent.

"I did," he admitted. "Oakley, you know the real me. I'm Pickett Hanson, that teenage boy who fell for you the moment he laid eyes on you. I just hoped that you might one day fall in love with me, nothing but a cowboy ranch hand."

"And I did."

Pickett pulled her close. She laid her hand on his shoulder, the two of them staring up at the ceiling. "Can you imagine what would have happened if I'd told Holden McKenna I was in need of a job with a name like Archibald Vanderlin Westmoreland the fourth? It was bad enough that I had no ranch experience. I was as green as spring grass, and Holden knew it. And yet, he took me on as if he knew how desperate I was for this kind of life, this kind of family. He's been like a father to me, Duffy like a brother, you...like a dream come true."

"When your father was dying, when you left, I was so afraid you wouldn't come back."

He kissed the top of her head. "That was never happening."

Oakley felt herself weaken as warmth spread through her chest. She loved this man. First as a friend, then as a lover. "How do I know you won't get tired of this life and go back to the other one?"

"I gave it all away. Well, most of it away. I saved enough to buy a piece of land, build us a house, make sure you and our kids have a safe, secure future."

"Our kids?"

She felt him freeze for a moment. "Tell me you want to have a passel of babies."

"Not sure how many that is," she said. "But I wouldn't mind having kids with you."

"Really? That mean you'll marry me?"

She couldn't help smiling. "Maybe."

He turned and dragged her to him and, lifting her chin with a finger, kissed her. There were fireworks and heat filling her with happiness like none she'd ever known. "I love you," he said as he drew back. "I'd risk my life for you."

"You already have."

"This mean I'm forgiven?"

She nodded. "Just never lie to me again."

He ran a finger over his chest to form an X. "I promise. There is one thing, though. You know the truth and Holden knows and probably Duffy as well, but I hope that's it. I'm fine with people thinking I'm just a ranch hand who lucked out and won the heart of a rancher's daughter."

"That would be funny if I was still a rancher's daughter."

"You haven't talked to your mother?" She shook her head. "I tried to call once, to thank her for sending her lawyer, but it went to voice mail. I'm sure she still blames me for everything, even though apparently she's no longer trying to get CJ out of trouble this time."

"What about Tilly's wedding?" he asked.

"She hasn't heard from Mother, either. As awful as Mother was to her, Tilly still really hopes she will respond to the RSVP on the invitation. She thought it would go a long way to mend the rift between the families. I know. My sister is a dreamer. But you and I will be there. My brothers Ryder and Brand have agreed to be ushers, so that's something. With a lot of luck, there won't be any blood shed at the wedding or the reception."

"You don't think your mother would try to stop it, do you?"

She stared at him. "I really wish you hadn't said that. She wouldn't, would she?"

HOLDEN KNEW THAT he was the last person on earth Charlotte would want to see. He couldn't imagine what she must be going through. His heart broke for her. He thought about his own eldest son. It would be so easy to lose Treyton the same way, given that he and CJ had been a lot alike, both always wanting more.

He'd hardly seen Treyton lately. He knew that Cooper was worried about him, suspecting he was up to something. Holden sure hoped not. He had enough to worry about with the upcoming wedding. He hoped it would bring the families together. He feared it might have the opposite effect—even with CJ behind bars.

CJ, he thought with a curse. He'd heard that he'd been planning on drilling for methane near the creek in a spot Holden knew so well. Had Charlotte known? He couldn't imagine that even hating him like she did, she would destroy the place that they'd loved.

Saddling up, he rode across his property to the creek that separated their ranches. As he neared the spot where the water pooled under the cottonwoods surrounded by large, smooth boulders, he saw the damage and felt sick.

It had been such a beautiful place. But now the trees were burnt black and grotesque, the creek cluttered with ash and charred limbs, the ground scorched.

He had so many wonderful memories of the time he'd spent here with the woman he still loved. Lottie must be as sick as he felt. Oakley had taken such a radical step to stop her brother from drilling and show what kind of man he was. He hoped it wasn't for naught.

As he rode closer, he saw Lottie. She had her head down, her shoulders slumped, her face crumpled in pain. It was all he could do not to rush to her as he desperately wanted to take her into his arms and relieve at least some of that horrible hurt. But he'd lost that right a whole long time ago. He knew she must be devastated. She had been devoted to CJ. She'd believed he was the future of the ranch.

Still, he drew his horse up short and dismounted, ground-tied his horse then moved toward the woman. Lottie. Once his Lottie. "It will come back."

She looked up, straightening, at the sound of his voice. There was such an emptiness in her expression as if she'd lost too much and could no longer feel the pain. "The grass will grow come spring," he said as he took a step toward her. "New cottonwoods will sprout along the creek bank."

"It won't ever be the same," she said, but not with her usual bitterness, not with her usual conviction, either.

"No," he agreed as he stopped within a few feet of her. "Things change. It's the nature of the universe. But not all things, Lottie."

Lottie. His nickname for her stabbed a hole in her already battered heart. She turned away to swallow the bitterness that rose in her throat. She'd known he would come. Wasn't that why she'd ridden out here today?

But she wasn't up for a fight. All the fight had been knocked out of her over the past twenty-four hours. Just the sight of this place where her daughter had almost drowned… CJ might not have been holding Oakley's head under, but he was just as guilty as the man he'd hired—if not more so.

"It will be all right," Holden said. Out of the corner of her eye she saw him step even closer.

She couldn't bear to look at him for fear that she would reach for him, grab him and pull him to her and never let him go. All the wasted years, all the ache, all the need, all the sleepless nights. All because she had never gotten over this man.

"Why are you here?" she asked, still not looking directly at him.

"Where else would I be? I'm so sorry about CJ. Also, I knew how much this spot meant to you, because it means so much to me."

She felt hot tears fill her eyes; sobs closed her throat. "Why?" she asked on a sob, knowing that she was asking how they'd gotten to this point. She felt his hand on her shoulder. A part of her screamed for her to shrug it off, to push him away, as she had for years.

But she was no longer strong enough. Instead, she reached up and laid her hand over his. It felt warm and strong, and wonderfully and painfully familiar.

"Does it matter all that much how we got here?" he asked quietly. "We're here, Lottie. Through it all, we're here."

She shook her head, that bitter, blackened part of her still fighting the one thing she wanted more than her next breath. "I don't know that I can ever forgive you."

"Let me help you try," he said and gently pulled her into his arms.

She rested her head against his chest, letting out all her anguish. Even as she cried, she told herself that she'd never be able to face him—or herself—after this.

It had been years since she'd let him see her this vulnerable. She had promised herself she never would again.

But right now she could do nothing more than hold tight to him, leaning into him, letting it all come out here in this spot where he'd given her such joy—and such sorrow.

THE SHERIFF HAD been relieved when after searching the Turner Ranch where Rory Eastwood's pickup had been found in the reservoir, his body hadn't turned up. He was hoping that the man was alive as he tried to remember what Abigail had said that day in the car.

He couldn't remember a lot of it. Shock? Trauma? Or just plain old fear? He had trouble recalling her exact words. Once she'd pulled the knife, things had gotten really fuzzy.

That was why the last thing he'd been expecting was a call from a landowner that his kids had been playing by an old well on the neighbor's property. When he went to make sure it was securely covered, he'd shone a flashlight down in there and he'd found what sure as the devil looked like a human skeleton.

Stuart thought about sending Dodson, but quickly changed his mind. He doubted the deputy would know the difference between canine bones and human. All the way out to the ranch, he kept hoping that the rancher was wrong.

He especially hoped that was the case when he realized how close the Stafford Ranch was to the abandoned well on a neighboring ranch to the south.

He was healing fine according to the doctors, but it was going to take some time to feel steady on his feet again. The cuts would leave scars, but nothing like the scars inside him. He'd almost died. Worse, he'd done something so stupid that not even he could believe it. He wondered how long it would take to trust himself again, as he reached the ranch and saw the rancher.

After climbing out of his patrol SUV, he walked over to where the rancher was waiting for him next to the hole in the ground. The west was littered with old homestead wells, dangerous to animals and humans alike. Because of that, it wasn't that unusual to find bones in the bottom.

Shining his flashlight down into the well, he saw the pile of bones. Leaning closer, he shone the light around the rocky bottom until he found the one thing that would convince him. The human skull.

He swore under his breath before thanking the rancher, saying, "I'll take it from here. I'd appreciate it if you'd keep this between us." Even as he said it, he figured it was too late. He thought about calling the coroner, but from the condition of the bones, even he could tell that they'd been there for a while.

Stuart called Deputy Dodson. "I need you to come babysit some human remains." He gave him directions. "Bring whatever you need for however long it takes. I've called state forensics but it's going to take them a while to get here."

"You have to be kidding. If they're human remains, they aren't going anywhere. Wait, who do you think they belong to?" Dodson proved that he was smarter than Stuart often thought. "Rory Eastwood? Wait, next to the Stafford Ranch in a well? It can't be. You think it's the missing husband, Dixon Malone. That's why you called in the state boys."

"Let's not speculate until we have more information," the sheriff said. "I just don't want anyone messing with what could be a crime scene."

"Right," the deputy said and laughed. "This is going to be good."

Not in any way was this going to be good, Stuart thought as he waited for Dodson to arrive at the well for babysitting duty. He'd already seen several pickups drive past on the county road. Word had gotten out. Speculation would run rampant. Most everyone would come up with the same conclusion he and Dodson had. Not that Stuart would ever admit it. He was just covering his ass in case this skeleton belonged to Dixon Malone, husband of one of the most powerful ranchers in Montana.

CHAPTER TWENTY-EIGHT

OAKLEY HAD NEVER seen Tilly so nervous. "You look beautiful," she told her sister as she joined her in front of the full-length mirror at the church. "It's going to be a wonderful wedding."

Tilly looked over at her, tears in her eyes. "Nothing is going to spoil it, is it?"

"*Nothing.* Our brothers are ushers. They will be watching the door. Duffy will also be making sure that nothing is going to spoil this day, and the sheriff is Cooper's best man. I'm sure he's ready for anything. Trust me. It's going to be the best wedding ever, I promise, because you're marrying the man you love."

"I do love Coop so much."

"I know," she said, handing Tilly a tissue. "My sister, soon to be an old married woman."

"I suspect you won't be far behind. I'm surprised Pickett hasn't already asked you to marry him," her sister said, turning back into the older, bossier sister. "Wait, has he?"

Oakley pretended to turn an invisible key on her lips, sealing them. She suspected he was waiting until after Tilly's wedding, not wanting to take away from it. "Right now we're dating. It's fun and interesting. I've known him for so long and it feels as if I've never known this man. Does that make sense?"

"No," Tilly said. "Except for the fact that you didn't really know him."

"I didn't know his background or his birth name, but I *knew* him from the time we were teenagers. I just didn't know him as a man. I realize that I've always thought of him and Duffy as the boys."

"Duffy is still a boy," her sister said. "He is never going to grow up. Why are we talking about Duffy on my wedding day? If you even mention Treyton—"

Oakley laughed. "At least now you're not crying and ruining your makeup."

"Cooper said his entire family was warned about what would happen if they misbehaved at this wedding," Tilly said. "Treyton especially. Cooper said Treyton's been skating on thin ice as it is with his father. He doesn't expect any trouble out of him. Now, all I have to worry about is Mother."

Elaine stuck her head in the door to announce that it was time. Her sister grabbed Oakley's hand, squeezing it hard. "Tell me Mother isn't going to try to stop the wedding."

"She's not. She wouldn't be caught dead at this wedding. Mother in a church? Never going to happen unless she gets married again."

"That's not funny," her sister said with a shake of her head, but she was smiling. "Let's do this. Try not to trip."

Oakley looked at her, aghast. "Now you know I'll trip and fall on my face."

Tilly quickly hugged her. "I love you."

"I love you," she whispered back.

PICKETT HAD SAT close to the church door so he could see Oakley the minute she started down the aisle. Also so he would be close by in case there was any trouble. He'd promised Oakley that he wouldn't let anything—or anyone—spoil her sister's wedding day.

As she appeared, his heart took off at a gallop. She was so beautiful. Her ash-blond hair was worn up and adorned by tiny white roses. Her emerald green dress matched her eyes and fell like a waterfall over her curves. She was breathtaking.

She gave him a smile and a wink as she passed, making a few people nearby chuckle. *This woman,* he thought, heart swelling. She was everything. He'd never been so excited about the future. He felt the small velvet box in his pocket.

Nothing could stop him now from asking her to marry him. He'd waited because he didn't want to take anything away from Tilly's big day. He was waiting for the right time to pop the question.

The two of them had been officially dating. It had felt strange and awkward at first. They'd known each other for years. But their dates had been fun, some formal dinners at nice restaurants in Billings, others picnics by the river after a horseback ride. They had been getting to really know each other. It felt as if he'd been peeling away layers, piercing the protective shell Oakley had built around her because of her mother and brother. He'd fallen more in love as each layer had fallen away, each of them opening up to the other.

As the music played, Tilly came out, looking beautiful as well, and followed Oakley to where Cooper and the sheriff were waiting. He saw the look on Cooper's face. He knew that kind of love, he thought as Oakley took her sister's bouquet and the preacher cleared his voice and the music stopped.

That was when Pickett heard the church door open and turned to find Charlotte Stafford standing there.

OAKLEY KNEW THAT she must have gasped at the sight of her mother. Charlotte hesitated, silhouetted against the brighter daylight behind her. For a moment she looked lost. A cool spring breeze blew in. At first, only a few people turned to see who had come in.

Then, within seconds, whispers began to circulate, and more heads turned until the whole church was staring at the figure standing in the doorway.

Oakley hadn't heard what the preacher was saying. It appeared her sister hadn't, either. Tilly was now staring at their mother as if afraid that Charlotte had come to cause trouble—at worst, try to stop the wedding. Cooper had tensed the moment he saw Charlotte at the back of the church. Oakley knew he would do anything to make this wedding the best day of Tilly's life—including escorting her mother out.

Ryder and Brand were on their feet. Both turned to look at Oakley as if waiting to be told what to do. She had told them that if their mother showed up to try to get her out of the church before she could make a scene.

They now looked from their mother to Oakley again.

It all happened within seconds. Oakley saw the way she was dressed—as if going to a wedding. But still, she wasn't sure what to do until her mother's gaze met hers. She could see how hard this was for her, coming at the last minute as if losing the battle to stay away.

Oakley nodded to her brothers and said, "Could you show our guest to a seat please?"

Everyone turned back around as Charlotte Stafford was led to a seat. Tilly reached over and squeezed Oakley's hand before returning her attention to the pastor. Smiling, her sister said, "I'm sorry, could you repeat that?" and reached for Cooper's hand as if to assure him. He looked worried, Oakley thought, glancing at her as if to say, "I hope you know what you're doing."

She'd made the only choice she could have, she told herself. This didn't mean that her mother approved or would ever accept the marriage, but she'd come, which to Oakley was huge. She knew her sister would feel the same way. She'd seen the change in her mother since CJ's arrest and the remains having been found in an old well close to the Stafford Ranch.

But still, she was glad when the pastor didn't ask if anyone objected to the marriage of these two people. She felt as if she was holding her breath and couldn't help the sigh of relief when the pastor declared Tilly and Cooper as husband and wife. "You may kiss your bride."

As they kissed, Oakley sneaked a look and saw her mother rise and quietly leave the church.

Little steps, she thought as the pastor introduced the couple as Mr. and Mrs. Cooper McKenna to those gathered. Tilly had married the man of her dreams. Oakley had never seen her look happier.

Her gaze went to Pickett as she felt his eyes on her. She smiled, close to tears, wanting to pinch herself, half-afraid something would happen to spoil not just this moment, but also this cloud she'd been floating on for weeks with Pickett.

CHAPTER TWENTY-NINE

DUFFY FELT LOST. Just as he'd known would happen, Pickett and Oakley were now a duo. Not that he didn't see Pickett on the ranch. Not that they weren't still best friends. But the three of them were spending less and less time together.

Dirty Business had suspended meetings—at least for a while. After what had happened with Oakley, the gas company had moved their operations out of the area—at least temporarily. Even the big news about Charlotte Stafford attending Tilly and Cooper's wedding had died down.

Most everyone was waiting to hear if forensics had found a match for the human remains found in the old abandoned well close to the Stafford Ranch. Rumors had run wild at first, but even those had died down. At loose ends, Duffy had been working with Holly Jo on her trick riding. He admired the way she continually pushed herself to get better.

"She's a natural," his father liked to say. "She's really taken to horses and the ranch." He'd seen his father's pride in her, which only made him wonder again about Holden's connection to her and her deceased mother. Not that he suspected his father would ever be forthcoming on that subject.

Just the thought of Holly Jo reminded him of the trouble she'd been having with that boy at school. He decided to drive by the school, which was about to let out for the day, and meet this Gus.

As he pulled up, the bell rang and moments later students began to file out like bees from a hive. Duffy climbed out of the pickup and walked toward the school, looking for Holly Jo. He liked the idea of surprising her with a ride home—and maybe a pit stop for ice cream at the store.

He spotted her about the same time that he noticed a boy standing off to the side as if waiting for someone. The moment Holly Jo cleared the schoolhouse door, the boy headed for her. Gus?

Duffy watched as the stocky blond boy stopped Holly Jo even as she tried to sidestep him. Moving quickly in their direction through the students still pouring out, he heard just enough of the conversation to know the boy was giving her a hard time.

"Excuse me," he said. "Is this boy bothering you?"

Holly Jo's face flamed red. "Duffy, what are you doing here?"

The boy started to walk away, but Duffy called to him. "Are you harassing my little sister?"

"N-no." The boy looked as if he was about to lose his lunch.

"What's your name?"

"Gus."

"Gus, what?"

"Gardner."

Duffy recognized the name. A ranch hand by the

name of Joe Gardner worked on the Montgomery Ranch. "I know who your old man is."

"Duffy!" Holly Jo cried as she looked around. A few of the students had stopped to watch. "You're embarrassing me!"

"I won't have you harassing Holly Jo. You understand?"

The kid nodded and took off.

Holly Jo wouldn't look at him. "I can't believe you just did that," she said under her breath, head down as she stormed toward the waiting school bus.

"You told me he was bullying you," he said as he caught up to her. "I came to check on you. I thought you'd like a ride home."

"You really don't know anything," she said, sounding close to tears. "Just leave me alone." She hurried to the school bus and disappeared inside.

Duffy stood, feeling confused. He'd heard Gus say something to Holly Jo like, "You better be careful. You don't want to cross—" He hadn't let the kid finish, but what he'd heard made him think Gus was threatening her.

So why had Holly Jo not been glad that he'd straightened Gus out?

Shaking his head, he went back to his pickup. It just wasn't his day. Hell, it hadn't been his year.

THE SHERIFF HADN'T been surprised when he'd gotten the call from the state forensics lab tech. The remains found in the well were those of Dixon Malone.

He picked up his Stetson and headed for the door. It was time to talk to Charlotte Stafford, the widow.

She hadn't been seen since the wedding. Stuart knew that she would have heard about the remains found in the well not all that far from her ranch. He figured she wouldn't be surprised as he drove up to her ranch house and got out.

Charlotte opened the door herself to his knock. He'd thought she looked different at the wedding. Like then, she held her head up high. A tall woman, her blond hair streaked with gray, worn in one long braid that fell almost to her waist. She appeared to have just either returned from a horseback ride or had been about to take one.

Stuart removed his Stetson. "Mrs. Stafford," he said with a nod.

"Sheriff Layton." She pushed the door open wider. "Please come in."

He stepped in, admiring her calm since she had to know why he was in her home.

"Can I offer you something to drink?" He shook his head. "Then please have a seat."

They sat in the living room. The house seemed strangely quiet. He knew she had staff and two sons who still lived at home. He tried to imagine what it might have been like growing up in such a lavish house, knowing that you owned land for miles in almost every direction. He couldn't even imagine it or why this woman was so alone. A house this big should be alive with noise and laughter—at least that was the way he'd always imagined it.

"I'm sure you've heard about the human remains found in a well not far from here," Stuart said. She said nothing, simply waited. "They belong to your…

husband, Dixon Malone." That, too, didn't seem to faze her. She'd obviously been expecting this news.

He pulled out his phone. "I have to ask you on the record, Mrs. Stafford…" He pushed the record button. He'd planned to get into it slowly by asking her when she'd last seen Dixon Malone, ask about the fight they'd had, and take it from there.

He looked at her as he said the date and whom he was interviewing. Then he asked, "Did you kill your husband and dump his body into that well?"

As PICKETT TAPPED at the den door, Holden McKenna looked up and smiled. "Come on in, son. What can I do for you?"

He felt like a fool for bringing this to his employer, but over the months since he'd left to go back east and had returned, he and Holden had grown closer. The man had been treating him like he really was his son.

"I'm going to ask Oakley Stafford to marry me," he said, getting right to the point.

"Good for you," Holden said. "If you're looking for my blessing…"

"Actually, I need your advice." He stepped a little farther into the den. "I've been wanting to ask her for weeks, but I just can't seem to decide on the right time."

The older man laughed. "It is always the right time, but I know what you mean. You want to make it special, right?"

"We've been…dating so I'm torn between a fancy restaurant or some music event."

Holden was shaking his head. "It's Oakley. You know her. Neither of those sound right, do they? Where is Oakley most comfortable, most herself? That's the place where you ask her."

Pickett laughed. "I think I knew that, but I want to do this right."

"Believe me, you'll do it right. I suspect she wants to marry you as badly as you want to marry her."

"I hope so. Thanks. I've got it."

Holden laughed. "I'm sure you do. Any thought as to where you'd like to get married?"

"Oakley and I haven't discussed it, but I'd love to get married right here on the ranch."

"Wonderful idea. If Oakley is agreeable, you can have it right here in the house."

WHEN OAKLEY ARRIVED at the ranch, Pickett already had the horses saddled. He'd told her they were going on a picnic. Spring had come early to the Powder River Basin. The sun felt warm against her face as she walked under a cloudless blue sky out to where he was standing by the two saddled horses.

A light breeze ruffled his hair, his dark blue eyes shining, as he smiled at her. It had been a while since they'd gone horseback riding. They'd spent as much time as possible together. While he was working on the McKenna Ranch, she'd been helping her mother at the Stafford Ranch.

Her mother hadn't mentioned Tilly and Cooper's wedding or their long honeymoon in Hawaii. Nor had she said anything about Oakley dating Pickett Hanson, even though she surely knew.

They'd fallen into a companionable arrangement as her mother let her help with running the ranch, taking over Tilly's duties. Ryder and Brand seemed to spend more time in the house when Oakley was there—and CJ gone. CJ's trial was still months away. Oakley noticed how her mother didn't mention his name. No one else did, either.

"Perfect day for a ride," she said to Pickett now as she gave him a kiss, he handed her the reins and she swung up into the saddle. This was where she felt most at home, she thought as he mounted his horse and they headed out toward the mountains.

They rode up to an outcropping of rocks and Pickett reined in. The view was incredible, but today it was breathtaking. The spring breeze smelled of new leaves and wild grasses. She breathed it in, marveling at this wide-open country as vast as the sky overhead. The river, the one constant in this basin, wound through it all, a glistening ribbon through the cottonwoods.

Oakley had been so busy looking at the country that she hadn't noticed that Pickett had dismounted and was now standing next to her horse. The moment she saw his face, she knew. Her eyes filled with tears. She had wondered when it would happen, how he would do it. She should have known he'd make it perfect, on the side of a mountain on horseback.

"Oakley Stafford, will you marry me?" he asked as he produced a small velvet box and held it out to her.

Her throat closed with emotion. She nodded, feeling tears trail down her cheeks. "Oh, yes," she croaked out and they both laughed, her through her tears.

He opened the box, took out the ring and slipped it on her finger. She stared at it for only a moment, the diamond glittering in the spring sunlight. "It's beautiful."

"You're beautiful."

She slid off her horse and into his arms. "I can't wait to marry you."

"I was hoping you'd say that because I'm not sure I can stand a long engagement." He kissed her, drawing her closer as the horses whinnied impatiently. "We've never talked about a wedding. If you want one like Tilly's—"

"No," she cried and then they both laughed again. "I want something small, simple, quick," she said with a grin.

"Holden said we could use the house to get married," he said cautiously.

"That would be perfect," she said instantly.

"What about your mother?" he asked, looking worried.

"We'll invite her. Who knows? She might come."

"I wouldn't count on that."

She smiled up into his handsome face. "I just want to marry you. Nothing else matters. I can't wait to become Mrs. Oakley Hanson."

He stared at her, his face filled with emotion. "I never thought I'd hear those words."

Oakley snuggled against him as they turned to take in the view. "About that passel of babies you want to have." She grinned up at him. "I can't imagine a more perfect day or more perfect spot than this one to start a family."

"I love the way you think, cowgirl," he said and kissed her.

* * * * *

Do you love romance books?

JOIN

on Facebook by scanning the code below:

A group dedicated to book recommendations, author exclusives, SWOONING and all things romance! A community made for romance readers by romance readers.

Facebook.com/groups/readloverepeat

RLRBPA0323